Praise for Denise Mina's
THE RED ROAD

Short-listed for the Theakstons Old Peculier
Crime Novel of the Year Award
Selected as one of the Best Mysteries of the Year by:
The Guardian (UK), *Wall Street Journal*, *The Independent*
(UK), *Milwaukee Journal Sentinel*, *Kirkus Reviews*

"If anyone can make you root for the murderer, it's Denise Mina, whose defiantly unsentimental novels are less concerned with personal guilt than with the social evils that create criminals and the predators who nurture them. *The Red Road* is as fierce a story as any Mina has written." —Marilyn Stasio, *New York Times Book Review*

"Mina's narrative is full of suspense, fresh dialogue, and sharp glimpses of all sorts of characters. Most interesting of all to watch is Morrow herself, who struggles to cross the gaps and fill in the blanks between past and present." —Tom Nolan, *Wall Street Journal*

"Along with being one of the finest practitioners of the criminal art, Denise Mina is also a social commentator of perception and humanity, as *The Red Road* reminds us....Mina is second to none in the creation of damaged female protagonists....Disparate elements are brought together with authority, intricately drawing us into a narrative that engages with a variety of issues, all equally provocative." —Barry Forshaw, *The Independent* (UK)

"Mina is a dab hand at constructing complex reads in which corruption permeates all levels of society and no one is left untainted, and *The Red Road* is no exception: unsentimental, unsettling, and very, very good." —Laura Wilson, *The Guardian* (UK)

"Psychologically astute.... *The Red Road* is heavy with guilt and bristles with tension."

—Carole E. Barrowman, *Milwaukee Journal Sentinel*

"Denise Mina rarely writes a sentence that doesn't induce dread in the reader or at the very least a serious case of shaky nerves. Mina clearly takes the view that a crime novel is supposed to provide thrills on every page—and she delivers the goods....It's a complex story told by Mina in prose that grips the reader by the neck and doesn't let go."

—Jack Batten, *Toronto Star*

"Mina's at the top of her game here, deftly unveiling the sad truths of the past and present to create a gritty must-read for fans of complex psychological police procedurals."

—Christine Tran, *Booklist*

"The plot is as compelling as it is intricate. Denise Mina grows in assurance and becomes more accomplished with every book; and this one is a cracker, beautifully worked out, every scene serving a purpose. It demands concentration from the reader, but the story is so gripping that you are likely to hurry along, eager to learn how the plot unfolds. Eventually you arrive at a splendid, abrupt, and laconic conclusion, which rightly leaves some questions open. Then I suggest you may want to go back to savor the details, for this is that rare thing, a crime novel that invites, and benefits from, a second reading....Crime fiction is entertainment, and Denise Mina is always entertaining."

—Allan Massie, *The Scotsman*

"Few authors know meaner streets than Denise Mina. Her fictional Glasgow is a vicious and soul-destroying place, and no victim is as chilling as fourteen-year-old Rose Wilson, prostitute and pimp murderer. Twenty-five years later, Detective Inspector Alex Morrow is faced with a new case, one that will reopen the Rose Wilson conviction and force DI Morrow to confront the ultimate dilemma of the ethical copper: when are justice and the law in conflict? One of Mina's most complex works." —Margaret Cannon, *Globe and Mail*

"Interesting, compelling, twisted, and true.... It's Mina's insightful and incisive view into human frailty that makes her stories so perceptive and astute." —Tracy Sherlock, *Vancouver Sun*

"Edgar-finalist Mina's fourth novel featuring Glasgow Det. Insp. Alex Morrow (after 2013's *Gods and Beasts*) is perhaps her finest yet, a brilliantly crafted tale of corruption, ruined lives, and the far-reaching ripple effects of crime." — *Publishers Weekly*

"Mina continues to enthrall with her astute perceptions and descriptions of Glasgow's underbelly....Her novels tell you more about the crime landscape of Glasgow than a host of sociological surveys." —Marcel Berlins, *The Times* (UK)

"A brilliantly plotted tale that segues between past and present, *The Red Road* is a 'tartan noir' police procedural to rival Ian Rankin's best work, as Mina blends the harsh realities facing Glasgow's underprivileged kids with the salubrious world inhabited by the city's legal and financial wizards. The chief appeal, however, is Alex Morrow herself, a meticulously crafted character of depth and substance who succeeds in a patriarchal environment by virtue of her intelligence, persistence, and humanity." —*Irish Times*

"I've read *The Red Road* twice, and the book is marked up like an eighth grader's English essay—and this is still the most confounding book I've ever read. And it's brilliant...more noir than noir itself." —Jeff Mannix, *Durango Herald*

ALSO BY DENISE MINA

ALEX MORROW NOVELS

STILL MIDNIGHT

END OF THE WASP SEASON

THE RED ROAD

PADDY MEEHAN NOVELS

FIELD OF BLOOD

THE DEAD HOUR

SLIP OF THE KNIFE

GARNETHILL TRILOGY

GARNETHILL

EXILE

RESOLUTION

OTHER NOVELS

DECEPTION

THE RED ROAD

A NOVEL

denise mina

BACK BAY BOOKS

LITTLE, BROWN AND COMPANY

NEW YORK   BOSTON   LONDON

Copyright © 2013 by Denise Mina
Reading group guide copyright © 2015 by Denise Mina and Little, Brown and Company
Excerpt from *Blood Salt Water* copyright © 2015 by Denise Mina

Back Bay Books / Little, Brown and Company
Hachette Book Group
1290 Avenue of the Americas, New York, NY 10104
littlebrown.com

Originally published in hardcover in the United States by Little, Brown and Company, February 2014
First Back Bay paperback edition, March 2015

Back Bay Books is an imprint of Little, Brown and Company. The Back Bay Books name and logo are trademarks of Hachette Book Group, Inc.

The publisher is not responsible for websites (or their content) that are not owned by the publisher.

The Hachette Speakers Bureau provides a wide range of authors for speaking events. To find out more, go to hachettespeakersbureau.com or call (866) 376-6591.

ISBN 978-0-316-18851-7 (hc) / 978-0-316-24001-7 (large print) / 978-0-316-18850-0 (pb)
LCCN 2013956654

10 9 8 7 6 5 4 3 2 1

RRD-C

Printed in the United States of America

THE RED ROAD

1

1997

Rose Wilson was fourteen but looked sixteen. Sammy said it was a shame.

She was alone in his car, in a dark city center street of shuttered pubs and clubs. Outside, the soft summer breeze stirred the silt of a Saturday night, lifting paper wrappers, rolling empty cans. Rose watched a yellow burger box crab-scuttle from the mouth of a dark alley and tentatively make its way across the pavement to the curb.

She was waiting for Sammy to drive her back. It had been a long night. A sore night. Three parties in different flats. She used to think she was lucky she wasn't freezing on the streets but she wasn't sure tonight. He was off arranging next week. Lots of dough, he said with a twinkle in his eye.

Rose leaned her head on the window. Sammy was full of shit — they weren't making a lot of money. She shut her eyes. They weren't even doing it for the money. He was doing it to make other men like him, so he had something they wanted. She was making them pay for what they were taking anyway. But they went through this pretense, like it was a big moneymaker, her being underage. He said the money was lower than he promised because she did look sixteen, but never mind, eh? She still had a good long time to make her money. The men weren't interested in her age. They weren't perverts. Rose knew all too well that those men just befriended some daft junkie cow with six weans and took it for free. The men Sammy fed her to were just normal men. They liked that she was young because they knew no one would believe her. Nothing easier than making a wean shut up.

But Sammy needed to lie to himself, pretending he was a businessman or something. He'd save the money, he said, and they'd live together when she was legal. It was about the money and he loved her, they loved each other. Whenever he said that he looked deep into her eyes, like a stage hypnotist she once saw at the Pavilion.

Before her mum died, Rose never went out. She hardly even went to school. She couldn't leave her mum alone with the young kids because she was always nodding out and dropping lit cigarettes, letting anyone into the house. But she went out that one time because she didn't want to let Ida down. Ida T. was their neighbor back in the flats. Ida was decent. She knew there were problems, more than normal. Thinking Rose's mum was like herself, but with loads of kids, Ida thought she'd feel better if she got more fun out of life, had a laugh. She bought two tickets for the late-night hypnotism show. By the time Ida came to collect her Rose's mum was asleep and looked like staying that way, so Rose pulled her coat on and went instead.

When the lights went down and the show started the hypnotist got everyone in the audience to press both hands together as if they were praying, and then told them that their hands were stuck.

In the dark theater Rose's tiny hands came apart easily. So did

Ida's. They both thought the trick hadn't worked until people began to stand up, lifting prayerful hands, laughing, baffled. They kept their hands together as they clambered over knees and bags, making their way to the aisle, and assembled on the stage, prayerstuck, beseeching the Almighty for a bit of naughty fun.

The hypnotist gave them orders, stupid things to do, and the rest of the audience laughed at them. Some of the people on stage were having sex with chairs, taking their tops off, snogging invisible movie stars; some of them weren't hypnotized. Rose could tell. They were pretending, so they could get up on stage and act stupid and get attention or something. It was a lie they all agreed to tell each other.

When Sammy looked deep into her eyes and said they were doing it for the money she pretended like she was hypnotized. Love you too. But Rose's hands came apart in the dark. She was waiting until she could get away from him, until she could find someone else, someone that she didn't need to lie to. You did need somebody to cling to, she knew that.

She looked out at the street of pubs and clubs, where pals and cousins and sisters and workmates had met and spent the evening together. Her brothers and sisters had been scattered all over, adopted into different families down in England. It wasn't even that long ago but she couldn't remember all of their faces properly. She didn't miss the responsibility, the weight of them all. She watched them leave, relieved. They wouldn't miss her, she was sure. Wherever they went would be better than where they'd been. They might do all right, in a new place. She let them go. Rose had been twelve and a half, too old for adoption, she knew that. People wanted to adopt fresh kids, and she wasn't that.

Everyone else had someone. They weren't even grateful. Mostly they complained about who they had. Rose hated kids at school whining about their folks. Moaning because someone demanded to know where they'd been all night, angry if they came home covered in bruises, smelling of sick and spunk.

Sorry for herself, she felt that familiar plummet in mood. She couldn't control the drop, or slow it, because she was so tired, it was morning, and she was heading back for a fight with the care-home staff because she had been out all night. She ran through the night staff rota in her head: that new woman was on, the tall one, so Rose wouldn't even be able to fall back on the old trick to get out of a grilling: she couldn't pull her clothes off and force the male support worker to leave the room. The staff were al-ways calm, she hated that. They never raised their voices or got excited or screamed because they loved you. Sammy screamed and shouted. Sammy's mood rose and fell, swooped and dived from extreme to extreme. That's what first made her notice him. He stopped her on her way to school and said she was beauti-ful and she got embarrassed and told him to fuck off. The next day he was there, waiting to see her, but now he was angry and told her she was full of herself, wake up, hen, you've got an arse the size of Partick. Then the next day he was sorry, he looked sorry too. He just wanted to talk. He felt this connection be-tween them, that's why he came back. Rose had kept her eyes down since her mother died. The first time she looked up it was for Sammy's bullshit.

Her mood was shifting now, swooping low, low, low, below angry. Random memories that echoed her mood came to mind: taking her pants off in a hallway stacked with bin bags; a grubby avocado-colored bath with yellow fag burns; four men looking up at her from a living room.

She'd never admit it to her psychologist, but she did use some of his techniques: she shut her eyes, breathed deeply and sum-moned Pinkie Brown.

Pinkie holding her hand, his big hand over her small hand.

Pinkie stirring a pot of food. Pinkie in their clean, wee flat. Pinkie holding a baby, their baby, maybe.

It worked. The breathing and the images shifted the tar-black mood. The psychologist said you could only hold one thought in your head at a time and she could choose that thought. It wasn't easy, he said, but she could choose.

Pinkie sitting on a settee watching a football match on telly, wearing joggers and no top. Pinkie's hand brushing his buzz cut.

The truth was that she didn't really know Pinkie Brown. She'd spotted him a couple of times when they fought with Cleveden, the other kids' home nearby. She saw him standing at the back, a head taller than everyone else. He was different. He was in charge. She noticed him cup the elbow of a crying child, his wee brother Michael, as it turned out. He'd be good with kids, she knew he would. He caught her eye twice, once in the street, once outside school. A girl at school said Pinkie had asked about Rose.

Pinkie Brown got stuck in her head and she made up stories about him: Pinkie was her childhood sweetheart. Sure, they both grew up in care, but they understood family, like those wee girls in the home with bad teeth: their mum walked all the way across the city to visit so she could spend her bus fare on sweeties for them.

In Rose's story she and Pinkie grew up together. They stayed true to each other. When they were old enough they got a wee clean house, had a baby. They wore matching rings from Argos. He never cared what she'd done in her early life either. He understood and she made good money. Maybe she'd stop it when she got older and could. Maybe she'd go to college and become a social worker, not like her social worker but a really good one, one who actually knew what went on, and could stop stuff happening to kids like her.

Better. A warm lift took the black edge off her. She felt the mood subside. Getting dozy, she sat up and bit her cheek to keep herself awake. She had to stay on guard because when she got in the staff would take her in the office and quiz her about where she had been all night. She must not say anything about Sammy or the parties or the men. They'd kill her. They never threatened her but she heard them talk. Easiest thing in the world, getting rid of a girl no one was looking for. And the staff: she didn't want them to know about this other world. The kids all said they hated the staff but there was something sweet about some of them, hoping they could help. She didn't want to spoil things for them.

So she opened her burning eyes, sat up and found herself looking straight at Pinkie Brown.

He stepped out of a dark alley, side-wall to ChipsPakoraKebab. He was looking straight back at her. Her pulse throbbed in her throat. He had come, as if her yearning had conjured him from the filthy dark.

Stepping out of the shadows, he kept his eyes locked on hers as he walked fast towards the car. Streetlights hit him and she saw his dark T-shirt was ripped at the hem, wet all down the front.

He reached forward, pulled the passenger door open. "Rosie fae Turnberry." He was breathless, skin glistening with sweat and panic. "Come on."

Elated, Rosie stepped out to meet him, and then she saw the red splatter on his neck, on his forearm. His T-shirt was soaked in blood.

He shut the car door behind her and pulled her deep into the alley. Heavy chip-fat air was cut through with the sharp smell of piss.

"'S that your blood?" she asked, aware that it was the first thing she had ever said to him in real life.

"Nut." The alley was dark. "Guys frae the Drum jumped us. Battered our Michael." The kid he'd comforted: his brother—he cared about that kid. "I'd tae get them off him."

"Was it another home?"

"Nut." He looked at her then, to see if she understood, and she did. When not-in-care gangs came, they were after all of you. Cleveden or Turnberry meant nothing to them. To them you were all care-home scum. They knew you'd get the blame for everything.

"Rose." Pinkie lifted a hand between them. "Take this?"

Not a ring from Argos. Instead, in his open palm, sat a Rambo knife, curved blade, ragged teeth. The handle was gaffer-taped silver, spongy with blood.

"Put it down your sock and I'll come for it later?" He raised the hand towards her face. "Gonnae hide it for me? The polis'll search Cleveden for sure. I need it but I can't keep ahold of it."

The bloody knife was inches from her nose.

He watched her expectantly but Rose didn't move. Her eyes brimmed with stinging tears. She kept staring at the blurry knife. She blinked and behind her lids saw yellow burns on a green bath. She opened them and a tear fell, landing on the dirty blade: a clean silver splash on the red.

"Don't be scared," he said, but Rose wasn't crying because she was scared. "You like me, don't you?"

Rose lifted her hand slowly and took the knife by the handle. It was wet and sticky. It didn't matter. She had touched worse.

Pinkie smiled, whispered, "Your prints are on that now."

A trap. Eight men in a flat, not Sammy's one friend. Drunk men, dirty bed, vodka to wash her mouth clean. Her hold tightened on the handle and blood oozed from the gaffer tape, like mud through toes.

He sensed the change in her and tried to soften it. "I like you too, Rose." But he said it flat, like "nice to meet you," like "it's for your own good," like "we're only trying to help."

Pinkie Brown had clocked her like she clocked punters with

cash and a conscience. She could read compunction like other kids read crisp flavors and Pinkie Brown had read her. He would never hold her hand or stir a pot or coo at a baby. There was no one in the wee clean house. There was no house. When she made up those stories about him, she had been pressing her hands together, convincing herself they were stuck. Well, they were unstuck now.

This was all there was. Dirt and piss smells and Sammy and filth. She shut her eyes tight.

"Rose, I've seen ye at school—" Pinkie's shadow was over her, his breath in her face.

Hope exhausted, she shoved him away.

Except she didn't.

She meant to shove him, slap his shoulder in a flat cold rage. But he had moved and she'd forgotten the Rambo knife in her hand. The sensations registered in her elbow: teeth catching in meat. Warm wet flecked on her cheek. Disgust and panic made her jerk her hand down fast, sawing through whatever she was caught on. Down and down, the knife ground free. She dropped it, heard the chink of cutlery on stone. She shut her eyes tighter, pressing her lips together so that nothing splashed into her mouth.

A suck of air signaled the weight of him dropping to the ground. She heard him land, heard him grunt with surprise. She heard a splash on cobbles. The rubber sole of his trainers shrieked as he scrabbled against the floor. Then he was still.

She couldn't look. The wet on her face began to cool.

Wary, she opened the eye closest to the wall. Normal. Dark, smelly, night. The stench of piss and fat. She looked down. The cobbles were molten.

Pinkie was on the ground and next to him lay the knife. He had fallen sideways, arms out, eyes half-open. He lay completely still except for something moving under his neck, a brief throb that caught the silver light.

Rose watched the beat slow. She stood, barely breathing, looking sixteen, feeling twelve. A slow dawning realization: a door had shut. She would never get away. They'd cut her up and leave her in a bag.

Keeping her hands on the wall behind her, she bent down, picked up the knife and tucked it into her sock like Pinkie said to. She slid upright against the wall, fingers sticky because her jeans and socks were covered with blood.

Rose blinked and turned off all her physical sensations, she knew how to do that. Then she clung on to the wall, moving backwards out of the alley, smearing bloody prints as she edged away.

She crossed the pavement to the car, not even looking to see if there was anyone there. Back inside the car she locked the door, pulled on the seat belt and sat still, looking blankly out of the window.

As soon as Sammy saw what she had done she was dead. Like her mum. A man on top of her. A fat, smothering man on top of her mum in the dark kitchen, heels kicking the floor, a fat man on top of her. She kept kicking, as if it would help. Kicking against air, looking for a thing to kick against. Rose closed the bedroom door and stood against it, watching the wee ones, praying that none of them would move or wake or make a noise. She stood behind the door until the man left. A drunk, fat, clumsy man, brushing against walls on the way out, never seen again, never found. Her mum had tried suicide many times, failed and was sorry she'd failed and yet she died kicking against air.

Rose sat in Sammy's car and thought about that for an hour or a day or a minute, she couldn't tell. Finally Sammy sauntered along the street. He walked up to the car, not looking in the alley. As he put the key in the door his plump belly flattened against the window. He would kill her. Or take her to the men who would kill her. Soon as he saw the blood on her she was dead, but he climbed back in without looking at her.

Sammy was bald at only twenty-four. He was fat too. He looked about fifty to her. She looked sixteen but he looked fucking fifty or something, disgusting.

"Fucking hell, guess what?" he said, looking out of the windscreen, his voice normal and loud and cheerful.

"What?" Rose asked, numb.

"Princess Diana's dead." He huffed a small laugh. "'Magine! Died in a car crash in Paris."

Rose couldn't see how that was relevant. "Fuck off," she said, mechanically.

He smiled at that and started the engine. "Aye. In a car crash."

"'King hell," said Rose.

Sammy flicked the lights on and pulled out into the deserted street.

"Wow," he said as he drove. "Makes you think." He seemed excited about the whole thing. "She was young to die. And those boys. What d'ye think Charles'll have to say about it?"

Rose wasn't used to discussing current events with Sammy, or anything with Sammy. It made the night feel even more strange, him being chummy, like they always talked about stuff like this.

He nudged her with his fat elbow as they drove down Bath Street. "What d'you think? Charles: what'll he be feeling?"

"Dunno." She had to say something. "Gutted?"

"Nah." He smiled as he took a turn at some lights. "Not gutted. He's free to marry that other one now."

He gibbered on about it, about the Queen and Prince Charles. Rose tuned out. She didn't know about politics. She was so deepdown tired that she forgot Pinkie Brown. All she could remember was that she was dead and there was blood. Death filled her consciousness like an ache.

They were drawing up into the mouth of Turnberry Avenue. She reached down to absentmindedly scratch away an itch from her ankle. As dampness registered on her fingertips she remembered: it was itchy because it was covered in Pinkie Brown's blood and she had killed him. She froze, bent double, her fingers touching the car floor like a sprinter on the blocks.

The kids' home was in a big Victorian villa at the heart of the posh West End. Sammy's eyes flicked around the street, checking for staff or witnesses.

"Good girl," he said, seeing her bent down, thinking she was hiding for him.

He parked two hundred yards further up the road, in the deep shadow under a big old tree. A branch sagged down in front of them under the weight of leaves, heavy, swaying, leaves flipping over and back in the breeze, silver, black. Orange streetlights winked through but dawn was already bleeding into the night. Rose stayed down.

Sammy was chatting away now, she thought he'd had a smoke or something while he was out of the car.

He said, "One day you'll grow out of me, hen, you know? You'll move on in your young life, but I hope you'll remember me kindly. I think the world of you, you know."

He waited for the responsorial lie—I'll never move on from you, Sammy, you're the only one in the world who gives a fuck about me—but Rose didn't say anything. She was thinking about air and kicking air and felt that same urge rise up in her.

Her eye fell on the posh flats outside, dark with curtains drawn. Sleeping in those flats were lawyers and students and dentists, refreshing themselves with warm, comfy sleeps. They'd wake up in a few hours, have calm breakfasts and then settle into Sunday.

They'd get dressed and start writing letters to the council, complaining about the children's home bringing down property prices.

"What do you want for yourself, Rose?" he said, repeating the tone, changing the sentiment. "From life, what do you want?" And then he pulled on the handbrake as if he was planning to settle in for a long conversation.

"Dough," she told the floor. She couldn't get up. He'd see the blood.

"Well, you're going the right way about that, hen." He laughed softly. "What ye doing down there?" He was looking at her now, his big stupid face kind of gawping.

What was she doing down here? The question howled through her. What was she doing all the way down here? Why was *she* all the way down here? The injustice of it struck her so suddenly and completely that she had to blink to warm her eyes. Why were other girls asleep? Why were they wearing ironed clothes and worried about the size of their thighs and learning piano and painting their fingernails and she was down here?

Rose looked back at him, her fingers creeping up her leg, drawing the jeans up with them until she felt the gaffer tape.

"You're in a strange mood—what's down there—"

She bolted up against the air, swung the knife at his neck, in and out. She'd kicked and now she shut her eyes, curled up knees to chin, cowering into the passenger door.

Wet gasps and thrashing. Rain in the car. Sammy kicking, feet scrabbling against the pedals. He grabbed her hair and yanked her down to the side.

Slowly, his fingers relented, slid down her wet arm and disappeared. Rose waited as the thrashing slowed. Like her mum, Sammy's legs were the last thing to still. The only sound in the car was a wet gurgle.

Sammy deflated, wilting onto the steering wheel, and the horn eased out a long droning blare.

Rose couldn't hide indoors, she was covered in blood.

She couldn't run away. When the police found the body of Sammy the Perv the first place they'd look was the children's home; the first thing they'd notice was that she was missing. Even if she got away from the police the men would find her.

She'd never get away.

She opened her eyes and looked out of a window filigreed with blood, deaf to the skirl of the horn.

Outside the car lights burst on in flats. Curtains drew back. Angry faces looking for the car horn ripping their Sunday morning. Rose watched the streetlights deferring to the dawn, flicking off, one by one.

She sat inside the bloody car and waited for the police to come.

2

Alex Morrow hated feeling this nervous. She hated it. A chair
scraped the floor beyond the door and her stomach sent up an acid
distress signal. She ground her teeth until they hurt, angry with
herself. She knew her nerves were caused by public speaking and
seeing Michael Brown again but knowing didn't seem to help.
Deep breathing didn't help. Eating bananas and avoiding coffee
hadn't helped. She hated this.

The witness waiting room was dull. The walls were lined with
yellow pine, the carpet navy blue. Six chairs, in matching pine
and navy blue fabric, and a low table with some magazines no
one would ever read. An empty water cooler gathered dust in
the corner. Morrow imagined an anxious witness, waiting, taking
drink after drink from the cooler to moisten a dry mouth and then
needing the toilet as soon as they stepped into the witness box.
Morrow's mouth was dry too. She chewed her tongue.

Usually when she felt like this it would make her wonder why
she put herself through it, but not today. She'd happily sit here,
heart hammering, every day for a year if it meant a longer sen-

tence for Michael Brown. She never wanted to have to interview that bastard again. He threatened her during interviews. He threatened Brian during interviews. He said he knew of pedophile rings who'd pay for the use of her children. He'd chanted her home address, goaded her about her sex life, he even tried to expose himself to her.

At first Morrow considered handing the interviews over to someone else. She was getting angry, felt soiled. But as they went on, as his pallor changed to prison white, as he lost weight and started wearing prison-issue clothes, she began to see him for what he was: a lifer in his death throes. He was out on license when they arrested him. He'd been done for murdering his older brother, Pinkie, when he was just a kid. When word got out that he'd been loaning semi-automatic guns to junkies, there would be a suspicion that he wanted to get caught and sent back, that he just couldn't cut it outside. The rest of his life would be shit if they believed that of him so he had to put on a good show, resist the firm hand as hard as possible. It was the lifer equivalent of final exams and Morrow wasn't the audience, she was a prop.

They knew what the finale was going to be: Michael Brown would try to escape from this court. His Dutch lawyer had just commissioned a refurbishment of Brown's villa in northern Cyprus. If he did manage to get there, she was sure, he would absentmindedly come back to Glasgow for something and get done then. They didn't know how, but they knew he was planning to abscond. A leap over the wall to the public gallery was a possibility.

She leaned back in her chair and thought her way through the security arrangements: a van of officers at the front and back of the court. Extra security staff downstairs. CCTV on every exit and a closed court. Two armed officers putting on a show in the lobby. The jury were sequestered for the full trial, kept in a hotel with heavy security. It was costing a fortune and there was to be no press coverage. Journalists would be allowed in, but only to make notes for later. It was easier than saying no, but effectively the same.

The door to the court snapped open and Morrow jumped in her seat. The macer, the court usher, looked in. She was slight, swamped by her black gown, dirty blond hair pulled back in a messy ponytail. She looked hassled and tired.

"DI Alex Morrow."

The macer disappeared down the steps and Morrow heard a silence fall in the courtroom beyond. Everyone in the court would be watching the doorway and every second's delay gave her a bigger buildup.

Morrow stood up, carrying her briefcase, wishing it wasn't so big. She couldn't leave it in the witness waiting room or in the car. It had her laptop in it and losing those files was a sackable offense. She had to take it with her but it looked as if she was going on a short holiday.

Through the door, down five steps and into the well of the court.

Wrong shoes. Her solid heels sounded like a slow handclap on the wooden floor. Michael Brown was staring at her; she could see his outline from the corner of her eye. She felt, again, intense discomfort at his presence and tiptoed up to the witness box. She kept her eyes on the well of the court as she bent to tuck her briefcase against the side of the dock.

Standing up, she looked around the room. The jury were already a comfortably coherent group, had notebooks and pens out. A roll of mints was being surreptitiously passed along the back row.

Everyone official looked to the noter, sitting just below the judge. He nodded to all that the recording equipment was working and they could start.

Drawing a breath, the judge led Morrow in the oath. She had said it a hundred times. She followed the prompts fluidly, taking in the room in her peripheral vision.

Michael Brown was sitting in the dock, staring at her, trying to catch her eye. It was important not to look back. None of her testimony should look personal and Brown made her so uncomfortable that it might register on her face. The jury would see that she was afraid of him. They might suspect that it had colored the case against him. It hadn't. The case was good, she knew that.

Most cops at her level knew to just hope for the best and expect the worst but Morrow was too deep into it: she wanted Brown to get a long sentence. She was surprised to see a journalist there, in the press seats which were provided with a flip-down table. He looked real too, not a camouflage-trousered crimezine journalist, but wearing a shirt and a jacket. She couldn't imagine why he was there as he couldn't print any of it.

Oath done, James Finchley, the prosecuting counsel, stood up and went over to the podium next to the jury. Taking his time, Finchley opened his manila folder, looked through two sheets of paper, turned a page over, making them wait.

Finchley was short and priggish. His black gown always looked pressed, his wig freshly powdered, his diction clipped. Morrow knew that out of court he was warmer than he seemed in court. He was thorough but dull to watch.

Anton Atholl for the defense was quite a different man. Atholl was a minor celebrity and an earl, but people liked him because he didn't use his title. Exploiting his flair for drama and loopholes, he gave angry interviews to the local news, drank prodigious amounts and wore his wavy gray hair too long. He would certainly appeal when Brown was found guilty. That's why Prosecutor Fiscal put Finchley up for the prosecution: thorough but dull.

Today Atholl seemed to have dressed himself while spinning around; everything was slightly askew: his wig, his gown, the papers in his file. Clever, thought Morrow. Atholl was the only interesting thing to look at in the room. He was contrasting himself with Finchley. Even she was looking at him.

Finchley looked up from his folder, asked Morrow to say her name, which station she worked at and detail her length of service. He asked the questions in lawyerese, curt and wordy at the same time, conventions of a profession which valued precision but billed by the hour.

And on that day in May, at what time precisely, could she say, was the warrant for a search of the premises executed, exactly?

Morrow said that they knocked on the door at seven thirty-five a.m. Some of the jury members glanced over at Brown, sitting in the dock. They were wondering if he would be up at that time, what sort of pajamas he wore, maybe, trying to picture the scene.

Brown watched her from the witness box and her eye flicked over him. He looked gray, not at all the suntanned bully they'd spent hour after hour questioning. But he'd already had four months in custody and was flanked by two burly security guards who had been outside enjoying the summer.

Too late, after her eye had left him, Brown tried to sneer. He glanced over at her now, trying to make eye contact, almost pleading with her to look back. Morrow kept her eyes on Finchley.

Finchley moved on to a series of questions about the search of Brown's home: on that date how many officers did she have with her? Seven other officers. Were some of those officers from the armed division? They were. Why were those officers there? It was suspected that Mr. Brown had firearms in his house.

She remembered the house vividly: a brand new suburban four bedroom with en suite this, en suite that. It was on a luxe estate in a shit area. Brown was living in one half of one bedroom, everything else in the house was untouched. He had kitted his living space out exactly like a Shotts prison cell: TV and single bed, small wardrobe, a table and chair. Brown grew up in prison. He'd only been out on license for three or four years.

Was Mr. Brown helpful during the search? Not at all, he refused to unlock the padlocked rooms and physically tried to restrain two officers. Did they find arms in Mr. Brown's house? Not in the house but they were found buried in grounds behind the house.

Was there proof that Mr. Brown knew they were there? They had his fingerprints on them. And they were in his garden? Yes, she said. They were in his garden.

Atholl smirked and scribbled on his notes. He knew she and Finchley were playing a game, implying that Brown knew. Possession of a gun, even without knowledge, now carried a mandatory five-year minimum. A postman with a parcel containing a gun could get five years. But guns buried in the garden didn't count as possession. Brown burying them in the garden was a response to cases the ink was barely dry on. Someone was carefully keeping abreast of the case law and she didn't think it was Brown.

Finchley moved it on: what else did they find, therein? A lot of money, shrink-wrapped. Why was that significant? It suggested that the money was about to be—

"Objection." Atholl was on his feet, muttering about conjecture.

Fine. How much money? Half a million in twenty-pound notes. What else did they find that was of interest to the police? Forty iPhones, still in their boxes. Where did they come from? They had been legitimately bought in a number of shops. Each had a receipt sellotaped to it.

Atholl was on his feet again: if the iPhones had been legitimately bought they could not be said to be "of interest to the police." He was wrong, and he knew it, but Finchley conceded. The Crown would have to present another case if they went into the iPhones, a complex case they knew about but had no evidence of.

Drugs money was moved out of the UK through international networks called hundi. A Scottish heroin dealer could visit a hundi man in Scotland and deliver three-quarters of a million pounds in cash. Within a few hours, or even less, the equivalent in Pakistani rupees would be delivered by the hundi contact, often via motorcycle courier to a dealer in Lahore. It was not always drugs transactions, though—sometimes perfectly innocent informal transfers of cash by people with no bank account or faith in conventional banking. But the innocent and the criminal were indistinguishable because the hundi networks had become so complex and fragmented: the cashier was now separate from the hundi man in Pakistan, debt enforcers were separate again and hardly knew who they were working for. Brown was one of many pawns and over the course of their interviews Morrow had become convinced that he knew nothing about who or what he was involved with. Someone knew though, and some lawyer was giving up-to-the-minute legal advice about guns and boundaries, about buying iPhones and sellotaping the receipts to them.

They knew that the forty iPhones would be sent to Pakistan as an end-of-the-quarter settling up between the two hundi contacts. They all knew Brown was the fall guy, the cannon fodder, holding the phones and guns. Only a disposable foot soldier ever held the guns. But they had no evidence and Brown had no interest in helping them lift the veil between the lawyers and the clients. He needed the bad-boy credit points for his triumphant return to prison.

Finchley looked slowly through his file and Morrow shuffled

on her feet. She didn't like being on someone else's turf. The formality, the wigs, the gowns, the archaic language, the accompanying solicitor to whisper to; all of that was designed to let everyone know this was their turf, they were the big boys in this playground.

The macer brought over an evidence bag for her to look at: a clear bag containing a single gun. Everyone in the court shrank back from it. Morrow agreed with Finchley that she had witnessed it being put into the evidence bag and that it was indeed an SA80 assault rifle.

SA80s were standard issue to service personnel in conflict zones abroad. They were automatics, had thirty-round clips, and sights perfect for snap shooting, which meant swinging around and blowing away someone you'd barely had time to look at. The guns had the ID numbers scratched crudely off the barrels but they sliced through the metal and found the number in the deep indentation from the stamp. They had all been lost during the conflict in Afghanistan, where 90 percent of the world's heroin came from. Someone was bringing them back and hawking them to gangsters. She was disturbed at how powerful the guns were, that and their history: they had all been used in the sand and dirt of a conflict zone. Morrow felt as though a little of that distant overseas chaos was seeping back onto her turf.

From the corner of her eye, Morrow saw Brown sitting up tall to see the bag.

The macer saw him shift too and stiffened, the security guards sat straighter, the judge leaned forward, everyone suddenly aware that this was the sort of firepower Brown had at his disposal. Brown sat back and Morrow imagined that he was pleased by the fearful atmosphere in the room. He relished the discomfort of others.

Finchley alone didn't flinch. He rolled through the weapon's specifications, asking her to agree with them as the macer put the assault rifle safely away. Everyone in the courtroom stood down a little.

Brown's fingerprints had been found on the money, the iPhones and the guns. Finchley only asked Morrow about her part in the evidence chain: no, Brown hadn't touched any of them when they were brought out. They'd ask the fingerprint expert to give evidence on the rest of it.

Finchley looked backwards and forwards through his notes, being thorough, being dull. Morrow stole a glance at Brown and saw him whisper to the guard next to him. He looked worried, spoke urgently behind his hand.

Finchley decided that he'd finished, packed his notes neatly into the folder. As he made his way back to his seat the security guard next to Brown beckoned him over and whispered something to him.

Lord Anton Atholl rose, took a sip of water and a small smile rippled across his face. He lifted a messy file and began to speak as he strode across the room.

"DI Morrow," his sonorous voice rumbled around the room, "can you tell me something?"

He sauntered to the jury's side as if he'd spontaneously decided that he wanted to go there and be near them. Actually, it was where he was required to stand. "How *long* did you say you had been in the service?"

Atholl wasn't looking at her, but at the jury. The jury, she was pleased to see, were not looking back at him. They were looking at her.

Morrow answered: "Um, coming up for twelve years."

He nodded, keeping it conversational. "I see. And in that *time* have you, yourself, ever attended a warranted search where the subject of the search was *themselves* happy, and willing, to facilitate yourself, or whomever else was conducting that search, to come into their home and/or place of business?" Atholl raised his bushy eyebrows, incredulous. He had a tic, she'd been told by another officer, of speaking quickly, sounding argumentative, trying to get you off balance. Morrow was good at this game. She did this all the time. She let him wait for the answer, pretending to ponder.

"Sorry," she said, "I'm not really clear what you mean."

From the corner of her eye she saw Finchley on his tiptoes at the bench, whispering up to the noter.

Atholl affected surprise at her statement. He gave a little laugh towards the jury, currying support. He paused and rephrased: "Is it *usual* for a person having their house searched at seven thirty in the morning, by eight officers, some of whom are armed and wearing bullet proof clothing, to simply *throw* the doors open and invite those officers in?"

She thought for a moment, and answered in kind. "In my experience, you really can't say what's usual or unusual. Every search is different."

He swung to face her. "A simple yes or no will suffice."

Again, she let him wait. She took a breath. "I can't answer that with a yes or no."

"It's very simple." He looked at her angrily. "Yes or no: at seven thirty a.m. do most people welcome a search, by eight officers, of their home or not?"

Atholl was making a mistake using this technique on a police officer with her experience. It was a member of the public question.

"Yes," she said, and left it.

"'Yes'?" He gave them suppressed outrage.

"I can think of instances where people have been welcoming when we arrived with search warrants. So sometimes: yes. Also, sometimes no, but you said I have to choose one. So I did."

Atholl looked at her then, a slow-rising eyebrow acknowledging that he'd been trumped. He liked her. She could tell.

"DI Morrow, I find that *very* hard to *believe*," he said with finality.

The judge gave Atholl a warning look, telling him to flirt in his own time. The jury were hardly listening: though they were trying to be discreet they were all aware that a message was being passed around the court. They watched as the noter put a slip of paper on the desk in front of the judge.

Atholl's performance wasn't for the jury, it was for Brown. He was putting on a show of a struggle. He was part of the fireworks display for the prison population. He opened his mouth to speak—

"Well," the judge interrupted, fitting the note into his file, "I think we'll stop there for a moment."

It was bizarrely abrupt. Suddenly the macer was at the foot of the stairs, gesturing to Morrow to come down quickly. Morrow's first thought was a bomb threat.

She hurried down in her noisy shoes and the macer pushed her elbow, turning her to the steep stairs for the witness room. She was barely up and through the door when the court were ordered to rise. As the witness-room door shut on a slow spring Morrow saw the judge exit swiftly, the jury being chased out by an usher and Brown being bundled downstairs to the cells.

The door shut softly on the scene.

Morrow found herself alone in the windowless room, the noise of the court muffled by the door. If it was a bomb threat then she should get out of the building. Normally they'd warn her but maybe they were assuming she'd know because she was a police officer. It was then that she realized she had left her briefcase in the witness box.

She had files in there, her laptop, a USB with other files about ongoing investigations. She had to get it. She lingered behind the court door like an eavesdropper, tried knocking softly but no one came. She could hear people shuffling about in the room, Atholl's rich voice sounded calm and light.

It couldn't be a bomb threat. They would have cleared the building.

She knocked again, louder, and heard someone approaching on the stairs. The macer opened the door and looked in.

"Sorry, I've left my briefcase in there," said Morrow.

"Oh, sure." The macer stepped back to let her in. Morrow tiptoed in her noisy shoes, down the stairs and across to the box.

The court staff were relaxed among themselves, Atholl's solicitor was chatting to the noter, the macer grinned at Atholl as he finished telling a story.

"'Get him OUT!'" said Atholl waving an arm, playing a part. "'Out of my hair!'"

The macer laughed at the punch line and shook her head sadly. "Auch, a great man," she said. "A funny man."

"Yes." Atholl had spotted Morrow climbing back into the box, bending over and reaching for the handle of the briefcase cowering in the dark corner. "Sad. And sixty-four seems young."

"Lungs collapsed, didn't they?"

"After a fall. He smoked so heavily, if it happened spontaneously I wouldn't have been surprised," said Atholl and called over to Morrow, "Did you forget your messages, young lady?"

Morrow stood straight in the box and glared at him. His accent had slipped down several social rungs.

"Well, that was condescending..."

A hush fell in the room. She shouldn't have said that. The convention was that lawyers and cops pretended to get on, they pretended they weren't on opposite sides or drawn from different social groups. The fiction was that they were all part of the same process.

She held the bag up. "My briefcase…" No one wanted to look at her. "Wasn't a bomb threat, then?"

They all glanced at one another, unsure whose jurisdiction covered the business of answering.

The noter took responsibility: "Someone has been taken ill," he said carefully, "and we may adjourn if they're not fit to continue."

Brown was sick. She'd seen him looking gray and passing notes. They didn't want to tell her, or let the jury see him vomit or pass out in case it made them sympathetic. It might still be a trick.

"If he's leaving the building," said Morrow, sorry now for her faux pas, "you need to notify the cops on duty."

The noter looked aggrieved. "We already have."

Morrow had insulted everyone. She wasn't popular at the station, the squad were nearly all new and didn't know her well enough to see past her curt manner and the negative stories attached to her: her old squad had been ripped apart by a bribing scandal, her half brother was a famous local heavy, she said the wrong thing almost always. And now even here she'd managed to piss everyone off. She mumbled a general apology. The noter accepted with a shrug and turned away, cutting her out of the conversation. "So, Atholl, if we do adjourn, are you going?"

"Yes. Want a lift?"

"Only if you're taking a taxi. I'm not going if you're driving."

"Technically, we could walk."

"Uphill?"

Morrow took the stairs down out of the box.

"DI Morrow, did you know Julius McMillan?" Atholl had stepped towards her.

She nodded, wary still. "Sure. Why?"

"He died."

Atholl's eyes were brown with startling yellow flecks around the iris. The whites were tinged yellow. She thought he probably drank too much. She realized suddenly that they were staring at each other.

She hesitated, wondering why she couldn't look away. "What did he die of?"

"Collapsed lungs," he said, and smiled inappropriately. "The poor man smoked sixty a day."

They were still holding one another's eye, each on the brink of a grin. Everyone else in the court was looking away, embarrassed to witness such blatant, honeydewed attraction between two slightly unprepossessing middle-aged people. They began to talk among themselves.

"I'm sorry for sounding condescending." He looked up at her, puppyish. "I didn't mean to."

Morrow hugged her briefcase like a shield. "Aye well, you've insulted me in public and now you're apologizing in private. I think that's a bit crap."

It was no more or less obstreperous than she would have been to anyone. They both broke into inappropriate grins.

Atholl was loving it. He called to the assembly, "DI Morrow: I APOLOGIZE." He stepped closer still. "If we have to adjourn will you come to the funeral party with me? It's in the Art Club. It's only up the road."

"This afternoon?"

"Yes." He took another step closer to her. "You can come in my taxi. We could have a drink."

"I can't. I'm working." She noted that she'd avoided saying "on shift" as she normally would and wondered if she was trying to sound less like someone who would leave their shopping in a witness box.

"I see." Atholl glanced to the side, seeing if they were being listened to. They were, but the others were disguising it well. "Well, that's a shame."

Alex dropped her briefcase to her side and met his smile. It was nice, talking like this, sweet and fun and unthreatening. She hadn't flirted with anyone in a long time. "I'll wait until you tell me if you're adjourning then?"

He took another step, tentative this time, and mumbled, "*After your shift…*"

He looked up, seemed surprised at himself asking her out. They both laughed at how ridiculous it was and Atholl slapped a hand over his eyes.

"God," he said to the ceiling, "after years you forget how painful…I need drink to…"

Morrow laughed. "You recently single?"

He gave a little nod. "Three months. Separated from my wife. I've got three teenage boys."

"I've got a lovely husband and one-year-old twins."

Atholl tipped his head at her, curious. He reached up and took his wig off, held it to his chest, like a gentleman. "Well, DI Alex Morrow, staggering maturity on my part: I find myself pleased to hear that."

She wanted to kiss him. Half laughing at herself, she turned and walked away up the stairs, realizing only when she got to the top that she had made him stare at her backside.

She shut the door behind her, leaned against the door and laughed silently. Ridiculous. He was an advocate and an earl. He probably pulled that act on every prosecution female. Still she smiled, enjoying the afterglow as she pulled her phone out of her bag: it was nice, though.

Turning her phone on she found a flurry of calls from the office. One message from DC Fyfe. Please call back asap.

Sitting as she was in the heart of the building, the signal was low but she called anyway and got Fyfe on a weak line that cut out every three or four words.

"Ma'am…erious problem: "Brown's fingerprints turned up… *last week*."

"What?"

Fyfe spoke slowly: "Brown's fingerprints were foun…at a murder committed…days ago."

Morrow stood still, shuffling the words into order. Finally she said, "*This* Michael Brown?"

Fyfe was certain: "Yes, ma'am."

Morrow couldn't quite take it in. "The one I'm here with now?"

"Yes." Fyfe's voice faded under a smog of crackle. "…prints at a murder…north division…ast week."

It made no sense. Brown was locked up in prison and had been for months. For a moment she found herself suspicious and angry at Fyfe for telling her something that simply could not be true. Irritated, she barked into the mouthpiece, "Wait on the line." And dropped the phone to her side as she strode to the exit door.

Outside the witness waiting room she passed an armed guard who had been waiting for Michael Brown to burst out of there. He turned at the waist to see her, his fingers tightening on the butt and barrel of his gun as she fumbled her wallet open to show her warrant card before backing out to the lobby.

Morrow was wrong: Fyfe was dependable and wouldn't have called to tell her this unless there was good reason. It wasn't Fyfe's fault. Morrow just didn't want to hear it. She had expected Brown to jump a wall or break a window to get out, not start an elaborate game to undermine bits of evidence.

She stood in the lobby and took a deep breath before lifting the phone to speak again: "I'm in a public place: be careful. Now, slowly, tell me that again."

"OK," said Fyfe. "Michael Brown's fingerprints were found at a murder scene in the old Red Road flats."

"The ones they're pulling down?"

"Yep. And the murder happened three days ago."

"Three days, for sure?" she asked.

"Definite. Because they're demolishing the flats they're check-ing for homeless all the time."

"Who's dead?"

"Guy called Aziz Balfour."

Morrow shut her eyes. "Well, he's in prison, Fyfe, there must have been a mistake on the prints, get them to check the match again—"

"They have, ma'am. They've checked and checked. The match was high confidence each time."

"*High* confidence?" Morrow squeezed her eyes tight, reluctant to hear the answer.

"High confidence."

She opened her eyes and found an armed officer, both hands on his assault rifle, staring fiercely at her. She didn't know if he was thinking about shooting her or waiting for an order.

She looked away.

The court lobby was new, part of an extension to the old high court. It was two stories high, one wall of glass, the other three had a mezzanine level running around them with a frieze of yel-low limestone on it. The entire frieze was carved with a jumble of words and letters in different textures, large, small, smooth, rough. Unthinkingly, Morrow read a nonsense phrase carved deep into the frieze:

TURNS OF SPEECH RIDDLES

"Is the dead guy anyone we know?"

"No. Balfour worked for a charity." Morrow could hear that she was reading it from a sheet. "Earthquake Relief. Good man, no record or previous. Three thousand attended his funeral."

"So, he's buried already?"

"Says here cause of death stabbing. Must have released him quick for burial...so that's..."

She was telling Morrow that the man was Muslim but didn't know if it was all right to say it.

Morrow tutted. "So, he was Muslim?"

"Um, yeah, probably. Says he's from Pakistan."

That caught Morrow's attention. Pakistan suggested a potential hundi connection to Brown.

But the prints were impossible. She found herself wondering whether they had been found on something planted there, something movable, a cup or a bit of paper? An accomplice could have taken his prints in. There would be an explanation. She would find it.

"Put it all on my desk." She hung up, slipping her phone into her pocket.

Brown wasn't jumping a wall but it was still a weak opening gambit. Morrow had expected something better. Maybe the lawyer giving him wily advice about inches beyond conveyancing perimeters had ducked out and this was a younger lawyer's advice. It was a change of tone, certainly.

She pulled on her raincoat and thought her way through some possibilities: visitors with cups, visitors with celluloid on their wrists, bribable officers.

She should ask to see the ACE-V report by the fingerprint analyst. The match may well have come up high confidence but there could still be a mistake in the reading. They had to do that now, show their workings, how they analyzed it, how they compared it, verify the points of confluence.

She looked up and saw Anton Atholl. He was walking towards her across the lobby, clutching a bundle of files tied with pink ribbon. She found herself irritated by him now; she didn't want to flirt anymore, her mood had shifted, her thoughts on other things.

Also, there was a duty of disclosure to Brown's defense. She didn't know the time frames or parameters of telling Atholl about the prints. If there was bogus mileage in it, Atholl was the last person she wanted to tell. The Fiscal's office were already pissed off about the cost of the trial and knew they weren't getting the major players. Brown was back in prison anyway and the trial was costing them a fortune. Everyone was on a budget these days.

"We are adjourning," said Atholl. "But we'll meet again to-morrow?"

She wondered suddenly if he already knew about the prints. Atholl might have had them put there, for all she knew.

"Yeah." Morrow wondered if Atholl was waiting for her to tell him.

"You all off to get steaming this afternoon, then?"

"Indeed," he said, nodding formally at his shoes. "It seems only proper in the light of a great drunk's passing. I did my traineeship with McMillan."

She was a little surprised he was young enough to have studied under McMillan. "You trained under him? I thought you were the same age, sort of..."

He tutted playfully. "I'm not as old as I look," he said, "I've just had a lot of adventures. No"—suddenly stern—"we must all go. Lend a little support to poor Margery. She's his wife. I'm sort of looking for people to go with..."

She wanted to leave, get back to the office right now but was worried that it would seem abrupt and arouse his suspicion. "Did they have kids?"

"One." He looked away, towards the wall of light. But for the daylight catching she wouldn't have noticed the thin tear brimming in his eye. "A son."

He had a nice profile, a good big nose.

"I have to go."

Atholl bowed from the neck and backed away. "See you tomor-row."

She walked off, slow-clapping herself through the metal detector. She took the revolving door and turned to the car park. From the corner of her eye she saw Atholl through the big window just as a white van pulled out and obscured her view. She walked on towards her car, glancing back to see if Atholl was still standing there, watching her.

He wasn't.

3
1997

It was half ten on Sunday morning and Julius McMillan was watching the television news. Princess Diana was dead. Great racking sobs spewed up from his abdomen like hiccups, his eyes ran, tears dripping into his open mouth; he didn't even know he was capable of such depth of emotion. He was crying so hard he couldn't manage to light a cigarette. His eighteen-year-old son, Robert, and Margery, his wife, were still in bed, either asleep or avoiding him. He couldn't let them see him crying. He wouldn't be able to explain why he was so upset. He was afraid that if they found him and asked him he might blurt something about the clients' missing funds: the disaster looming on his own horizon.

Diana, betrayed and alone, always pictured alone. Betrayed but hopeful, still looking for love. She still cared about other people, about landmines and AIDS patients. She loved all the people. She had boyfriends, was still looking for love. But no one thought about how she felt. No one cared how alone and overwhelmed she felt. No one knew how frightened she was sometimes. Diana must have had staff who loved her—they couldn't know her and not love her—but Julius had no one. He was in a bind, needed money and Dawood McMann was circling, hinting that he knew about his situation, offering a way out. *Help me to help you.*

What Dawood wanted would be illegal. He was a strange character—Julius couldn't see his endgame at all. He floated from one set to the other—lawyers, city councillors, union leaders—never settling, never belonging. But he was half Scottish, half Pakistani, maybe he was used to straddling and that's just what he did.

Julius knew one thing though: Dawood was picking him because he knew he was desperate. The investment firm looking for their money back must have told Dawood about it, that they were one week away from starting a legal action against him. *I want you because you know people.* Julius knew everyone. *This will need a number of people.* He kept saying it—a number of dedicated, loyal people. *It is a long-term thing, a good thing. Help me to help you, Julius.*

But Julius couldn't. Anton Atholl worked for Julius, he knew McMann wanted a deal. If there was a whiff of a deal between them, Anton Atholl would tell the police. Atholl had a thing about Dawood McMann. He told Julius not even to talk to the man. He had *heard* things about him, wouldn't go into detail. Atholl hated McMann so much that Julius felt he'd do time himself, just to fuck McMann over. Julius explained it to Dawood: Atholl won't go along with it, he just won't. Let me help, said Dawood. A week later he gave Julius the photograph. A Polaroid. Atholl drunk. Very drunk. It was revolting but not illegal. It didn't help Julius at all.

The phone rang, jagged and loud. Julius jumped up to get it, afraid they'd hear it upstairs, come downstairs and catch him crying.

A murder case at Stewart Street station. Juvenile, a girl, care-home case, found in a car with a dead man, saying she did it. Could he come in?

Twenty-five minutes, he said and hung up, glad of something to think about other than Diana dying in Paris, alone.

He went to his downstairs bathroom. No one else used it and he kept his shaving things and his toothbrush in there, so that he didn't have to disturb his son or his wife. They all kept out of one another's way as much as possible. The bathroom was in an awkward part of the house, through the cold-floored utility room. Black spots of mold flourished on the silicone seals around the never-used bath. One of the bulbs over the mirror had gone ages ago. He had to shave in virtual silhouette.

He ran the water until it was warm and put the plug into the sink before looking up at himself. Red eyes, a weak, twitching mouth and he saw what Diana had seen the night they met.

It was years before, at a charity ball, a dreary affair in the Royal Academy in Edinburgh. She sat at a distant table, a blond smudge next to other smudges. Julius didn't care much. After dinner they gave the loyal toast. Julius crossed his fingers as he drank it and then lit a longed-for cigarette. Diana stood and read a faltering speech while Julius smoked and calculated his journey back to Glasgow.

Somehow they all came to be standing as she left the room. She came past Julius's table and stopped.

"I saw you smoking," she said.

"I was gasping," he said, his mind still on the journey home.

She smiled right at him, taller than him, luminous. "*Gaspers,*" she said. "Terribly bad for you." Terribly bad for you. Not carping, not like that, tender, as if she was concerned.

Then, quite suddenly, Julius was in the room, in Edinburgh, with Princess Diana. She was beautiful. Long necked, a choker of small pearls, six or eight rows of them, such a long neck. She wore a purple dress, sleeveless, the skin of her arms was bronzed and flawless.

She left, gliding through the assembled tables, but Julius stayed in the room with her. He never told anyone how he felt about that. He would have been ashamed. He was a Republican, anti-Royalist by instinct and tradition. But he couldn't deny it to himself: the sensation that he had met someone much, much better than him and that she had cared whether or not he smoked.

Now she was dead.

Julius saw the footage of people sobbing at the gates of Kensington Palace, strangers clutching one another, lucky not to live in cynical Glasgow, a city exhausted of sorrow.

He lathered soap on his cheek and scratched it off, aware that the blade was wrong, that a flaw was scratching tiny welts in his skin, but too sad to stop. He splashed water on his cheeks, washing the soap off his sore face and patting it dry. The towel smelled faintly sour.

Defeated, he lit a cigarette and examined the grief-stricken face in the mirror. You could tell, just looking at him.

He would tell the police officers that he was hungover. He took the cigarette out of his mouth, lifted his shoulders as if his head hurt. He lowered his eyelids into a half wince. A hangover. That's what he would say. If Diana came up he'd say he'd heard about it and then move away. He couldn't discuss her with any of them. He just couldn't.

Julius finished his cigarette in the corridor outside the holding cell interview room. He glanced in at Rose Wilson through the wired glass in the viewing slot.

The glass was scratched on the inside, almost opaque, but he could see that she was tiny. She was sitting at a steel table. When they found her she was covered in blood and her clothes had been taken as productions. The prison issue hung off her, as if she'd shrunk in them.

Julius dropped his cigarette and stamped it out, nodding to the officer on duty. The cop came over and took out his big brass key, fitted it in the door and opened it.

She looked up at him.

She had been covered in blood when they found her. They'd given her a basin to wash in but no mirror. Her face was washed with watered blood. Every future furrow, every crease that would one day be, picked out in dried crimson. It was in the folds of her forehead, the laughter lines around her mouth, the prophetic tracks of sorrow under her eyes. This newborn ancient looked up at Julius with the eyes of a disappointed mother.

Aware that he was stalled at the door, he dropped his chin and forced himself to walk into the room, taking in what he could bear to look at. She wore a baggy gray T-shirt and a pair of gray track-suit bottoms, rolled up at the ankle into a fat rim. Her hair was brown, quite short. It looked as if she had cut it herself because it was shorter at one side than the other. She was miniature enough to evoke wonder, like a baby's fingernails, but these fingernails were black with dried blood.

The door scraped shut behind him, the lock crunched closed as he sat down opposite her. He didn't want to look up. He busied himself getting a notebook and pen out of his pocket, putting them on the table, straightening them.

She was looking straight up at him. "The fuck are you?"

"I'm Julius McMillan. Mr. McMillan. I'm your lawyer."

He had brought her a bar of chocolate. He always did with young offenders. He brought fags for the older kids. That was all it took, a cheap gift made them loyal customers for life. That's why he liked young offenders, they kept the office number and used it again later, and there nearly always was a later. He had clients he'd been representing for twenty years. But Rose Wilson didn't look as if she could be bought by chocolate.

"So, Rose, what's the story here?"

She looked at the wall. She raised a hand and scratched her cheek, flaking off a dusting of rust. He saw then that she wasn't old, didn't look old. She was nothing special, just a child. He picked up his pen.

"What age are you?"

She smiled at the wall but her smile looked bitter because of the lines on her face. "Fourteen," she said. "But I look sixteen."

She looked a hundred today.

Julius wrote it down. "And where do you live?"

"*Live?*"

"*Stay,*" he said, using the vernacular. "Where do you *stay?*"

"Turnberry." She watched his notebook, waiting for him to write it.

"The kids' home?"

"Kids' home, yeah."

He wrote it down for her. "And how long have you been staying there for?"

"Two year."

These were questions he could answer with a glance at her file but he was trying to get her talking as a warm-up to the difficult events of the charge. When she got going he would be able to jot it down, put in a guilty plea, get out and think about this Dawood situation.

"You like it there?"

She raised a shoulder. She was looking at the wall again.

"Is it OK?"

"Mm."

"Like the staff?"

She shook her head a fraction. "Mm."

"Chocolate?" Julius put the Dairy Milk bar on the table and pushed it over to her with his fingertips.

He watched her looking at it. She wanted it but didn't take it. Instead she looked at the door, suspicious. He followed her eyeline. She was making sure the viewing slot was open. She looked at the chocolate again, wanted it again, but shook her head and shrank back from it.

"I'll leave it there in case you change your mind," said Julius casually. "Do you smoke?"

She shook her head. "Makes me chuck." She was very suspicious now and sat further back in her chair. "You smoke. I can smell ye. Spark up if you want."

"So, what happened to you last night?"

"Went out..."

McMillan didn't say anything.

"Went out..." she said again, waiting for an interruption that never came.

"OK." He put his pen down. "Let's start with what you have told the police about what happened last night."

Desolate, her mouth hanging open, she stared beyond him to the wall. "Nothing..."

"You've said nothing? They've questioned you, haven't they? Brought you into an interview room and taped you talking?"

"Found me in his car." She was shocked, drawling. "Haven't been taped."

He knew then that they had so much overwhelming physical evidence against her that they didn't need a confession. "Did you tell them you did it?"

"Yeah."

"Did you do it?"

"Yeah."

"What did you do?"

"Stabbed him."

"Where did you get the knife?"

She fell back into shock. Slowly her forehead rose to meet the map of bloody wrinkles.

Julius put his fingertips on the chocolate bar and pushed it closer to her. "Eat that now."

She picked it up and fumbled with the wrapper, her fingers unfocused. He took it off her and undid it, pulling the entire wrapper off and handing it over to her. "Eat at least half."

She did eat half and he watched her. She didn't swallow because her mouth was dry but kept chewing, waiting for her saliva glands to start working. The habit of compliance. She had been ordered around a lot.

"You've been in care for a few years since your mum died, haven't you?"

She looked up at that, dutifully chewing dry mud. "Julius McMillan," she said, rolling her chocolate-stuck mouth around the strange name. She flicked a finger from him to herself. "What's this?"

"What?"

"This." She flicked again, faster. "The point of this."

"I'm here to help you."

A sharp smirk, quick as a blink. "Help me? How's my life not going to be shit anyway?"

He looked up. There was no self-pity, no real sorrow. Rose Wilson was resigned to desolation. She had fully, without rancor, surrendered to the pity of life. He saw her next to the car in the Paris tunnel, shrugging. He pictured her at the gates of Buchenwald with her hands resting in her tracksuit pockets, sorry about the queues of women and children, but accepting. He saw her through every catastrophe in history, standing at the side, an impassive witness.

He asked her, "Did you hear about Princess Diana?"

She fell back in her chair, shrank into the tracksuit and whispered in a voice channeled from elsewhere, "She was young to die..." Her eyes brimmed with trembling tears and she said, "And those boys..."

They sat at the table, heads bent as if in prayer. They stayed there for a while. When he looked up Julius saw wet tear tracks on her cheeks.

Quite abruptly, because of the tears maybe, Julius recognized her. He had seen her before. She was *the* girl. Of course, Samuel McCaig, the deceased, it was Sammy the Perv. Of course it was her. He never thought he'd meet her face to face, but she was sitting here right in front of him. She could make everything all right for him.

"What age are you, again?"

"Fourteen."

Fourteen. Illegal. It was perfect. And he had her here, in his sole and exclusive power and he had the power to keep her close.

"I can help you," he said, not certain he could but certain he wanted to. Confused by his adamance, he said it again, "I can help you."

The flashing smirk again, softer now because she had been crying. "You gonnae give the judge chocolate?"

"This," Julius lifted a finger to the room, "I know how to work *this*." His turn to whisper. He said it as if they were conspiring children.

Intrigued, she nodded him on.

"I knew Samuel. I know what sort of man he was."

"He was a perv."

"That's what they called him, wasn't it? Sammy the Perv."

She nodded.

"He had a string of convictions for sexual offenses against young girls. Did you know that?"

"Yeah. "'S how they called him Sammy the Perv."

"OK, Rose." He put down his pen. "Rose, this could end in a long sentence for you or a short one. Either way you'll get detention, understand?"

She nodded, listening intently.

"The *way* we tell the story is what will decide if it's a long or a short sentence."

She leaned in. "Get a short one."

"Yes, we want to make it short. So here's the story we need to tell: you didn't know he was called Sammy the Perv. You didn't know he had a string of convictions. You thought he was a friendly man, you're a lonely child, be a child on the stand, in interviews, OK? No more swearing. They don't want that. No more 'my life's shite anyway,' no one wants to hear that from a child."

"What do they want?"

"They want you to hope."

"Hope what?"

"To have hope."

"What kind of hope?"

"Hope you'll be a pop star, hope you'll be a vet, find true love, things like that."

She looked at him for a moment, hardly believing him, and barked a startled laugh. "Mr. McMillan—"

"That's what people want from children. You need to act like that. If you don't know what to say, say nothing. And try to cry."

"I don't cry."

He loved her for that, because she had cried over Diana.

"Just think of something that makes you cry and do it."

Looking into a distant corner, she thought about it for a while. "How long do I need to keep that up for?"

"Long as you can. After the trial anyway. Can you do it?"

She held her hands up in surrender, palms scarred with a thousand years' hard labor. "I'll try."

"Here's our story: you were lonely and you met Sammy and he was friendly. You got in his car and he attacked you, OK?"

"OK…"

"I'm not going to ask about your relationship with him. If anyone else asks, you only just met him that night."

Julius looked at her, waiting for the questions. None. He looked at her and saw suddenly how long her neck was and a rope of blood around it. He took out his cigarettes and lit one with his gnarled old hands and looked at the second half of the chocolate bar, nodding her to it.

She picked it up and put the whole thing in her mouth, smiling through shit-smeared teeth. He smiled back and they sat across from each other, he smoking, she chewing hard on the rest of the chocolate. She was going to save him, make everything all right.

"I'm going to make everything all right for you, Rose Wilson," he said finally. "I'm going to give you a second chance."

She threw her head back and looked down her nose at him, wary, angry. "What you asking back?"

"I want us to be friends for a long time. I'll visit you in prison, stay close, take an interest."

"Right, I'm not fucking you or anyone else, I'm done wi' that."

"As a friend."

She swallowed her chocolate and considered his offer. "OK."

4

Robert McMillan had hired a castle on the island of Mull because he didn't want to die at home.

Sitting alone in his car, heavy rain thrumming on the roof, he looked up, disappointed. Really, it was more of a Gothic mansion. It wasn't big enough to count as a castle.

His phone was in the passenger seat. He had turned it off as he left Glasgow. He couldn't bring himself to listen to the messages from Uncle Dawood. *Come home*, that's what the messages would say. *Come home, we miss you, we're worried, your mother is worried.*

Uncle Dawood had phoned six times before Robert left Glasgow. He didn't know that Robert had looked in the back safe, didn't know Robert understood what they'd been doing. When the police found Robert dead the messages would still be there. Robert wanted them to go and see Dawood after his body was found.

The fact of his death ambushed him again, horrifying, absolute. Robert held tight to the steering wheel, fingers stiff, palms prickling with sparks of sweat.

He glanced at the digital clock on the dashboard. The funeral had started, they'd be singing at the crematorium. Uncle Dawood would give the eulogy. Charity work. All those trips to Pakistan. Kind man. Sugared lies. Robert wondered if it started with Dawood, was it his idea, but it didn't matter who it started with. It started. That was all.

Valiant windscreen wipers were engaged in a futile war with fat raindrops. Wipe and ruin, wipe and ruin. Robert found himself charting the hopeless struggle for order instead of looking beyond it to the view. Narrow focus. He was angry with himself. If he had done this a long time ago, looked closer, paid attention to minutiae, he wouldn't be here now. His father had only told him about the safe in his delirium, but there must have been other clues. He should have paid attention.

He turned off the engine and sat for a moment, mouth slack, swollen eyes itching, feeling the heat of the engine seep away. The funeral service might be finished already, he wasn't sure how long these things took.

Afterwards they would mill outside and then go back to a hotel or something; his mother wouldn't want people in her house. They'd drink and talk about what a great man he was, how funny, how charming, how community-minded. No mention of Robert or his absence. Margery would get drunk and the gathering of strangers would pretend it was because she had lost her husband. They'd all know, really, that she had an unhappy history with drink.

Rose would be ushering the kids down the aisle, Francine walking behind, two steps behind. Sometimes, he felt as if Rose and Francine were the real couple, as if he was working to finance their life together.

The car was getting cold. His buttocks were damp from sitting in the warmed seat on the long drive from the ferry. The rain got heavier suddenly, stealing the light, turning the inside of the car blue and green. Cadaverous, he thought, a coffin car.

The women would have dressed the kids in appropriate clothes: suits for the boys and a dress for Jessica, black but good quality. They could wear them again for his funeral.

A sharp knock on the side window made him jump in his seat. The worn crotch of a pair of pink jeans was eye-level with Robert. He flinched away from it. Rather than bend down to look in the window, the owner of the crotch stepped back as if he had a bad back and didn't want to bend.

He was an old hippie, had long gray hair pulled back in a ponytail and he was holding a woman's umbrella, white, frilly and yellowed at the edges where it had been wet and dried.

"Yeah, McMillan?" The low voice was muffled through the glass.

Robert sat for a moment, watching him. The rain ran down the window, melting the hippie's face over and over. Robert thought, this could be the face of death. This hippie could be the one they'd sent to kill him. But he'd probably just have shot Robert through the window if he was. The man's face was in the shadow of the umbrella but Robert could see his mouth quivering through the rain and saw him try to make a warm, welcoming smile. It withered instantly to a baring of teeth. He wasn't used to smiling.

The man's eyes narrowed over the roof and then he looked back, suspicious. "You McMillan? D'you hire the castle?"

"Yes, sorry," said Robert through the window and waited. The hippie didn't shoot him. It was time to get out.

He opened the glove compartment, pulled out the envelope full of money and opened the driver's door. He swung a leg out into the lashing rain, watching his suit trousers and the upholstered interior of the car door getting wet. He turned his torso and brought the other leg out. The rain hit the back of his neck, cold, fresh.

He stood up, shut the car door and handed him the envelope. "That's the money," he said.

The hippie took it, squeezed it as if he could count it by feel and put it in his back pocket.

Robert found himself looking away from the house, at a path into a deep forest of Scots pine, the floor thick with ferns glittering with silver tears. Even to him, it looked quite beautiful.

"So, yeah." The hippie was happy now. He swung a loose hand at the house. "Brolly?"

He was a good deal taller than Robert. Robert stood in the rain, rolled a shoulder, mentally simulating the ungainly walk of a tall and small person sharing an umbrella.

"No," he said, "let's, just, go inside."

"Yeah." The gangly man set off for the steps leading up to the grand storm doors.

The doors opened into a stone porch with a glass door beyond into the hallway.

In the shelter of the porch the hippie put his umbrella down and turned back to the steps, shaking off the rain by flapping it open and shut. It smelled stale, and as he flapped it the whiff of mildew billowed back at them.

Robert looked out at the view. An angry sea battered the white sands below. High sheer cliffs on either side, topped with high hills, green as felt. The rain was so heavy it flattened the grass on the lawn, bounced five inches off a long bench looking out to sea. And yet, beyond the bay, a wide slanting column of sunshine out at sea.

"Yeah, so, come in?" said the hippie, opening the door.

Robert did as he was told and the hippie shut the door behind him.

The castle was lovely inside. The hallway was painted a cheerful yellow, walls hung with muted, cheerful pictures of no great
value. At the end of the short hall a stairwell curled up, the banister a sensuous sweep of warm cherry wood. The hippie must have
prepared for him coming and put the heating on because it was
warm. A small fire was set in a pink drawing room to their right.

"Warm," muttered Robert.

"Yeah." The man held a hand up to a corridor leading off the
hall. "Kitchen."

Robert walked where he was told. The hippie followed and
rolled through a series of facts: here is the fridge. This is the ther-
mostat. Here is an oven.

Robert watched him. The man was wearing a woman's green
velvet knee-length coat over an orange suit shirt. Velvet seemed
an odd thing to wear in such bad weather. And it was a woman's
coat: he could see the breast darts. It was good lush velvet, the rain
had spattered over the hem, sinking deep into the material and
one of the sleeves. When he reached over to point at something
Robert saw that the lining was pink silk with tiny hummingbirds
on it, as if the man had pulled a tiny exotic garden around himself.

"This one's our cupboard so please don't use the stuff in it.
This is yours." He opened the cupboard next to it. The shelf was
lined with used goods left by other holidayers: bottles of ketchup,
Waitrose teabags, salt from Morrison's, fancy herbs for cooking a
special dish—lemon pepper, allspice.

"You live here?" asked Robert.

"Downstairs. Please don't come down unless something goes
wrong. I don't like being disturbed. I, uh, do meditation."

Robert couldn't let it go. "I thought I had exclusive use of the
house."

"You won't see me again."

"But you'll be downstairs?"

"I'm the housekeeper." He walked away. "The TV room is down here."

Alarmed, Robert followed him down the corridor. He found himself in a small room with a crappy TV in the corner.

The hippie pointed vaguely at a table. "The remotes are in that drawer."

"Look," Robert said firmly, "I needed the house to be empty. That's what I'm paying for, for exclusive use."

The man looked at him for a moment, his mouth hanging open. Robert sounded too fervent, he knew he did. He could see the man run through the possibles: you're going to hang yourself in my kitchen. You're planning to burn the place down. Robert saw him decide to be firm and grind his teeth in preparation.

"No. I live downstairs," he said unequivocally. "I'm the house-keeper."

"You live here?" Robert pointed to the floor. "All the time? It was my understanding, from the conditions in the lease, that I would have sole use of the castle for the duration of my stay here."

The hippie was looking at Robert's mouth, trying to process what he had said. "I live downstairs," he repeated. "I'm just there if there are any problems."

"What sort of problems?"

"Boiler can be a bit tricky. The wood might run out."

"I wanted sole use of the castle."

He processed the thought. "D'you want your money back?"

"No. I want *you* to go *away*."

The lights were off and they stood in the dark of a faux night, looking away from each other.

After a while the hippie sidled past Robert to the corridor, careful not to touch him, and continued with his speech. "There's a toilet there. The flush is sticky but just give it a good yank. The library is in here."

He went through a large door. Robert followed, his heart racing. The hippie couldn't be here. Men were coming to kill Robert and they'd kill a housekeeper or a gardener without a thought.

The library was a newer addition to the building, a large square room with double height ceilings and windows that peeped around the shoulder of the house to the sea. Floor-to-ceiling bookshelves were built from a red wood, not terribly nice and hardly varnished at all. An upright piano sat in the corner, next to a large mahogany writing desk. The fireplace was huge, flanked by well-loved couches and a large square table between them with drawers for keeping games in.

The hippie pointed out the wood basket for the fire and the matches, the newspaper kindling.

"There's extra wood outside."

"Couldn't you go away?" said Robert desperately. "If I pay extra?"

"No."

"Why not?"

"Don't want to."

"I've got cash."

The hippie looked very suspicious now. He glared down his nose at Robert. "When are the rest of your party coming?"

He clearly thought Robert was ill and was hoping someone else would come and look after him.

"Probably tomorrow," lied Robert.

He grunted, looked out of the window as if he hoped to see them there, unexpectedly early. "Suppose the afternoon ferry'll be canceled because of the storm."

The hippie turned away then, heading back for the hallway. Robert followed him. As the hippie slunk down the corridor Robert saw him reach out a hand without glancing around, his fingers running across an ornament on the window sill. Robert hurried after him and, glancing down, saw a small brass statue of Pan. The furry-trousered god was blowing two pipes and skipping a dance on a gray marble plinth. The patina of the statue was black except for one hoof which was rubbed a shining bronze; it caught the light from the kitchen. The hippie had been here for a very long time. Robert thought suddenly that he must have grown up here.

He was waiting for Robert at the bottom of the stairs. "The bedrooms are upstairs," he said, and set off.

Upstairs he pointed to two doors. "Master bedroom. Bathroom adjoining."

He opened a door and Robert followed him in. A four-poster bed with a tester covered and canopied in blue toile and a matching bedspread. Windows looking out over the castellated entrance porch and beyond to the bay. The patch of sun at sea had gone, nothing but gray rain. The white sand of the beach had a filthy black rim.

"Are you the owner?"

The hippie seemed uncomfortable at that. He pointed at a door. "Bathroom." He hesitated then, and turned away, leaving the room.

Robert watched him walk away, noting the slight blush on the back of the man's neck.

Out of the window the dark hills glowered. Whoever they had sent to kill him might be here already, they knew where he was all the time. They might have caught the ferry before him and could be out there now, on the hills, watching the lights flick on in the rooms, tracing their movement through the house. Robert wanted to shout out to the hippie, tell him that if he stayed here he would die. He should run, get out, visit a friend or a relative, just get out. But if Robert did that the man would call the police. Robert couldn't have the police here. Worse, he might call a doctor—Robert did seem strange, he knew that already. He hadn't changed his suit in two days and he had been drinking. He probably smelled odd. They would take him to the local hospital, they'd hear that his father had died. They'd mistake his terror for grief and sedate him, so that he couldn't even think for the last few hours of his life. And then the murderer would kill whoever else got in their way.

As he processed these thoughts the hippie stared at him from the corridor. The house was terribly silent.

"Why do you want to be alone?" he asked.

Robert didn't know what to say. "My father's…" He didn't know what to say. "Just died."

"Oh." He looked at the floor and then pointed at another door. "Twin room."

Robert looked out of the window. He could hear the hippie padding around the house, now outside the door, now on the stairs. Robert didn't move. He watched the sea claw at the beach. He watched the sky bicker with the land. He watched the opposing cliffs growl at each other. He had tried to remove himself, to make it safe for other people. He could just as well have gone to a Premier Inn by a motorway and paid with a credit card.

There were family pictures around the room. Robert registered it as the home of a nice, old-money family. His parents' house wasn't old money or nice money. His family home was a big Bearsden status symbol but inside was dirt and chaos, misery running down the walls, dripping from the curtains, everything sticky dirty because Margery met the cleaning woman at the door twice a week and paid her to go away.

In moments of calm like this Robert knew that he was at a crisis point in his life. He was drinking too much, like his mother, making bad decisions, like his father. A lot of men went through a nihilistic period in their lives, when they wanted to die, he was sure. But in it, right in the eye of the storm, he felt certain it was true and that the periods of his life where he had hoped and loved and felt connected to other people, those were the times when he had been pitifully deluded.

He couldn't honestly remember the ages of his kids. Nine, eight and seven, was it? Was Jessica seven yet? He hoped she was. Give me the man until he is seven, as Nietzsche said.

He didn't see that much of them. He got in from work after they went to bed, left for work before they got up. He worked most weekends. He didn't know them.

Every year they went on holiday to his father's villa in Nice. It was like going away with cantankerous strangers. Robert remembered the holiday this year, sitting on that sun lounger at the edge of a hotel swimming pool. He was sitting in the sun, pretending to read the same shit book that everyone else was reading that year, minding the children in the pool while Rose and Francine went shopping. The kids were screaming at each other, pushing each other around, the seven-year-old (was she seven yet?) was shouting "You're *ugly*" at her brother. Robert knew he should do something, take control, get in the pool and make them behave, but he looked at them and realized he didn't know these people. A waiter, a stranger, would have had more sway over them. He didn't know them. He sat there, listening and wondering if he was lying to himself, if he just couldn't be bothered getting up and was making excuses. He wasn't. He didn't know these people. He'd started to cry, just quietly, and then he realized the children weren't shouting anymore. He looked up. They were staring at him, waiting for him to tell them to shut up. And everyone around the swimming pool knew that he was in charge and he'd done nothing, and now that he was crying.

Better this way. His father and himself gone within weeks of each other. A sad story for later in their lives but the stain dealt with in a short brutal swipe. He half hoped they would make it look as if he had committed suicide, so that the story would end with his funeral instead of dragging out through an investigation and possibly a trial. He had seen those families worn thin by the long slow process of a murder trial, seen them wait and hope and dream that they would feel better soon. He had witnessed the crushing fury at the end: the sentence was never long enough, the culprit never sorry enough. They all made the mistake of thinking the trial was for their benefit. Arrogant in a way, the assumption that all the institutions of State would whir into action to lessen their loss.

Tomorrow, probably. The storm was gathering strength. Even if they hired a private boat they would have trouble getting over tonight.

This would be his last night then. He thought of final meals, watching TV, building a fire, a good sleep. He didn't really want any of those things. He didn't want anything but for it to be over. He was ready to die.

He looked out of the window at the fierce waves trying again and again to claw their way up the sheer cliffs and he took comfort in the knowledge that though he would die, he'd be taking the right people with him. The hippie was annoying anyway. He didn't do meditation, Robert guessed he was smoking cannabis down there. He probably grew it himself. He talked like a stoner too: delayed speech, odd clothes, and he hadn't even left home. So better him than the kids or Rose and Francine or his mother, or the people in a local hospital.

He was damp. His suit was sticking to him. He had a poly bag in the car with other trousers in it. He went downstairs, feeling in his pocket for the car key.

"Hey." It was the hippie. He was in the drawing room, standing in front of the small fire, as if he had been there a good long time, waiting for him.

Robert touched his damp jacket. "I need to..."

The hippie pointed to a small table standing at the elbow of a comfy couch. Sitting on it, glinting invitingly, were two large crystal glasses. In each was a finger of dark amber liquid.

"Whisky?"

"Aberlour. Twenty-five years old. Take it. Drink."

Robert forgot the damp prickle of his clothes; he kept his eyes on the whisky and went into the warm pink room.

5

Darkness was falling, winter-early, as heavy rain stole what was left of the day. The Bath Street traffic crawled respectfully around two black Daimlers parked outside the Glasgow Art Club.

Passing drivers craned to see the funeral party, the sleek solemnity of the big cars, the blackness of the mourners' dress. They slowed for a glimpse of the memento mori, briefly remembered how sad it was that death was always happening to strangers, before driving onwards towards bland lunchtime sandwiches and afternoons squandered as if their own lives would go on forever.

Rose stood by the car holding a big umbrella over the door. The children scrambled out, giggling at the frantic rain ricocheting off the pavement, nipping at their ankles.

The Art Club was in an elegant Georgian townhouse in the center of the city. A broad staircase swept up from the street, furnished with cast-iron boot scrapes. It led up to twin doors of elaborate carved oak, branches to frame the heavy leaded glass looking into the club's lobby. Margery had booked it for the funeral drinks. Rose didn't see why. It meant that they had to go all the way back into town from the crematorium, with three frustrated children, to a room full of already quite drunk lawyers. Rose did not like her kids there, in a room like that. It felt unsafe; small people near big, drunk people. She didn't like the company either, their phony, aggravating cynicism, barks of laughter that depended solely on the speaker's status. It was exhausting remembering who she was supposed to be with them.

She clucked and harried her gaggle up the steps to the door. They were only here to imprint them with the memory of the event. They didn't need to participate in the party. She guessed thirty, forty minutes would be long enough. Fifty, if there were speeches. Please don't let there be speeches. She didn't want to be here a minute longer than she had to be.

From the shelter of the doorway she turned back to see Dawood, Francine and Margery coming out of the front car. Dawood hung back, watching as Margery walked slowly to the steps. She took hold of the handrail, sighed and began the climb. She was only sixty-three. Francine held on to the opposite handrail, paralleling. They walked up the steps in tandem, brackets around the chasm between them.

Behind them, through the veil of gray rain, Rose saw the funeral cars skulk back into the stream of traffic, panthers returning to the hunt.

Margery arrived in the porch. As the Art Club member she was the only one who could press the buzzer and be let in, but she made them wait. She stood in the oak porch and critically appraised the children, then Francine. Francine stood with her hands passively at her sides until Margery was finished, too tired to resist. Only Dawood escaped the inspection.

"You," aloof, Margery pointed at Rose, "you wait here. We'll go in first. Wait for a moment, then come in."

Rose dropped back on her heels, enveloped by the dark corner.

She looked down and found Jessica grinning up at her, baring her gappy teeth, too young to be embarrassed at her granny belittling the staff. Hamish, ten years old and young enough to believe in fairness, glared at his grandma, his mouth tight and furious.

Margery didn't care; she had turned away to press the buzzer and put her flat hand on the ornately carved door, waiting for the lock to snap. The door dropped open, a growl of chat and laughter yawned out at them.

Margery, matriarch of her clan, entered her club. Francine followed behind, eyes radiating fervent apologies back at Rose. Rose gave her a reassuring blink and cupped the back of Hamish's head as he passed her.

The door shut between them. Keeping her face neutral for the children, Rose watched them through the fingered glass. The family of Julius McMillan assembled, braced themselves and processed into his funeral party.

The slight stung. They shouldn't treat her like that. But then, she countered to herself, they were bereaved. Julius was a terrible, shocking loss to them, and Robert might be dead for all they knew. Plus, Margery was Margery. She was a doll in her day, Mr. McMillan used to say. Though her charm and looks were gone she still retained the mannerisms of someone with massive social cachet. She treated all women, even seven-year-old Jessica, as a potential rival.

So although Rose was slighted and upset and scared, she knew that she had been those things before. She had been those things very recently and she knew she wouldn't die of them. She could choose the thoughts in her head. She decided to use this time alone to remember who she was here. It had been a hard week, confusing, sore and busy. I'm a nanny, she thought. She corrected herself and smiled—I'm *the* nanny. I don't go out. I don't meet people. I'm the nanny. The shy, nearly thiry nanny. I don't have hobbies. I have no past. I'm the nanny. The persona came over her like a cassock. Her shoulders rolled forward, her eyes dropped, her jaw loosened.

So she knew who she was, and still there was time to waste. She glanced around and found herself alone, quite invisible to the passersby hunched in the heavy rain. She could remember Mr. McMillan. Rose took a step out towards the darkness of the street, shut her eyes and raised her face to the sky.

Small rain speckled her cheeks and forehead. She saw Mr. McMillan, his face, his baggy old eyes, his tar-yellowed teeth and fingers. She saw him and she said a prayer to him, in her own accent, her old accent: thank you, Mr. McMillan. Thank you for your kindness in this shitty fucking dump of a world.

Mr. Julius McMillan, LLB (Hons), sprinkled soft rain down on her and smiled. She saw him opening a chocolate bar. She saw him smoking a fag. She saw him weep because Diana was dead. Because of Mr. McMillan she didn't think compunction was a weakness anymore. She didn't see it as a chance. She saw it as a state of grace, a window for redemption. Not that he was the best man who ever lived, but Mr. McMillan was her redeemer.

The Art Club door opened at her back, catching her heel. Two men, not with the funeral party, were coming out, a little tipsy, smiling. Rose caught the door on the back swing.

Inside, she kept her eyes to the floor and tracked the murmur of the funeral party. Through a grand hallway and a large door, across a bar, through a small door. She had never been in here before and stopped at the threshold to take it in.

It was a gallery room. Two stories tall and as wide as the town house itself, and the ceiling had a long window running the full length of it, lending natural light to an exhibit of paintings. In the center of the room sat a black grand piano with its lid down, slick and glossy as the funeral Daimlers.

At each end of the room, echoing each other, stood tall, dark, wooden fireplaces. A sign on the wall declared that the fireplaces were by Rennie Mackintosh but said that they were too early to show his later, bolder style. An insert panel had a broken clock, in the other a beaten metal panel of a woman in profile, chin tilted upwards, gorgeous hair billowing out behind her.

The party was thin and almost exclusively male. The one or two women were dressed like men, in business suits and heels. Lawyers. Julius and Margery had few friends; they didn't socialize as a couple because of Margery's depression.

Rose lingered by the door, reluctant to enter and be among them. She looked for the children but couldn't see small scampering bodies tumbling around the wooden floor. She raised her eyes and looked for Francine, saw her standing by the near fireplace, nodding as a man monologued over her head

Francine reached out and took Rose's elbow as the man talked. He was glassy-eyed, reciting a story about fishing or something. It was full of obvious signifiers that Rose didn't get· *Deeside...*, he said, *three rods...beats.* And names, as if they would know them, Jonny Blahblah, Gunter Blah Von Blah, as if they all knew the same people and cared about the same things. Lost in his own frame of reference, he was good enough to glance down and notice that Francine's attention had been lost, that Rose was waiting to talk to her. He broke off and floated away.

Rose touched Francine's elbow. "Lots of doors. Did you get in OK?"

"Fine. I'm sorry about Margery," said Francine, looking to the far end of the room. "They're through that door."

Rose stood on tiptoe and kissed her cheek gently. She went off to find them.

The kids were having a carry-on in the bathroom. She could

hear them from outside the locked door. She rapped once, heard Jessica squeal and felt a thump against the wood.

"Open it," she ordered. The latch slid back, the door fell open. The floor was wet. Hamish had washed Angus's hair in the basin and stood, shamed and smirking by the wall. Angus's shirtsleeve was soaking wet.

Rose sighed and pulled a towel off the wooden rack, wiping it hard against Angus's arm to dry it.

"Silly," she muttered, not wanting to make a big thing of it, not today.

She squeezed the towel around his arm, trying to get the worst of it out. Jessica was at the sink, showily washing her hands, to be the good one, because Rose was always nagging them to wash their hands.

Hamish stood by Rose, his arm pressing against her side. Assuming he wanted reassurance she said, "I'm not very happy with you at all."

"Grandma was rude to you," he said, deflecting blame.

She stood up, folding the towel to find a dry spot. "It's been a bad day, Hamish." But she was pleased that he said that.

She rubbed Angus's arm again, squeezing his collar with the towel. The shirt was half-see-through but if they left his jacket off it would be dry soon enough.

She stood up and looked at the trio. "Right. We're going out there together. We're going to behave really well. We're going to speak when spoken to, tell people how old we are, and in twenty minutes we're going home to hot chocolate and a DVD. Is this agreed?"

They all nodded.

"But only for good behavior," warned Rose.

They went back out. The children saw trays of sandwiches and mini brownies on a far table and galloped off. Margery was sitting on a sofa under the broken clock, sipping white wine, in the middle of a group of men performing for her benefit, talking too loud across her as she listened. One of the men, sitting on her left hand, wasn't focused on Margery. He was staring at Rose, at her face.

She knew him, actually: £45k to Quetta, 7.5 percent fee, quarterly. She could feel his eyes boring into her. She knew the needful look but chose not to look back. Making a mental note to check the book, to see if he was due or owed, she pictured the back safe and it brought to mind the overwhelming store of chores she hadn't managed yet. Here, she was the nanny and she was shy and she knew no one.

She strode across to the children. They each had a plate in their hands and a white linen napkin and were behind a stout man, waiting for access to the brownie tray to clear

"'Two each," she said, seeing that the cakes were small and dry and probably wouldn't be very nice anyway.

Jessica groaned in complaint. The stout man turned to Rose.

"Hello."

She nodded a greeting back, not really looking at him, but he persisted. "D'you remember me?"

She felt her bowels drop: but she was a nanny here. She looked up, it was fucking Monkton. He'd ballooned but still fancied himself. Rose gave a nondescript smile, looked down. "I don't, um..."

He held out his hand. "I'm David Monkton."

"Oh, hello." She was pinned in on either side by the swarm around the buffet and had no option but to shake his hand. Suddenly Dawood was next to them.

"Lovely, what you said about him," she said, hoping he was here to take Monkton away. They didn't move to leave. Dawood and Monkton stood so close to her in the buffet scrum that she couldn't see past them. She was worried that the children were slipping away from her.

"Rose, we met years ago." Monkton was insistent. "Do you remember? With Julius."

She didn't answer. He shouldn't be talking to her, he must want something. Or know something. And if he knew something he would use it because that's what Monkton did: found things out and used them.

"So, David," said Dawood, reining his doggy in, "how did you get here?"

She should have known this would happen. Julius dead, Robert missing and suddenly everyone was misbehaving. She'd need to find out what they were up to. But not now.

"Sorry," she whispered, dipping her shoulder to squeeze through the forest of suits. She was just in time to witness Jessica cramming two squares of brownie in her mouth while she had two on her plate.

Rose reached over to her, took the plate out of her hand and dropped it on the table. She held Jessica by the back of the neck, guiding her through the suits and out of the crowd. In the clearing beyond the scrum, Rose found that her hand was trembling. It wasn't about Jessica.

Jessica wasn't worried, she was laughing and little boulders of brownie tumbled down her black dress. "Come on, Jessica, I said *two* only."

The buffet-hungry crowd were behind Rose, a dark forest of suits, but in front of her was Jessica, laughing, her black eyelashes intertwined, top and bottom, crumbs of dry chocolate sponge raining down her chin. Rose leaned in so that Jessica's opalescent pink skin filled her vision. She watched the girl chortle, saw spongy crumbs bounce off her little chest and she felt overwhelmed by love. Here was all goodness, and sweetness, and brutal honesty. Rose felt, not for the first time, that she wanted to uncouple her jawbone, fit her mouth around the top of Jessica's head and swallow her whole.

She stood up and pushed Jessica away from the food. "Move it."

Seeing her set on her way, she dived back into the crowd for the boys. She found them by the table. Angus had dropped his plate and was looking on the floor for his brownies. Hamish had done something wrong, she couldn't tell what, but he stood stiff with a plate of two brownies, looking shifty.

"Right," she said. "That's it." She had a boy on each hand, was pushing through the crowd, when she looked up and saw them: Uncle Dawood and David Monkton still standing together when they shouldn't, staring at her when they shouldn't. Rose looked straight back at them defiantly, heart hammering, guts churning. They used to be frightened of her. Not anymore. They knew what she'd done, that she was a spent force.

She stared, expressionless, until they looked away. She wasn't done. There was nothing to link her to Aziz Balfour. She still had the book and the contacts, she was Julius's heir and she would make them pay for the impertinence of that look. She couldn't do it again, though, she just couldn't do that again, ever. But she didn't need to do it again, she could pay someone else.

An innocent, glancing bump on her shoulder spun her around, ready to fight. The boys slipped her hands, took their chance and escaped.

"Sorry!" A smile, unsure, his hands full of a double whisky, a plate piled with sandwiches draped in a napkin shroud. "Beg pardon. I'm so greedy, it seems to have occluded my vision."

It was Anton Atholl. He laughed at himself and she found herself laughing too, a mad, drunk sort of release. Atholl laughed louder along with her, as if he was frightened and needed it too.

He was the best of them, Atholl. Julius always said so. The only decent one among them. She was glad to see him.

Atholl held his plate of small sandwiches out in apology. "Egg and cress?"

Rose shook her head and backed away.

"You must be Rose," he said innocently. "I remember Julius telling me about you." He was taking a chance, talking to her. He might know what Dawood and Monkton were doing.

Making a funny play of them not knowing each other, Atholl looked at his hands, found them full and instead held out an elbow, grinning. "I'm Anton Atholl."

"Nice to meet you." She met his elbow with her own and they shook, smiling just enough. She looked away.

"*Rose, you meant so much to him.*"

If she met Anton's eye now she would cry. She kept her eyes down. "Thank you."

She moved out through the crowd, giving herself leave to gather the children and get out.

"Have you seen Robert?"

It was Atholl, he was behind, following her. She shrugged, back in character. "I'm afraid Robert won't be here. He's not well enough to attend."

"Oh. People are asking..."

He didn't look chaotic now, or hungry or funny. He looked serious and leaned over her.

Rose muttered, "I'll tell him."

"Seriously, Julius *loved* you," said Atholl again.

Drunk already, she thought, and felt her lip curl.

"*Loved* having you around."

She smiled at her feet and whispered, "OK."

Atholl was swallowed by the swell of the crowd but still she didn't look up.

She needed to get out before they drank more. She scanned the room, spotting the kids beneath the far fireplace. Hamish was sitting on the couch, ostentatiously eating his last bit of cake. Angus and Jessica stood in front of him, watching covetously. Rose hurried over, keeping her line of vision high to avoid eye contact with anyone else.

She smiled to herself: the centerpiece of the fireplace was a beaten metal relief of a woman in heroic profile, hair billowing, chin tilted up, eyes shut. Her finger was pressed to her lips.

Rose dropped her eyes and bowled over to the kids. She couldn't wait to get home and shut the door on the world.

6

Alex Morrow sat in her boss's office and stared at the printouts on his desk. They were both dumbfounded. Riddell, a slim, pale man with slightly gray teeth and acne scars on his cheeks, opened his mouth and then shut it again. He frowned at the papers on his desk, his eyes running from the printed fingerprint sample taken at the Red Road crime scene to the neat little row of Michael Brown's ten fingerprints, taken from his criminal record.

Brown had been locked in a prison cell and simultaneously halfway across the city, touching things and murdering a man in a deserted block of flats. It was too much of a coincidence, the prints being found right now, just when he was about to go down for a long time. What was even stranger than his teleporting stunt was that it wouldn't get him out of prison. Brown plus others had staged this baffling, elaborate hoax and neither Morrow nor Riddell could work out what the pay-off was to them.

They'd run through possibles, Morrow suggesting, Riddell dismissing:

Distract attention from the person who actually did it? Too complicated. They'd use prints from someone who might actually have been there.

Draw attention to the dead guy's link with Brown? But the dead guy had no link to Brown.

Send a message: but no one would ever know Brown's prints were found there unless the police went about telling people and they had no interest in doing that.

Riddell said that those higher up wanted the fingerprints issue cleared up thoroughly and quickly. Priority. Put other cases aside. Morrow felt sure that the urgency came from the need to minimize costs to the Fiscal's office. No one wanted to be left looking like an idiot when the prefect badges were handed out next year.

Riddell cleared his throat. "So what are you thinking, DI Morrow?"

Then he sat back, with a hand over his mouth, and waited. He was a lazy man. He was asking her how she was going to sort this out for him. He wasn't a bad man or a bad cop, he was just lazy.

"Well, sir, I keep coming back to a move by Brown to muddy the fingerprint evidence in the court case. If not in this case then on appeal. I think he may have either planted his own prints there somehow, or paid someone to hack into the database and change his prints."

"Yes, I see," said Riddell as if that was his idea, "and so you're going to…?"

"I've called in an InfoTech expert to go through the system with me and explain the weak points."

"Yes, good, yes, do that. Do we have to pay for that?"

"No."

"Yes, good, do that then."

Morrow could see why he'd been promoted over her. He was

no trouble at all to management. She was more problematic: her background, her attitude, her brother.

She gathered the papers from his desk, thanked him for his help and left for her own office. She didn't hate Riddell actually. He was bland enough not to be offensive and he was a good buffer between her and the politics of the higher orders. When she asked him how he was he always told her who he was annoyed with. He was too lazy to vigorously implement all the new, sometimes contradictory reforms being brought in because Riddell was waiting for the new single Scottish police force to be formed in a year's time. It was a game of statues, everyone holding their breath, hoping someone else would fall over first.

She sat down at her desk and looked at the papers scattered over it, all urgent, all complicated. Being in court with Brown was exhausting. The adrenalin rush made her peak too early in the day. The rest of her shift was spent recovering.

She reached for the phone but stopped herself. Brian was getting annoyed at her calling every time she missed the twins. Her craving for contact seemed to be on a twenty-minute timer. Whatever was happening in her day, unless she was right in the middle of a meeting with senior officers or chasing someone down a hill, every twenty minutes her mind flipped suddenly to the boys, to their smell, the astonishing movement of their tiny hands, toes, faces. Her first son, Gerald, had died abruptly, and she wondered if it was insecurity that made her want incessant contact. But it didn't feel like part of that sadness. It felt like craven joy. She shut her eyes and allowed herself two seconds of the twins seeing fireworks for the first time. She and Brian held one each, and they stood at the kitchen window with the lights off and watched the boys seeing white fire-chrysanthemums bursting in the sky.

The truth was that even at home she missed whichever twin

she wasn't looking straight at. She was spread so thin that she could feel her hard-won career running through her exhausted fingers.

She forced herself to open her eyes. Paperwork. Maybe she could eat something, but she wasn't hungry. A Kit Kat or something small, just to break the tedium.

Cursing to herself, Morrow shut her eyes. Everything felt like a bloodless administrative chore. She had said as much to Riddell and he laughed and said maybe she was ready for promotion. It was no mistake, he said, that no one got any power until they could be trusted not to do anything stupid with it. She'd wanted to slap him for saying that. She couldn't stand the thought of the rest of her career being a careful, backwards tiptoe to the door, telling the right lies to the right people.

The thought of lies made her think of her brother, Danny. He'd offered her a loan of money. At that, she smiled. Her brother was a gangster, he was offering money made through criminal enterprise and she couldn't call him on it. Danny's life was mired in fictions: he cared about the community, he loved his kids, he was basically a good man beset with troubles. Danny was far from a good man. Danny was a bad and violent and greedy man. She couldn't say that to him—she used to be able to but now they had this lie between them, like a bastard child they had conjured from river water and mud.

She charted a biography of the lie as she sat in her office with the door closed, avoiding her squad. At the beginning she could mention his "work," ask him for tips, which he gave, and he could ask for tips which she didn't. They could joke about it. For a brief, gilded interlude they were honest about who they were. That lasted for a few months. Then she began to flinch at the sparks of hurt in his eye and avoided mentioning his big car, his cheap clothes, his empire. Tenderness prompted her to stop and slowly those truths became unmentionable and slowly, drip by drip, she was drawn into the lie that he was a service provider, doing his best in a bad economic climate. She knew, of course, that he wasn't, but just saying it, for the sake of peace, made it become the story they told themselves. Now, they were so far into the fiction that Danny could offer her a wad of cash with a straight face and she couldn't call it what it was. Small lies, layered, tenderly conceded, had changed their world.

She missed her old team. Personnel were shuffled from division to division all the time but higher up had been especially keen to move everyone under Morrow after a nasty bribery scandal was uncovered. Not her fault, she did all she could, but the only one left from her old squad was McCarthy. Every cop had a favorite team they had worked with and she worried that Harris, Leonard, Gobby and Wilder had been her best of times and, worse, she hadn't really noticed while she was there. She'd met plenty of nostalgic old cops who carped on about their glory days. She knew they were never happy again.

Too much change. Personnel change, forms changing, computerization of everything and now the service was being turned into a Scotland-wide service. They could all be moved anywhere at any time, that's what the union were warning. Scare tactics, probably, but Morrow felt every change as a nudge towards the door. Her new squad didn't know her well enough to like her. She didn't exactly exude sunshine.

Brian said it didn't matter whether she liked her job or not. The twins were costing a fortune, they needed two brand-new somethings every month and they'd had to take out a crisis loan on the pretext of fixing the roof to pay the heating bills. She had a job and plenty didn't, so shut up. He was right.

She sat up and looked around the dull room. The InfoTech

wouldn't be here for an hour. She took out the case file on Aziz Balfour.

It had been faxed over to her from DI Paul Wainwright in the north. It was his case and he was allowing her to see everything. He was a good man, Wainwright. They knew each other from their patrolling days, had never been close or anything, but she liked him for his genius at sidestepping the negative politics that plagued the police. When anyone began to gossip or whine he changed the subject or walked away. When she asked Wainwright how he was he told her who he fancied on *X Factor*.

The scene of crime photos showed a man lying on his left side. Next to his head a faded red girder rose out of the gray concrete, coated in black fingerprint dust. It was on that surface that they had found Michael Brown's fingerprints, high and low, holding tight, sliding off, partials and complete. Infuriatingly, although someone, not the dead man, had been violently sick nearby, they couldn't use the vomit to get a DNA sample: it was contaminated with dust and blood in it. Also a workman had stepped in it.

She looked at a photograph of a woeful dried puddle with a perfect footprint in the middle of it.

The dead man had been stabbed several times and had bled out all over the floor, the spill of sticky blood trapping dust and feathers from the many birds who had taken up residency since the block had been abandoned. She looked for a closer view of his hands. It was the right hand, the upper hand, or else she might not have noticed: the back of the hand had a deep, aged bruise on the knuckles, yellow and swollen.

The dead man, Aziz Balfour, was twenty-five. Originally from Pakistan, he had come to Scotland working for a charity that was raising money for the people left homeless after the 2008 earthquake. He was a posh boy, had a degree from back home and clearly came from money. He had been studying for a master's in Overseas Development at Glasgow and had married a Scottish girl last year. All his paperwork was good.

The Scottish family were interviewed. None of them could believe he'd been murdered. They said he was a "great guy." He didn't drink or take drugs or gamble, he did nothing but work and gave a fifteenth of his earnings to charity, even though he was expecting his first baby in two months. A photo of him showed a handsome guy at a party, holding a small girl in a preposterously frilly red dress. He was grinning, had a James Dean quiff and sideburns, exaggerated enough to be cool and ironic.

She looked at the death pictures, the slack face with half-open eyes, bathed in the cold light of the photographer's flash. Aziz was heavy, his backside and thighs rounded. He wore a gray three-quarter length coat and it had ridden up behind, showing pudgy hips straining against a belt. The back pocket of his trousers showed the imprint of a wallet, which meant he wasn't robbed. His shoes were patent leather slip-ons with leather soles.

It was telling her nothing. Morrow put the photos back in the envelope, opened the door to the corridor, forcing herself out.

She looked in at her team. They were working phones, checking computers, filling out forms over an ongoing surveillance case of a car dealership. They looked young, energetic. She could hardly remember their names. DC Brigid Daniel looked up at her standing outside the door. Morrow actually did remember her name. It was so bullishly Catholic and yet Daniel hadn't been given a papish nickname. It was a good sign, Morrow had thought, a sign of good change.

"Daniel." She flicked a finger for her to come out.

Daniel did so. "Yes, ma'am." She stood at ease, hands behind her back, eyes straight. Her polo neck and trousers were deep, lint-free black without a single washed-out splatter of baby sick. She ran, Morrow remembered; she looked fit but her thighs were splayed with fat and the tops of her legs rubbed noisily against each other when she walked.

"You find anything?"

"No, ma'am."

Morrow looked back at her desk. She had asked Daniel to check criminal records for anyone associated with a particular car dealership. Her desk looked very tidy. "Did you check the financial records?"

"Yes, ma'am. There's a couple of big transfers but they seem to be accounted for. Found bank receipts and everything."

"OK, come in here a minute."

Daniel hurried into Morrow's office with unseemly enthusiasm.

Morrow looked back in at DS McCarthy sitting at his desk. "Anything?"

"No."

"What are you thinking?"

"That the old guy's telling the truth and we're bastards."

That was her fear.

The car dealer had been in business for twenty-three years, selling luxury cars. They only became aware of him because a gangster's fat, spoiled son was seen driving a Lotus that came from his shop. CID went in looking for evidence that the fat son had paid with dirty money and found a wee old man who claimed that the boy came in, said he was taking the car, would bring it back when he was ready to, and simply drove off in it. The car dealer knew who the boy was. He was far too frightened to object. It sounded true but CID still had to order a thorough search for the money: if they didn't rip the business apart car dealers all over the city would be using the story within a week. So they had been through all of his records, frozen all of his bank accounts, trawled the accounts of all his family and friends for evidence of money laundering, looking for unusual purchases, mortgage pay-offs, bags of money in cupboards. They found nothing, which meant the old man was probably telling the truth, which in turn meant that he had been victimized twice: once by the fat son, once by the frantic search for the proceeds of crime. It was the burning crime question: where the hell was all the money going?

"InfoTech's coming to see me," said Morrow, trying to be conversational. "Talk through the fingerprints."

McCarthy nodded.

She nodded him back to his desk. "Keep going. We might not be bastards."

Daniel was sitting opposite Morrow's seat waiting to be spoken to.

"No," said Morrow, waving her to sit next to her facing the computer. "I want fresh eyes on something."

They shuffled around awkwardly in the small office until they were both facing the computer. Morrow called up the fingerprint database IDENTI.

"OK," she said, "talk me through the database and how a match is found."

Daniel nodded, took a breath and when she spoke it sounded like she was reciting a handout from her training: "Prints found at a scene of a crime are lifted, photographed and uploaded into the database as unidentified. Ten-prints taken at the point of arrest are uploaded into a separate but related database, adding the criminal record number if you have it. Searches can be run locally or nationally. It runs through the database of unidentified ones. Matches come back high or medium confidence and show you the date of birth and family name, so you can check it's the right guy."

Morrow nodded. The DOB on the matching set was right for Brown. "We've got prints at a scene from someone unknown.

They match someone they couldn't possibly be from. Let's say he's dead. What do you think?"

"It's a mismatch then," said Daniel. "If that's right then one of three things have happened: the ten-prints are wrong, the unidentified prints are wrong. Or the match is wrong."

"No, it's high confidence. Been rerun several times. And the DOD's right."

Daniel nodded and thought about it. "Well, thinking rationally, could the database prints have been changed?"

"That's what I thought."

Daniel suppressed a grin.

"Thanks, Daniel. You can go back now."

Daniel stood up, tried to think of something to say and then left.

"Shut the door after you."

The InfoTech expert, one Clare McGregor, arrived thirty-four minutes late for their appointment. Because she was late Morrow would not be home to give the boys their tea or get to bath them. But McGregor didn't know that, Morrow reminded herself, forehead pressed to the back of her office door. It was not deliberate. There might be a very good reason for it. She took three deep breaths and opened the door, heading out to the lobby to meet her.

She reminded herself of the questions: how could someone get prints into a scene or how could a database mismatch prints.

Morrow opened the door and walked into the lobby. The moment she saw McGregor she knew this would go very badly indeed.

Clare McGregor was furious. She leaned on the front bar, legs wound around each other, arms crossed, cheek-chewing. In her midtwenties, she was slim, pretty and dressed in comfortable trousers, a gray silk shirt and high-heeled boots. McGregor had never been in uniform, she was a civilian and wasn't dressed like someone who needed to stay dry while working for twenty hours, be able to run, and/or sit in a car for four hours.

"I'm DI Alex Morrow." She held her hand out. "Are you all right?"

McGregor uncrossed her arms but refused to shake Morrow's hand. She muttered a stark "yes" as if they were in the middle of an argument.

"Is there a problem here?" asked Morrow.

"No," said McGregor. "I'm the InfoTech. You *asked* me to come."

Morrow held her hand out insistently and McGregor gave in, pinching Morrow's fingertips in response.

It was clear to Morrow that Clare McGregor was having strong feelings about her and wanted them acknowledged. She was late, angry. She had probably rehearsed arguments, articulating her objections to Morrow all the way here. She wanted to be heard.

In compensation for missing the boys' bath, Morrow allowed herself the luxury of not asking. "Please come through." She turned and led the way to her office.

Showing McGregor in, she pointed her to one of the two seats facing the computer screen. While Morrow had been waiting for her to arrive she had checked out her pay grade to see how susceptible someone in her position would be to bribery. She was making thirteen grand more than Morrow, and her qualifications were transferable.

"OK." She took the neighboring chair. "I've asked you here to talk me through something." Morrow flicked her mouse to waken the screen and the IDENTI fingerprint database appeared suddenly.

"We've got a problem with a case: we found fingerprints in a place they couldn't possibly be. I need you to tell me how the database could make a mistaken match—"

"It can't," said McGregor.

Morrow looked at her. McGregor stared at the screen, mouth pinched tight.

McGregor was wrong. They both knew she was wrong. They sat in silence for almost a minute. It was too early in the conversation for Morrow to stand up and chase her out.

Morrow took a deep breath. "There are some gray areas to explore: prints could be complex marks or wrongly identified as not complex, isn't that right?"

"Complex marks" was a technical term for crap fingerprints. It carried with it a different set of obligations. Three examiners had to look at the prints independently. They had to submit reports with their conclusions to show their working. With noncomplex marks a superficial match on the database could be followed up with just one examiner and a standard report.

McGregor stared sullenly at the screen as if she was watching a boring TV show.

"Clare, couldn't there be gray areas in identification? It's not an absolute science, is it?"

McGregor was finding it hard to be wrong. Morrow thought that she must have been quite good at her job or they wouldn't have sent her over. Either that or she was a nutcase and they wanted her out of the office. She gave a sharp little nod at the computer, as if she wanted to head-butt it. "Gray areas... Yes."

"Could someone access the database and change an accused person's ten-prints?"

"Yes, if digits have been lost or scarred, you can change them. But you need a high level of clearance and it would be traceable. Every time a file is accessed it's traceable. Here..." She flicked through a couple of screens and drew up the file history detailing who had been in there, what their ID number was and when they were there.

Morrow watched carefully. "What about scene of crime prints? Can you go into the database and change them?"

"No."

Morrow knew they could change them.

"Are you sure?"

McGregor blinked. She was wrong and she knew it. "Not anymore," she conceded.

"*Anymore?*"

"Used to be able to if you were working on a partial and you got a better set, for example, but they changed that seven years ago. It's all traceable now."

Morrow sat back. "So, you *can* but it's traceable?"

"Yes." McGregor clicked through three screens. "See there?"

Up on the right-hand corner in vivid blinking red was a notification of the date of when an entry had been changed and the IT officer's number.

"OK."

They could be changed. Michael Brown could have found a bent IT officer to change his prints and give a match.

"Could you hack in and alter them remotely?"

"No. You'd need access to the building, to the servers that are capable of accessing the database..."

She didn't believe McGregor now, because she'd bullshitted before. Morrow made a mental note to ask someone else and tuned out as McGregor talked her through access codes and passwords, who changed them and when.

As a final test Morrow asked an obvious yes prompt: "Could someone have put in the wrong prints in the first place?"

"No," said McGregor.

Morrow sat still, letting the idiotic "no" echo around the

room. They sat there, together, until the untouched page on the screen dulled for a moment like a sleepy eye half shutting. Then it went off.

Morrow stood up. "That's all I need from you."

McGregor got to her feet, shoving the chair back noisily. "Cousin used to work in this division."

This was the pre-rehearsed argument. Morrow asked, "Who's that then?"

"DC Harris. He used to work here."

Harris was as close as Morrow had ever come to a friend on the force. He'd been done for taking bribes and was currently in prison. Morrow was so disappointed in him that she had punched him and broken his nose. She regretted it. She missed him.

McGregor was so angry she was losing her breath. "And *you*"—she said, bubbling at the nose and mouth—"are just the sort of…"

But again Morrow wasn't listening. She was blinded by visions of Harris standing in a dark street taking a punch and letting her punch him again, because he knew what he had done was low and shameful.

"Harris pleaded guilty."

"Your brother's Danny McGrath."

Morrow found herself shouting. "If you can't function in the service because of your family history you should leave and get another job."

She opened the door and held it as the other woman slunk through it. McGregor's was a good job, an easy job, and they both knew it. She could see McGregor was worried Morrow would report her, make up an allegation and she'd lose her position.

McGregor looked back at her. She didn't look anything like Harris but Glasgow was a small city and the service was even smaller.

"Tell Harris I was asking after him."

McGregor responded automatically, "Will do."

Morrow slammed the door. Everyone knew about Danny now. It came up all the time and even when it didn't she felt the shadow of that association hanging over her, tainting her moral authority.

McGregor would go home and sob. She'd worry about her job for the next few months, but eventually she'd forget that it ever happened. Morrow wouldn't forget it. She missed Harris every day.

Thoughts of what she missed made her check her watch: she was too late for the bath but if she hurried she could still get them to bed.

She opened the door and called DS McCarthy over.

"McCarthy, you trained to use a mobile fingerprint ID?"

"Yes."

"Get one and bring it to the high court at nine thirty tomorrow morning."

McCarthy was surprised. "We're taking his prints *again*?"

"If he'll let us." She turned away to get her coat and bag. "I suspect he'll be very keen to."

7

The moment Rose Wilson heard the buzzer she knew it was the police. It was typical of Margery to be so deep in denial that she'd call the cops in when Robert ran away. Francine wouldn't do that. Still, Rose reminded herself that was normal, that's what people did when someone went missing. The cops might even get a handle on where Robert was. She'd checked his credit card online. He hadn't paid for anything in the past two days. She'd checked his "find my iPhone." But he had turned it off. At least no one else would be able to track him that way.

She looked at the video phone screen. Two men in cheap suits at the gate, both of them slightly fat. One had thinning dark hair and spoke into the camera, telling her they were Strathclyde Police, could they come in for a moment? The other cop looked at the house, mild puzzlement on his face. She knew what he meant. The house didn't work.

She pressed the button for the gate and opened the front door for the officers.

The security gate was low and leapable. The drive was shallow. Realistically, the householder could look out of the window and get better definition and a clearer idea of who was out there. But the gate and camera were cheap copies of actual security. The developers knew that anyone paying a million pounds for a house would look for certain features, like security gates, sauna, double garage, so they had crammed them in. Sometimes, if she got up in the night or approached the house from the wrong angle in the street, she saw it all afresh, a chaotic jumble of pointless totems.

The cops looked over the building, their eyes confused by the small, ill-matched windows on different levels, some cutting across the floors to create minstrels' galleries. A gray, overhanging roof dominated the white facade, the entrance portico had too many columns.

The house looked outside how the family felt from the inside: disjointed, overembellished, nervous and busy.

"Hello," she said, as the two men approached the front step. The bald cop smiled at her.

"Strathclyde Police," he said, smiling again, showing her his ID. "We're here about Mr. McMillan?"

"Please come in." She opened the door.

They stepped into the hallway, looking around awkwardly, trying hard not to gawp.

It was a big hall, wide but low. A pine staircase lurched up the wall and veered away awkwardly. The ceiling was too low for the eighteen halogen downlighters punched into it. They hit the eye like consecutive searchlights. She offered to take their coats. They demurred politely but Rose's attention was drawn by the whispers of children on the upper landing.

They weren't supposed to be playing up there. Angus had a bad tumble down the stairs once and she'd told them not to play there.

She shut the front door and stood tall. "Hamish! Angus! Not there."

Two small faces peeked around the head of the stairs, Angus smirking behind his brother who was too interested in the police to mind being in trouble.

"I said not there, Hamish."

Hamish raised a finger. "Who are they?"

"Don't point at people," she said.

The bald policeman smiled up at the children and said "hello."

"Who are they?" smiled Angus, still shielding himself behind Hamish.

"Hamish, what do you say?"

The boys paused for a moment and ran through all the things she nagged them to say. Hamish hit the jackpot with an obligation "hello" but Angus said "thank you."

"These men are policemen."

"Are they here about Daddy?" asked Angus.

She didn't want to look at them. "Yes," she said, hearing the hiss in her voice reverberate around the cold hall. "You two go upstairs to the playroom. You can play on the Wii for twenty minutes."

They bolted off upstairs as Rose held out a hand towards the kitchen door. "Would you like to come through?"

The cops walked through to the back of the house and she followed them.

The kitchen was narrow with tottery stools around a breakfast bar. The dining room had a big table and chairs but she didn't want them to be comfortable, to linger. She offered the cops a seat, watching as they climbed up, gracelessly yanking their jackets out from under their bottoms. They settled and looked at her, as if expecting praise for getting up there.

"Can I get you tea or coffee?"

"No," said the bald one, "no thanks." He put a nasty plastic briefcase on the clean worktop. A greasy sheen on the handle caught the light. Rose thought she could see crumbs, possibly from biscuits, caught in the zip. It looked disgusting. She imagined licking it, felt sick at the thought of it and forced herself to look away.

"I'll get Mrs. McMillan for you. She's lying down."

"Hang on," the dark-haired one spoke for the first time, "you're not Mrs. McMillan?"

"No, I'm the nanny. I'll get her."

She had already turned away when he said, "Sorry, what's your name?"

Rose knew that tone. The tone denoted interest, suppositions about complications. He'd be wondering about Robert, about affairs and unreciprocated crushes, about fumblings in the middle of the night. She heard the tone from Robert's friends, from Francine's occasional forays into the world of other mothers, from workmen who came to the house. She wasn't offended by it, not anymore. Most people couldn't even begin to understand the closeness between her and Robert. He was her brother. Her naive older brother.

She turned back. "Rose Wilson."

The cops exchanged glances. "Maybe we could interview you first, Rose?"

Rose didn't want to but it would look strange. She turned back and sat down on a stool, hands clasped in front of her on the table, facing the cops.

"Sorry. It's been a heavy day. Family funeral."

The dark-haired one unzipped his briefcase and pulled out a form. "Julius McMillan's funeral? Was it this morning?"

"Still going, I'm sure."

"I met McMillan once," said the baldy one. He waited then, openmouthed, for a prompt.

Exhausted, Rose gave it to him. "Did you?"

"Yeah." He smiled at the table. "When I was a young cop I arrested some care-home kids and McMillan was their defense counsel. Even back then, and that was ten years ago, you could tell he'd been brilliant and here he was defending a wee—" He looked up, remembered where he was. "You know. Well, you know how he did those defense cases "

Rose cleared her throat. "Look, um, I can save you a bit of work if you'd like. That's how I met him. I was one of those cases. He defended me when I got in trouble."

It took a moment to register. Then the dark-haired one dropped his voice to confidential. "What sort of trouble?"

"You don't need to whisper. It was a culp hom." She noticed that she'd dropped her own voice. "The family know, well, the kids don't know and I'd rather you didn't mention it in front of them…"

The cops were too uncomfortable to write it down.

"Culpable homicide?" The dark-haired one repeated it to give himself time to take it in.

They'd go straight back to the office and check out her record. They'd see the guilty plea and the details. Were the photos in that file? If they saw the photos they'd be horrified. Julius McMillan showed her them. He wanted her to see them, take it in, get over it. She could recall them in detail: Sammy slumped against the wheel like an empty costume, blood everywhere. Black and white, color. Mug shots of her, encrusted with dried blood.

The balding cop cleared his throat. "And you stayed in touch?"

"He did. He helped me out when I was released."

"That was good of him." His eyebrows were high on his forehead.

"Yes. He was a better man than most people knew. I can understand Robert wanting to be alone. He'll need time. Julius is a terrible loss to all of us."

"He was very ill, wasn't he?" The baldy one was building to something.

"Julius?" she said, trying to anticipate his next move. "Yes. Yes, I'm afraid he was. Lung condition. Could have happened at any time. He wasn't in pain."

"So it was a mercy, really?"

She shrugged. They looked at each other. And though Rose kept a straight face she was thinking that the bald cop had never been with anyone when they died. Rose knew that death was never expected or accepted, no one went gently. There was always a futile kick against the kitchen floor. She dropped her eyes to the table and repeated the palliative lie for him, "It was a mercy, yes, I suppose."

He smiled at her for saying that. "But Robert doesn't see it that way?"

"He didn't show it but I'm sure he's very upset."

The dark-haired cop was busy studying her. She didn't look the part, she knew that. She dressed like a middle-class graduate: good quality jeans, big belt, baggy cashmere jumper. They were all things that Francine had bought her or replacements for worn out things she had bought her. And she had that ease and arrogance that confused people, the steady eye of someone who knew exactly who she was but who spoke with a low-class accent.

"We need to fill out the forms."

He took her name, her age: twenty-nine; her address: here; and her job. She was a nanny, had an HNC in Early Education and Childcare from Langside College.

He pretended to be pleased. "Did you do your HNC when you were in prison?"

"After. Francine and Robert were expecting their first baby, Hamish. They offered me the job before he was even born."

"That's very community minded." He looked to his partner to see if he would concur in the lie. "We don't always hear stories like that, you know?"

Rose smiled politely. "I know. They're good, Christian people."

"Oh!" he said. "They're *religious*."

She smiled but didn't confirm or deny it. They both seemed satisfied with that as an explanation of why a professional couple would hand over their firstborn to someone convicted of murder. The truth was that Francine was the one who wanted her. Rose and Robert liked each other, felt very close in many ways, but it was at Francine's insistence that Rose got the job. She trusted her. You know how to look after people, she said to Rose, in secret, because Robert didn't know yet. I'm going to need you. Can you keep a secret? They were all consumed by the need to protect Robert.

So, could she tell them when she last saw Robert McMillan?

Rose told them it was the night before last. She told them he seemed fine.

And, they asked, how did Robert seem, recently?

She told them that Robert had been calm when his father died. He spent time at the private hospital and was there with his father when he died after the operation to reinflate his lungs.

Did she get on with Robert?

She said she didn't really see that much of him. He worked for a big law firm and spent most of his time at work. He rarely managed to get home for family dinners and she was always busy with the kids. When he was around her job was to attend to the kids and let Robert and Francine spend a little time alone together.

It was true in a way; she didn't know what films he liked or watched or enjoyed. She didn't even see him eating that often. But she and Robert had known each other since they were children, herself only four years younger than him. Two sides of a coin, Julius called them. She'd loved that when she was younger.

Suddenly, she found herself back in remand, in the dark, a fourteen-year-old, her skin dry from the dusting of blood. She kept scratching her head and finding red dust under her fingernails. Her scalp was raw by the time Mr. McMillan came to see her. Though she was fourteen and looked sixteen she was still small, too small for the clothes they gave her to change into. She sat across the table from him in the interview room, a small, flattened thing at the end of her life.

Not here. That memory did not belong in this house but she couldn't shake it and knew that she was frozen at the table, staring, exciting interest.

With a furious energy, she managed to make the memory ebb, kicking it down through the kitchen floor. She looked up at the cops.

"Sorry," she whispered, hoarse. "It's been quite a shock, really, all of it. Everyone's been very upset. We knew he wasn't healthy but it was still an awful shock. Awful."

The coppers nodded, as if they knew anything. "You said you became very close?"

"Mr. McMillan visited me in prison. I wasn't going to appeal the sentence. It was five years for culpable homicide, he did a great job, the court was very kind to me. He visited me though and encouraged me to study while I was in there—he took an interest."

"And when you got out he gave you a job?"

"No, when I got out I was doing nursery training at Langside. I was living in supported accommodation. Francine was pregnant and he got me an interview. Three kids later I'm still here."

And how did she get on with Francine?

She wiped her nose, listening for noises from the hall, mentally mapping the children's positions in the house. "I love Francine. She's like my sister. I just love her."

Did she have a boyfriend?

No.

That seems unusual, a pretty woman her age. They smiled at her. She didn't smile back. They persisted.

Was there someone recently?

No.

She couldn't pretend like they wanted her to. She couldn't giggle at the compliment or make up a history. There was no one. There never was anyone. She never wanted there to be anyone. Every night she got into bed and before she fell asleep she remembered that no man had touched her today, and smiled.

They wrote something on the sheet and she could see them thinking she was having an affair with Robert, or Francine. Or both. But she looked at their doughy cop faces and guessed that their imaginations probably wouldn't stretch to both. Not unless they watched a lot of pornography. You could tell when a man did that. It gave them a lot of strange ideas about people.

They filled out the bottom of the form and asked her to go and get Francine out of her bed.

Rose stood up, reviewing her performance. It was OK. "Officers," she said, "are you sure I couldn't get you a cup of tea?"

She sounded imploring, mostly because she was upset but she saw them respond to the suggestion of respect and care as a child does to love. They looked at her and their faces blossomed warm and soft. Them and us. Us and us.

"No, thanks, Miss Wilson, if you could just get Mrs. McMillan for us."

She turned back to the hall, keeping her head down so that the children wouldn't see her looking upset.

Francine was reading in bed. She had a throw over her legs and a folio edition of *The Mill on the Floss* open on her knees. She had been crying.

Rose walked over to the bedside and looked down at the book. She was on page four. Rose sat down.

"Is that the police downstairs?"

"Yeah."

"They want to talk to me?"

"Yeah."

"Did they ask about you?"

"Yeah."

"What did you tell them?"

"Everything."

Francine reached out to Rose and held her hand for a moment.

"Once the police leave, I need to go out," said Rose.

Francine squeezed her hand.

8

1997

Julius McMillan sat in his small office, tapping his pen on the desk, and considered the situation. It was a bad situation. She had killed two men in one night. He had their story for Samuel McCaig. That was a good story. Rose had just met him, he tried it on, she panicked. Fine. Culp him, self-defense. So that was fine. But the Pinkie Brown murder, that was bad.

He lit a Rothmans and sat back, climbing inside the story, looking for the chinks of light. Pinkie brought the weapon. Pinkie had a record of violence. They could claim that he tried to rape Rose but that would undermine the Sammy the Perv defense. They were at school together. It was difficult. Julius couldn't see a break in it. There was no way out. The significant thing so far was that she hadn't been charged or even questioned about Pinkie. But she would be, eventually, if he didn't do something.

She was an astonishing little animal. McMillan had defended kids, women, people in extremis, but he had never met anyone like her before. She had no one: no family, no friends, even her social worker changed every six months. She'd never even been fostered and she didn't have friends at school. Her pattern seemed to be that she had one person in her life at a time and that person was her all. Her mother, first, an all-consuming mess. Then no one for a year, then Sammy. Absolute fidelity. McMillan saw it in her. When she pledged her loyalty to him he saw the rest of the world die in her eyes. But it wasn't that she had a naive belief in him, she wasn't stupid. She saw something in him, he knew she did.

He picked up the phone and called Dawood McMann. They arranged to meet in a car park, which seemed a bit melodramatic to Julius.

He was careful not to tell his receptionist, Mrs. Tait, where he was going. He was sure she was leaking information to Anton Atholl.

DC David Monkton was in the locker room, hanging his T-shirt and jeans neatly onto a hanger. He had a half smile on his face, half listening to the chat among the other officers. He felt self-conscious about that smile because it wasn't genuine, he knew it wasn't. He was trying to convey belonging and yet not belonging, being somehow above the rest of them and yet not making a big thing of it, but the smile kept slipping. The joke among the men was going on too long and it wasn't really that funny.

"Hey, Monkton." The officer speaking to him was standing in crumpled underpants and his blue shirt and he was fat and hated Monkton.

"What?"

For a short moment they looked at each other across the heads of the others with undisguised loathing and then the fat man turned it into a smile. "You been ironing your cock?"

Everyone laughed at him. Monkton knew the expression to make: unconcerned, also amused, but he just couldn't get his facial muscles to do that today. He looked sick, he thought, so he changed it and then worried that he looked hurt. He turned into his locker and hung his clothes up for the end of his shift and thought to himself, one day I will be your boss.

"I'm just asking," said the cop, "because you've got a seam down the front of it."

He hadn't seen David's cock, The laughter was less cheerful this time, wary. Someone said, "Nah, man." Monkton came back out of the locker. The cop was still glaring at him.

Monkton met his eye, raised his eyebrows. Everyone looked away.

"What?" said the cop, thinking he was squaring up to fight him.

Monkton said nothing. He was remembering the man's face for later, further on in his career. He turned and walked out of the locker room. He was just outside the door when he heard the guy say, "Who does he think he is?"

Monkton wanted to run back in and punch his lights out. But he didn't because he was controlled, because he knew what he was doing and scum like that couldn't stop him. He was going right to the top. That's what they couldn't cope with: his ambition. And he would one day be running divisions, running squads full of grunts like him and he wouldn't have to put up with their crap, their humiliating, belittling crap.

He walked up the stairs to the office he was sharing with his DS. He was in an office with the fucking DS because he actually had ambitions. He was already ahead of the game and that's why they hated him. They were jealous. His phone rang in his pocket as he reached the landing. He took it out. It was a tiny phone, they could make them so small now.

He answered it and found Dawood McMann on the other end. A warm sensation flooded through him. A call from McMann meant money. Cash to spend, cash he *had* to spend because he couldn't bank it.

"What can I do for you?"

"It's a bit more complicated than the usual. Can we meet?"

Monkton looked around. No one who mattered was anywhere near him. "Sure. When?"

"Now? Outside?"

It was a Range Rover, the cabin was warm and the seats were made of leather. Monkton shifted in the chair, even the steering wheel was covered in leather, pale leather, his hand lingered on the seat leather, brushing it, feeling it, loving it.

"So it would be a step up," said McMann. "But are you ready for that?"

"How much?"

Dawood didn't answer so Monkton looked at him. He was a strange-looking man. Half Pakistani, he had a mustache when no one in Scotland had a mustache. It was a big one too and his hair had some sort of preparation in it that made it look wet, the tracks of his comb still in there. He wore jewelry as well, big gold rings and cheap string bracelets around his left wrist that looked dirty.

"Fifty thousand."

He savored Monkton's reaction, watching the wide easy smile spread across his face, looking at his teeth as if he was counting them, reflecting the smile back at him.

"That's a hell of a lot of money."

Dawood smiled. "I'm asking a lot. It's not just a bit of information this time. Find someone, make it stick. That's all."

They smiled at each other, wider, unguarded. Monkton didn't mind the dirty bangles or the wet-look hair. He didn't care about the gold filling in one of Dawood's incisors or his strange way of nodding his head that looked like yes and no at the same time.

9

Morrow's eyes fell on the house, the warm light in the front window, the scraggy grass on the sloping lawn to the road, the mossy hedge. She glanced at the roof, worrying herself. It did need to be done but they'd spent the money already and had to hope that the roof would see the winter through. Even as she was fretting she was still smiling because she was so close to being home. She puckered as she turned into the cul de sac, rehearsing a smother of kisses for her boys, already feeling the tickle of soft baby hair on her lips. Then she saw him. Her brother, Danny, was parked outside her house, waiting for her.

She drew up sharply, bonnet to bonnet with Danny, a car space between them, and switched the engine off. They looked at each other in the dark. As if it was happening in slow motion, she saw him realize she was pissed off that he was there. She saw him glance down, decide to ignore it and look up. He forced his face into a passive smile.

She stayed where she was, watching him. Danny McGrath letting an insult go. With her cop's head on she knew it was ominous. Danny was a predator and he was after something.

His car bonnet loomed over hers but she sat, looking up, not matching his smile. He must know the things she knew about him, the broken legs and burned-out shops, the wash of money and the army of muscle.

Danny ran half the taxis in Glasgow, since he had magically acquired a license despite his reputation and all his previous convictions. Alex knew what went on with the taxis, how much money was being cleaned through the cash business. She sat in her car and remembered the dapper old car dealer weeping in his office as they bagged up the files of his decades-long business. She blamed Danny, though the family that did it were rivals of his.

She got out, grabbed her bag and walked over to his window. It rolled down smoothly and Danny smiled at her.

"How are you?" he said.

Morrow chewed her cheek. "What you doing here?"

Though the act of tolerance was choking him, he rallied: "Just visiting my godsons in there. How are you?"

He waited for a pleasantry back. She didn't have one for him. She looked over the roof of the car. "Look, um, don't come to my house when I'm not here."

Danny wasn't used to that, to people being sharp or abrupt with him. He was a powerful man. He had been in knife fights, he'd kicked people in the face. He huffed an indignant laugh at the windscreen and looked at her, amused and puzzled.

She said it again, "I don't want you in my house."

"...My godsons," he said, smiling but the anger showing in the set of his eyes.

They stood in the dark, looking away from each other.

Finally Morrow spoke. "Danny, this isn't..."

"This isn't *what?*"

She didn't want to get into a discussion.

"Am I not good enough?"

She looked at his face, at the scar on the chin, at the lies in his eyes. He wasn't good enough to be near her kids but they were so mired in bullshit that she couldn't say that. "Dan, I think we should have a break for a while. I'll call you." She walked away up the path to the door.

"Alex." He was out of the car and coming after her. He'd put on weight, eating takeouts every night, and the tracksuit wasn't doing him any favors. "Wait."

He caught up with her, reaching into his back pocket and pulling out an old photo. "This is why I came. I only wanted you to have this." He handed it to her. "Nineteen seventy-six."

The photo was old, in the faded pastels of the 1970s. It had been ripped almost in half and sellotaped back together. Two girls, their arms around each other's shoulders, wearing shorts and cheesecloth smock tops. Alex recognized her mum's hairstyle: a Farrah Fawcett flick with a Debbie Harry dye job: brown at the back and blond-flicked fringes. The other girl was Danny's mum, still recognizable even without the broken nose. She had a matching hairstyle, cheaper, the flick less defined.

Morrow hadn't known their mothers were ever friends. The two girls each had a baby just a year or so after the photo was taken, both to the same nasty man. Danny and Alex. They started school together without knowing they were half brother and sister. They had a mutual crush in their first term at school, until their mothers met at the gates and set about each other. There was no mystery about Danny and Alex's relationship then, just shame and fascination.

But here their mothers were so young and fresh and hopeful. Photographed smiling, standing on waste ground, the earth hard and dry. There was a heat wave that year, she remembered her mum talking about it. Her mum's legs and forearms were sun-burnt pink in the picture.

Danny hated his mother. When he was very young, thirteen, fourteen, she couldn't remember, he'd been arrested for battering her. It seemed unfair to Morrow at the time. It seemed unfair to everyone at the time. His mother was no stranger to a brawl and if Danny hadn't come off the worst it was probably to his credit. He loathed the woman. Yet here he was, smiling over Morrow's shoulder at the photo, head tilted just so. Danny did nothing un-less it served him some purpose.

"I wanted you to keep it," he said. "For the boys, for later. So they can see how close they were. It wasn't always bad..."

She looked at the photo. The lies were rigid between them now. She looked at the photo and wondered what they were doing, if they were lying to each other or to themselves.

"Lovely." She backed off a step. "You got a copy?"

"Yeah." He took a hopeful step towards her.

"Thanks." She turned away, fitted her key in the door and shut it firmly between them.

She was in another world, suddenly looking at the stairs her waters had broken on, the Christmas stairs, the birthday stairs, the stain where baby Dan was sick.

A sour tang of milk sick was carried to her on the heat of the house. She took off her coat and let her senses engulf her.

"Alex!" Brian called from the front room. "Alex, get in here!"

She looked in the door. He was holding Danny on his knee, holding a cupped hand full of stinking white vomit in the other.

"A cloth! A cloth!"

The boys were falling asleep. Alex had given them a second bath and put them to bed while Brian took an hour to himself, sitting and watching football. Neither boy was hot or spotty and they didn't look as if they'd be sick again. It was one of the fleeting bugs they kept picking up. Small wonder. They put everything they got hold of into their raw wee mouths.

She stood at the door, smiling, and watched them battle to stay awake, getting to their knees and dropping back, punch drunk from the day. The cots were pushed up next to each other because they liked to hold hands through the bars.

She watched them until they fell asleep, listened to their snuffling until her feet were too sore to stand any longer. She turned the intercom on and tiptoed down to the living room.

Brian was slumped on the settee. All around him the carpet had scrubbed stains from glories past.

"We'll need a new carpet," she said.

"Hm." Brian kept his eyes on the TV. "Not yet."

She sat next to him, gently kicking his feet over for a share of the footstool. Brian fought back, gaining ground and losing a slipper. She took her feet off and then he made room for her. Their feet formed a tidy row and they smiled at the telly. The football match was between two teams neither of them cared about. Fifty minutes in and the score was nil nil.

Her foot nudged Brian's. "What was Danny saying?"

"He was only in for a minute. He was all smiles. Trouble at his work."

"Sort of trouble?"

Brian shrugged. "Just fed up, I think. Hard for everyone at the moment. He was here to see you."

"Well," she felt tired suddenly, "he saw me."

He sat up suddenly. "Oh, guess what…" He stood up and left the room, coming back in with a cardboard wine carrier with three bottles in it. He held it up and grinned. "Eh?"

"Where's that from?"

"This afternoon. The boys were asleep for twenty minutes and the door went and a market researcher came to the door. Fancy a glass?"

Morrow smiled up at him, calculating whether saying yes would mean she'd have to stand up. "Aye, go on then."

He smiled as he backed out of the room, returning with two small glasses. It was pleasant wine, sweet but crisp.

"That's quite nice," said Morrow to the television.

"Yeah, it's all right, isn't it? I'd prefer beer, really."

"What was the research about?"

"Holidays."

She took another sip.

"Have we got to go to a presentation or anything?"

"No."

"Did they go around the other neighbors?"

"I don't know."

"Man or woman?"

Brian tutted. "For heaven's sake, Alex."

"I'm just asking, Brian."

"You're very suspicious."

"Hm. Man or woman?"

He smiled. "Woman, OK?"

"For a twenty-minute chat, she gave you three bottles?"

Brian grunted but she wasn't sure if he was talking to the telly or her.

"What did you tell her?"

"We can't afford a holiday."

Morrow watched the millionaires jog around midfield and thought about what they were all prepared to settle for now. Free wine. Enough to eat. The absence of civil war.

10

Though she had a key Rose rang the buzzer. She wanted to give Atholl the impression of courtesy, so that he would think she was in one mood and she could wrong-foot him with quite another.

The block of flats was made of orange and yellow brick, a modern take on a tenement building, Ten years old and it was wearing badly. Someone's buzzer was stuck and the intercom gave off a perpetual hiss. The ground-floor windows were always roughly curtained, as though the tenants were sick of being stared in at by other people's visitors.

Atholl's voice crackled through the fuzzy intercom.

"Me," she said into it. The door fell open.

Inside, the stairs were steep and thin, carpeted to minimize sound. It was a noiseless place.

Atholl called it "Lonely Mansions" and "The Wound-Licking Station." He said it was full of separated and divorced people, some with kids, some with bottles. No one wanted to know anyone else. No one heard anyone else. It was a recovery room, he said. The flats were as much as they legally needed to be and no more: the bedroom could fit a double bed, but not the space to walk around it. The ceiling skimmed the scalp—and thank God the builders hadn't used Artex. Atholl liked describing things. He'd told her once that he'd wanted to be a writer.

She jogged up the stairs, three floors, six flights, and knocked on his door. He opened it and she could smell immediately that he was drunk. It wasn't the smell of vodka that hit her, it was his sweat. He gave off a strange odor that reminded Rose of her mother's melancholy smell. She took a deep breath and stepped inside, shutting the door behind her.

"This isn't the time," she said, meaning for drunkenness, but it was too late for that. Anton Atholl was bouncing off the walls on his way to the sitting room. His shirt back was caked in sweat.

Holding on to the door jamb, he managed the turn into the sitting room and she followed him.

Atholl slumped in a low armchair, half bottles of vodka cluttering up a table at his side, three glasses, different sizes, all dirty with orange juice. Behind him, through a long picture window, was the Clyde, a black mile oozing towards the sea, and beyond it, on the far bank, small windows into other lonely lives.

She didn't want to go into the room. She leaned on the door frame, tucking her hands into her hoodie pockets. Self-pity hung in the room like a smoker's fog.

Atholl attempted a smile. "You hear about Aziz Balfour?"

"What about him?"

Anton Atholl shrugged. Rose felt sick again and looked around the room. He hadn't taken much furniture when he left his wife and kids. He wasn't a man for going to John Lewis and picking out fabrics for sofas. He had a leather chair, a table for the drink, and a radio for the cricket. Luckily, the flat came furnished with a washing machine.

So Lord Anton Atholl sat on his one chair with nothing but his misery for company. Rose imagined his wife and kids, who she'd never met, over the other side of the city, laughing and sitting on different chairs, using crockery and napkins, reading books they'd had for ages, with chests and beds and sofas, laughing as they thought about the fat old man in his empty flat. Lonely Mansions, right enough.

She honestly thought that Anton would be the one to go to the police one day. When Julius died Atholl was her first concern. He was the weak point, they'd always thought that. She'd always believed that he didn't report them to the police out of loyalty to Julius. But now Julius was dead and still he hadn't made any kind of move. She looked at him, sitting in his ruin; the fact that he'd done nothing made her think less of him.

She cut to the chase. "Where the fuck is Robert?"

Atholl looked into the far distance as his eyebrows rose in panic and confusion. She watched as a sob seemed to roll from his belly, through his chest and come screaming out of his mouth. He covered his face with both hands and cried. He didn't know where Robert was.

She watched impassively from the doorway. She couldn't leave before she knew who was doing what. "What's Dawood up to?"

"I don't know. I don't know—" He broke off to sob. "... Work out what's going on ... Julius was the one who knew everything."

"I thought Dawood knew everything."

"Julius made his own contacts, recently. He's..." He lost his breath and sat crying, not messily like her with the cops, not out of control. It was funeral crying. He was trying to make her stop asking.

She watched him for a while. She wasn't entirely unsympathetic but she knew it was at least amplified by the drink. Julius warned her never to waste time talking drunks around. He said it was like trying to stand jelly on its nose.

She watched him for a while. Just when she'd decided he probably wouldn't stop soon, had rolled her shoulder into the hall to
leave, she heard his breathing change. She looked back. Wet faced
and red, Atholl looked up at her.

"I'm sorry."

She didn't understand. "What for?"

He started to cry again, a hand over his eyes. Rose tutted.
"Have you done something?"

"Not me. The office safe is *locked*. The keys are *gone*."

She froze. The safe. She should have gone there but she hadn't
had time. "What did you just say?"

"The keys are gone. Can't get in."

It was secondhand information. The safe didn't take keys.
Atholl was passing on information from someone else.

"Who told you that?"

"Dawood."

Dawood and Monkton. Looking for the contacts book, looking
for the accounts. That's what it was. That's what they'd been
planning.

Rose watched him sit forward, pick up a half bottle with an
inch left in it and drain the vodka. Rose felt her gums wither just
watching him. "What did Dawood expect to find in there?"

In the distance, somewhere across the water, a car alarm called
plaintively.

"There's nothing in there. More importantly, have you found
Robert's laptop?" asked Atholl.

Rose shook her head.

Atholl took a deep breath. "Robert sent a money-laundering
report to the Serious and Organised Crime Agency—" He heard
her sharp intake of breath and held a hand up, turning away as if
he couldn't bear her shock. "St— don't! Dawood caught it. It's
OK, Dawood caught it."

"The fuck are you talking about, 'caught it'?"

Atholl considered the angles and then just shut his eyes and told her, "Robert sent it on his laptop through the firm's Wi-Fi after he looked in the safe. Dawood has a ten-minute delay built into the computer system. He scans all the emails and he caught it. It never got sent."

Rose's mind was having trouble taking it in. Robert finding the safe, Robert looking in the safe, Robert reporting the contents to SOCA. And Dawood having access to all of the firm's emails.

"Did Julius know Dawood had that?"

Atholl shrugged. "Does it matter now?"

It didn't. She hoped no one had ever sent emails about her. They must have, though—her case was heard in late 1997. Everyone had email then, didn't they? But Julius wouldn't have said anything indiscreet about her in an email. He didn't even use a mobile phone.

The car alarm was still whining across the river. It made her feel afraid, brought back faint, uncomfortable memories. She wanted to get out of here.

"Well, Robert's laptop isn't in the house."

"And it's the laptop you need to find. The safe isn't important. He could have sent the report through another email system."

Not Robert. He did everything in a half-assed way because someone else was always there to sort out his fuck-ups for him. She stood straight, about to leave, when it occurred to her that she had come for information and given it instead. Even pissed and desperate, Atholl was clever. She could hardly remember why she'd come but then it came to her. "Atholl, why the fuck is Monkton talking to me in front of people?"

It was Monkton's seeping wound, the deal done with Dawood all those years ago to get her off. Julius told her that Monkton had arranged it all, found the boy, set it up. He wanted her to know so that she had it over Monkton, as insurance. Monkton had never spoken to her before, ever. Though they had passed each other in courts, been near each other in Julius's presence, though he had attended the christenings of all of Francine and Robert's children.

Atholl shook his head, looked as if he might cry again. It was a ruse to stop her asking again.

"What's making him so cocky? Why's he so sure nothing's coming up?"

He cried again, pressing his fingers into his eyes; it looked painful. He'd been crying before, when he knew she wanted to ask something. He panicked when she asked about Monkton. The SOCA report was alarming but it had been stopped and had nothing to do with the safe.

"Could there be something else in the safe?"

He shrugged. "No. The safe's...there's nothing in there. Robert's put the keys somewhere daft, that's all. He ran off because of the SOCA report."

Rose watched him touch the collection of half bottles at the side of his chair, looking for a mouthful. She hated vodka. She hated the smell of it, the greasy look of it, the acrid tang of vodka sweat. She looked at Atholl's face and saw it then: regret. He wasn't looking for mouthfuls of vodka left in the bottle, he was averting his face. Atholl had done something terrible. He had done a thing that he could never forgive himself for, something that would come to his mind in his death throes. She wondered if the thing he'd done was kill Robert.

"Is Robert dead?"

"What?" Still looking through his collection.

"Robert? Is he dead?"

"I don't know. Not yet, maybe."

Rose wanted to cry then. Her rarely used tear ducts yawned a painful ache. She sucked in a sharp breath, ordered them to

stop and turned and walked out of the desolate
goodbye. She shut the door carefully behind her out ‑

The cold night enveloped her so she pulled he
tucked her hands back into her pockets, tramping up and
the train station. hill to

Robert was a lovely person. She had seen him grow
a few years ahead of her, and she loved him as his father
they both saw in him the innocence and loyalty of a good n.
He married a nice girl from uni, he had nice children and a nice,
clean house. And when Julius got her to do a nannying qualifi‑
cation and mind Robert's kids it was always understood that she
was nanny to Robert as well. She was the buffer, because Julius
needed two things: a pair of soiled hands, and an heir. But if she
and Julius were ruined, Robert was their hope, their humanity.
She had failed to protect him. She had failed Mr. McMillan.

She cried for all of them, letting her tear ducts have their child‑
ish way as she walked through the quiet suburban streets to the
station. She formed her defense: if anyone asked her she'd say he
was crying for Julius.

A SOCA report meant that Robert had found the back safe.
How the hell did he get in there? He didn't even know the room
was there. Would Dawood have told him? He couldn't have, he
couldn't have been sure Robert would send the email from the of‑
fice.

Robert must have gone into his father's office and looked at ev‑
erything. Everything, otherwise it was just a pile of money and
no explanation. Rose felt the loss then, a sudden death. Not like
Julius, not just sadness. She had wanted better for Robert. She felt
herself sag, the weight of his innocence dragging at her, slowi
her feet.

Ahead of her in the lane, the bright lights of the static
through the inky dark. But Robert filled out a money-lau

what he saw and was indignant. He was fighting
report, ing, he didn't accept it, and that was hopeful some-
again e had to do now was get Robert out of a mess and she'd
how. a hundred times. No one knew where he was, that was
don
go
eered, deciding that it was the smell of the vodka, the SOCA
rt, the malicious reach of Dawood that got her so down, Rose
ied her face with her sleeve. She took the underpass to the plat-
form and waited with her hood up, facing away from the direction
the train would come from so that no one on the train would see
her when it drew in.

Then she thought back to Atholl. He didn't know where
Robert was, she felt certain that was true. Atholl was good at his
job, she reflected again, he could steer a conversation any way he
wanted. Three times, he told her not to bother with the safe. Then
Rose shut her eyes and processed his answer through her gut.

There was something in the safe.

11

Morrow and DC Wheatly were parked in the Red Road at the pitiless start of the morning rush hour. Wainwright had sent word that the health and safety paperwork was through and she could come and have a look at the murder scene, but she would have to come early.

Wheatly's meaty hands gripped the steering wheel and his farmer's neck craned to follow a chamois-faced early riser hurrying down the hill. They were all making their way towards the city, out of here, clustering at bus stops, smoking and waiting. They glanced in at the car, spotting Morrow and Wheatly, knowing they were cops because he looked so square and pinched-mouthed and policey.

"You could lose the mustache, Wheatly," she said, continuing a conversation they had been having intermittently for a week.

He wanted to do more undercover work but his face wouldn't let him.

"I've done that before." Wheatly stroked the black 'tache b towards his lip with his forefinger. "I still look like a recr poster."

Morrow shrugged and looked up at the flats. The body was gone and that was good. A body was always a distraction at a murder scene. It tended to draw the eye and evoke sparks of empathy, or, for Morrow at least, distracting ponderings on why she wasn't feeling empathy. The site was so spectacular, it would be hard enough to focus on details.

The Red Road flats were twenty-seven stories tall, five hundred yards wide and being stripped for demolition. All the walls, the casing and especially the windows were being removed before the explosives were set, to avoid a glass storm. They couldn't get into the scene of the murder before this morning: without health and safety paperwork she couldn't even pass through the protective fencing. Morrow didn't like heights terribly much.

Early in her career Morrow had policed the crowd when the high flats in the Gorbals were demolished. The officers had to stand with their backs to the show, watching the crowd for three or so hours. People brought food, drinks, things to sit on. The fevered atmosphere was unsettling. Morrow watched the crowd swell and grow boisterous, scanning for drunks and trouble and pickpockets. Over the afternoon she listened as people tried to explain away their excitement. It's a bit of history, they said, history of the city. But that didn't satisfy, it didn't explain the buzz of anticipation running through the crowd so they began to falsify complaints against the high flats: we had damp, my auntie died there, I saw a man go out a window. Excuses, because they knew there was something venal about their lip-licking excitement. It was a modern public hanging. They were there to see something bigger than them die, to participate in an irreversible act of destruction.

Morrow got out of the car. Cold rain pattered on her head and looked around the road, cut off at the end by a high fence. Her van was parked by some garages, presumably for the workers. At the base of the demolition site, still open for business, was a chemist. It must have been running a methadone dispensing program, keeping the locals dozy, or the council would have shut it down by now.

She climbed back into the car and told Wheatly to drive around the block to the other side. They pulled out and went up the hill, took a right at the roundabout and another right to the front entrance of the flats. Wheatly was looking hard in his rear-view.

"A white van's been following us," he said. "Stopped down there behind us, just moved off and went on up the hill."

She didn't really know what to say. "D'you get the reg?"

"Aye." He parked up carefully and jotted it in his notebook. "I'll check it when we get back."

The road was blocked off ahead by fencing and a complex of shipping containers with the demolition company's name stamped on them.

Morrow got out on the exposed hillside. Buffeted by the brutal wind and horizontal rain she pulled her coat tight and walked over to the chicken-wire fence. What used to be the central stairwells were being used as rubbish chutes to funnel the stripped rubble to the ground. At the bottom a digger was pulling lumps of plaster and brick away from the opening, tidying it into dunes.

Wheatly got out and came over to her side of the car. Beyond the wire gate they watched a hard-hatted workman come out of a shipping container. He approached the gate and checked their warrant cards before undoing the padlock to let them onto the site. He pointed them towards the container he'd come out of. It was made of blue corrugated steel with a window and door cut into the side.

They took the metal ramp to the door and knocked. It was answered by a small energetic man with a carefully mended har

She held out her hand. "DI Alex Morrow."

He shook it. "Farrell McGovan," he said, his top lip sliding on the diagonal.

He stood aside, welcoming them into the overheated metal room. It was carpeted, had chairs and two desks and a wall chart but it was still very obviously a metal container.

Standing with a DC was DI Paul Wainwright. Tall, dark and ugly, Wainwright smiled, shook her hand and nodded hello to Wheatly. She nodded at his DC as Wainwright introduced him, forgetting his name instantly.

"Nice to meet you," she said, feeling guilty. "So, we going up there?"

McGovan nodded. "I need you to sign this waiver, saying we're not responsible for your safety. I can't take you all up, there's only me, so I can only take two of you. Health and safety."

Morrow and Wainwright nodded their assent. He gave them the forms, long and legalistic, already faxed to their superior officers and OK'd. Morrow and Wainwright signed them and handed them back.

"Also health and safety: you need hats and high-vis vests on."

They nodded again and he opened the door out. "You two all right to wait here?" he asked the DCs. They looked to their bosses for permission to sit about in the warm office while Morrow and Wainwright climbed eleven stories of bare concrete.

She strained to think of a job for Wheatly. Finally she said, "Call that reg number in and then, um, just sit there."

Wainwright laughed softly next to her.

They shut the door behind them and followed McGovan to another container next door, filling the journey with pointless pleasantries: how've you been? How's the north? Will we all be getting moved next year? Morrow didn't really believe it would happen but the current custom was to fret about it.

McGovan welcomed them into a manned room, much colder

than the office, with a wall of yellow hard hats on a shelf and a rack of bright yellow waistcoats.

He found one to fit each of them. As they put them on Morrow considered why they needed to be highly visible; if it was so they could be seen falling, or spotted lying dead under a ton of rubble. McGovan led them out of the door towards the building. Wainwright made a weak joke about the Village People and Morrow laughed, because she liked him, not because it was funny.

"This is, um," Wainwright looked fearfully up at the building, "a bit hairy, really…"

Across a hundred yards of broken glass and wooden splinters, they walked into the rotting remains of a housing revolution.

The corner stairwell steps were bare concrete, the cladding on the walls stripped off. They climbed, slowing to catch their breath, following McGovan. On the sixth floor the banisters disappeared. On the eighth floor the outside walls were already down and the wind swirled dust around their knees, brushing it from the upstairs landings into their eyes, down their collars. Birds flew past their ankles. Each time her head rose above another landing floor Morrow saw the giant thrumming city afresh. The confusion of scale left her sick.

The girders were whining, the whole edifice swaying slightly as it caught the wind. The building felt as if it was crumbling, a skeleton dosed in lime.

Morrow's awareness of the sheer drops heightened until they were all she was aware of. The stairs became nothing but a series of mortal edges, hypnotic and terrifying. A braying wind buffeted her towards them, her muscles lost faith in her, resisting, tightening. Images of specks jumping from the World Trade Center drew her muscles tighter still until all of her movements were stiff and ineloquent.

Losing her breath, she had just decided that she couldn't go up any more when McGovan shouted over the wind that they were there.

Hands out to steady herself on a flat surface, Morrow was glad to turn away from the sheer drop and walk into what had once been flats. Not now. A five hundred foot long stretch of concrete and beyond that another mesmerizing drop. McGovan led them three girders down, to a dark patch and a girder whose dusty redness was marred by smears of black fingerprint dust.

No buckets of water had been carried up eleven terrifying floors to wash the mess away; the pool of dried blood was still there, undisturbed.

Morrow stood at what she supposed were Aziz Balfour's feet and took it in. They were thirty feet from the outside edge, from the front of the building, close enough to keep her stomach queasy.

Why eleven floors up, was what she was thinking. Why would anyone go to the trouble of bringing him up here? It was hard to imagine anywhere more godforsaken. Maybe this space meant something important to someone.

"Who last lived here?" she shouted at Wainwright, trying to be heard over the wind and the creaking steel.

"Asylum seeker," he shouted back, his voice snatched by the sharp wind. "Somali." He held up three fingers. "Three kids." Two hands in surrender, a frown and nod. "Couldn't be nicer." He pointed out to the north. "Lives there, now. Alibi. Nice woman." He repeated the surrender, using made-up, garbled sign language.

Morrow reciprocated, rolling her hands around each other. "Before that?"

"Empty for a long time..." shouted Wainwright, stumped for a gesture.

He hadn't looked into previous tenants and that was fair enough. It was his case and he had the right to decide which lines of inquiry to pursue.

"What's your thinking?" She wanted to sound deferential but it was a bit too subtle a tone for the circumstances. She held her hands out in a question. It was stupid, like a tourist shouting because someone didn't understand English.

Wainwright knew what she meant though. "Balfour's charity has its office over there." He nodded vaguely to the northern sky "They chased him from it, up here. Footprints"— he flattened a hand and slid it on the level—"running."

They gave up trying to talk and each looked around the site. Morrow wondered again why they'd chase him here, it had to mean something. Or nothing. They may have thought he'd never be found. The flats were due to come down soon but a pair of peregrine falcons had nested on the twenty-fourth floor, laid two eggs and couldn't be moved because they were a protected species. But a human wouldn't choose to be up here. She saw McGovan glance back to the stairs.

Wainwright turned his wrist towards his face without actually looking at his watch. He was thinking about time.

"OK." She waved a hand towards the stairs.

"Enough?"

She nodded.

McGovan looked at both of them, saw they were ready and shuffled around so that the wind would carry his voice to them.

"Now, I warn you," he said, perfectly audible, "the way down is a bit scary."

A sudden gust of wind carried a puff of dust and they closed their faces to it, tucked their chins into their chests and walked back to the stairs.

McGovan was wrong. The walk down wasn't scary, it was terrifying. The steps were coated in rubble and the dust that rose up from below. Wainwright wasn't enjoying it either, he was in front of her and she saw his back straighten, his feet feeling for the step in front. One foot slipped, skidding a millimeter in an unexpected direction and she read the sudden horror in his posture. He looked down, concentrating on the steps.

They arrived back on the floor where the sides of the building rose around them. Two floors further down and a banister appeared and they clung to it, grateful, as they were swallowed by the dark and followed the stairs down.

The tension didn't leave them when they got back to earth; Morrow and Wainwright still felt for their steps with their toes, still kept their hands out to steady themselves, until they got out of what was left of the doorway.

The sunlight and steady ground were a blessing they could hardly remember. Morrow was sweating under her hard hat, and exhausted, every muscle in her body had been taut for half an hour.

She followed McGovan. Wainwright fell into step next to her.

"Health and safety gone mad, eh?" he said.

Morrow grinned and rolled her eyes at him. "How many times you been up there?"

Wainwright winced. "Five times. Gets worse every time."

"Thanks, Paul, I'd no idea that was so..." she struggled to think of a more heroic word and gave up, "scary. Aziz Balfour seemed like a nice guy."

"By all accounts, really. Funny guy. Devout, kind, got married last year, first baby due in a couple of months. He came here after the 2008 earthquake to help run a relief charity."

"Why were they up there?"

Wainwright looked back up. "He was in the office, really late at night," he nodded to the north again, "then he was up here. We think he ran, trying to get away. He came up the central stairwell. There are skidded footprints all the way up, his soles."

"Just his?"

"And others, trainers," he said. "They're small, size six. They look like a kid's foot."

"Some wee guy?" She was thinking of a minor player, a young gangster trying to impress a boss.

"Could be. They were lone prints though and Adidas trainers." No one wore Adidas anymore.

"Take a pretty determined wee ned to chase him all the way up there. Bloody shame. Balfour was a real hero back home. He was involved in the rescue effort in the '05 and '08 earthquakes. Came from a lot of money, corrupt military family, but he walked away. He was a really good guy." Wainwright shuffled his foot, frowning, troubled by his engagement with the victim. It didn't help to feel that way.

"What about his hand?" Morrow held out her own fist. "In the photos it looks like he punched something a day or so before he died."

"That we don't know. Wife has no idea. She saw the bruise but he said he'd banged it by accident at work. That was a day before he disappeared."

"Bruises were yellow…"

Paul looked down at her. "D'you think going up there helped you?"

"It's more complicated than I thought. Aziz makes no sense. The Pakistan connection is interesting though. I thought it was a setup by Michael Brown, but he's not that smart. Mind you, he's getting very complex advice from someone…"

Wainwright nodded. "'S what money does for them. Crim's a crim but a crim with money, that's a different fish."

Morrow nodded. "Aye, Paul, you don't need to tell me about that."

"Oh, sorry, Alex, I didn't mean your brother—"

"No, no..." She waved his discomfort away, and looked back at the building. "I just can't see how they did it. I was hoping Brown's prints were on something movable."

They walked on for a few steps, enjoying the new fluidity of their muscles.

"Well," Wainwright stood tall, looking over her head, "back to the glamour."

"So, what's on your board?"

"Got this," he nodded back at the flats, "got another murder, a domestic. Got two big lassies that stabbed a pal with their jaggy heels at a club. And a missing person." He leaned over her, smiling. "The missing person's a lawyer."

"Aye? What does that mean?"

"Nicer biscuits," he said, and they laughed loud and long because they weren't dead.

12
1997

Glasgow shut down on the Sunday Princess Diana died. Garage flowers were left in a directionless pile in George Square. Cars drove slower. It rained. The city closure was not, like London, a natural response to crippling grief, but rather an awkward pause. The city cast its eyes down and stood to the side, waiting for the moment to pass.

By teatime DS George Gamerro had been working hard all through the quiet day, getting his own paperwork up to date and coordinating other people's. Now he was preparing to question the suspect in the Pinkie Brown murder.

He was sitting in the canteen, eating the sandwiches his wife made and drinking soup from his flask. Outside the window the sky was gray and glowering, grim, the early evening sliding imperceptibly into night.

It was nice when cases were this straightforward. George was late in his career, long enough in to see everything as part of a pattern. This was an easy clean-up, he would leave his desk tidy at the end of the day. Plus, it was satisfying to get someone who was like that off the streets at fourteen, before they could do any more harm.

Some uniformed colleagues came into the canteen, saw him at the table and came over and sat with him or near him, got their own sandwiches out. They formed an encampment in the big empty room and took their time. Everyone was getting proper long breaks today because of what had happened in Paris. No shoplifters because most of the shops were shut. No football trouble because there was no football.

Someone said it would hot up later, when the drink kicked in. They nodded. Foretelling disaster was a deeply embedded cop habit but they all knew that the city wouldn't get Saturday-night wild, not even Sunday-night annoyed. Everyone was a little bit stunned. Really dedicated alkies would be asleep tonight, having had a good clean run at the drink all day. Social drinkers would be sitting indoors watching the telly, waiting for the day to pass. The chat turned to the car crash in Paris, everyone said where they were when they heard, as if trying to insert themselves into the event, and then the stories petered out and everyone felt slightly confused.

George put the lid on his piece box and screwed the top back on his flask.

"Right." He stood up holding his belly and said what he always said after lunch, "That was nice soup."

"Don't you make your own soup, George?"

"Aye. It's fucking lovely."

They chuckled and George smiled as he made his way to the door. He jogged down one flight of steps to the office, heavy on his feet, old knees protesting at the jauntiness of his gait.

Four of them shared the office, their desks turned to the walls as if they'd all been naughty. Three of the desks were empty but DC David Monkton was sitting at his. He was waiting and broke off to smile up at George.

"She's in there now," he said.

Monkton was newly transferred to their section. He had asked to neighbor Gamerro in the Pinkie Brown questioning. He needed the experience, he said. He was planning to do his sergeants' exams soon.

Monkton was young, slick, ambitious. He seemed to know senior officers Gamerro was intimidated by, nodded to them on the stairs, smiled knowingly at the mention of their names.

George was an old cop, and he understood the formal systems of power, rank, seniority, qualifications. He also knew there were informal systems. He didn't really understand those. In his younger day, when he was ambitious, he'd thought about joining the Masons. He'd be embarrassed to admit that now. No one was really in the Masons or the lodge. The real informal power systems were invisible—at least they were to George.

So Gamerro felt uneasy with Monkton, who made it plain that he understood those informal systems. Monkton's voice was never moderated or deferent, he spoke loudly, always expected to be listened to. Another reason George didn't like him was that Monkton had bought a house. He was single. It seemed the height of decadence to Gamerro, a man of another generation, who had lived with his parents and handed in his wages until he married. He disapproved of Monkton, either for his abandonment of his parents or for coming from the sort of family who didn't expect their children to contribute.

But the real reason that George didn't like Monkton was that he made Gamerro feel old and clumsy. Gamerro gave advice as he always did with young officers but Monkton seemed to know everything already. He listened patiently, he was superficially respectful but he knew it already. The entry exams were more stringent now. The new intake were a different class than in his day. George found himself thinking about bringing his retirement forward. His cousin had a paper shop and wanted him to come in with a half share.

And yet George Gamerro was too experienced a cop to distrust his discomfort with Monkton entirely. He found himself seeking Monkton's company, the way he might return time and again to a lying witness.

"OK." George put his flask down on the desk for later. "You ready then?"

Monkton stood up. "Aye."

They walked down to the cells together, taking their time, walking in silence as they got their heads ready.

Questioning a child about a brutal murder would be draining. George's own children were in their twenties and he couldn't help but remember the unformed putty of them at fourteen. He comforted himself with the thought that it should be straightforward: in the car with Monkton and Harry, the kid had already confessed to the murder. They just needed to get it on tape for corroboration. If they didn't get it there would be plenty of fingerprints. The alleyway was wallpapered with smeared handprints.

The lighting in the corridor was dim and contrasted sharply with the hard white light in the interview rooms. George had often thought that it gave interviewees the subliminal sense of being marooned.

He and Monkton hesitated at the door to the interview room, looked at each other, gathered their thoughts. George opened the door to the startlingly bright room and his pupils contracted suddenly, a painful twinge as the light slapped his retina. His eyes watery, his vision blurred, he guessed his way to the seat at the table, following the route his legs remembered from a hundred other interviews held on a hundred other rainy evenings.

He didn't look at the boy at the table. Neither he nor Monkton greeted either him or the woman sitting behind him. It wasn't deliberate rudeness. They had to get the tape recorder working before anyone said anything, so that everything would be on record. George was aware that it must seem rude, or cold, or something, but they had procedures to follow and it was important that they saw them through. He was aware also of performing well for Monkton, showing him how it should be done, proving he wasn't past it. For a moment, as his backside made contact with the chair, he felt like a memory of Monkton's, from early in his career, a story being passed on to the would-be cops who were now in primary school, the boys who'd become the men who'd make Monkton feel old and out of touch.

Sitting next to the wall, blinking his vision clear, he put the tapes in, turned on the machine and gave the date, place and a list of those present. Then he started.

"Michael Brown? Is that your name?"

A whispered "Aye."

"Well, Michael, as you heard me saying to the tape there, I'm Detective Sergeant George Gamerro. I'll be leading this interview."

The boy didn't look up. He was small for his age, thin shouldered, wearing a dirty yellow Nike T-shirt. His eyes were swollen.

"Do you understand, Michael?"

The boy gave a tiny nod to the table.

"Do you know who this lady is behind you?"

He didn't say anything.

"Yvonne's a staff member at Cleveden House, where you live, isn't she?"

The boy nodded again.

"Would you mind speaking, Michael, so we can get it on tape?" George was being as gentle as he could but the boy didn't speak.

"OK. Now, Yvonne isn't here to give you legal advice or anything like that. She's just here to make sure you're all right, isn't that right, Yvonne?"

Yvonne looked up at George and nodded, half smiling, almost as shy as the boy. She was just a kid herself, a slip of a thing, she wouldn't be any trouble.

George's eyes fell on the boy's T-shirt. Dirty yellow. Not muddy or anything, dusty with dirt though, as if he had rolled around on dry ground. George caught himself. There was something wrong about the T-shirt. His glance fell to the boy's face.

The boy was facing the table but he was staring up at Monkton, and for a moment George thought his eyes weren't swollen from crying but from hating Monkton. He looked tiny, sitting with his hands on his lap, shoulders dropped, eyes straining through his eyebrows.

Aware of the tape, George lifted a bit of paper so that the pause would sound as if he had been looking through notes. But he kept thinking about how the T-shirt was wrong. He knew why suddenly: there was no blood on it. But this kid was in care. If he had come from a chaotic house and changed out of a bloody T-shirt there might not be a clean one to put on, he might have grabbed a dirt-dusty top from a floor. George didn't rate group homes as a way to bring kids up, whatever they came from, but homes did keep them clean. He had to give them that. They laundered their clothes and their bed linen, they cleaned the mud from their shoes and their knees. There wouldn't be a dusty T-shirt lying around a group home.

George put his hand on the table in front of the boy to get his attention. He dragged his fingers back, pulling the boy's focus with him. The boy looked at him and George softened his face.

"Michael, are you planning to speak to me?"

He was being much softer than he normally would. He could

feel Monkton bristle next to him, sucking his teeth, shift in his chair.

The boy was looking properly at George now, reading him.

"Is that your T-shirt?"

Confused, the boy ran a finger on his chest. "Bought it."

"Which shop did you buy it in?"

The boy lowered his brow, the look he had been giving Monkton on him now. He thought George was asking if he'd stolen it.

"Because," said George, "my niece was looking for a yellow T-shirt with Nike on it."

The kid tutted at the weak ploy, making George feel foolish in front of Monkton.

"OK," he said, his voice colder, "*when* did you put that T-shirt on?"

The boy looked left, anticipating an angle, he looked right, looking for a reason not to answer. He couldn't find one. "Yesterday. In the morning."

He'd put it on before the murder. George believed him. Monkton, however, gave a small sigh that would be inaudible on the tape. George was afraid he had missed something, that he was making a fool of himself. He decided to change the subject.

"What happened last night?"

But the boy didn't answer, he just stared at Monkton.

"This is your chance to tell us your version, Michael."

Nothing. Angry stares. Monkton was smirking at the table.

"How do you think it'll look when we go to court and you've refused to answer any questions? A jury will think only a guilty person would refuse to speak."

The boy was shifting in his seat, as if he was playing with something in his hands under the table.

"Hands on the table," George ordered and the boy did it.

George tried another tack. "Michael, just tell us. You've already told the officers who brought you in that you killed your brother."

He was fingering a cut, that's what he had been doing under the table. They were small hands, slightly puffy. The puffiness drew George's attention. He looked and suddenly saw swellings, scratches, welts. The injuries were not on the promontories of his knuckles, not where they would have made contact if the boy had hit someone. The cuts and bruises were in the soft valley of his knuckles, on the flat plains of the backs of his hands. Someone had hit him. His big brother had hit him and Michael fought back, and it got out of hand. George felt relief. Here was the reason, an excuse for compassion.

"Hey, those bruises on your hands," he asked, fingering his own knuckles, "how did that happen?"

But the boy didn't speak. He didn't blurt an excuse for killing his brother. He sat dumb, looked at Monkton's hands, at breaks on the knuckles there. George looked as Monkton covered the bruised hand with the other one. His relief deflated: Monkton had battered the boy and now he was sitting through the interview to stop the child saying anything about it.

George could do one of two things now: he could ask the question again and the boy might say that Monkton had hit him. The other course of action was to ask about something else. If he did ask about his hands then it would be on the tape. Even if George didn't report it, the person transcribing the tape would have to.

George was old enough to know what would happen to a cop who did that to another cop. He thought of Monkton's relationship with powerful men, the small knowing smiles at the mention of the chief, the DCI, the handshakes in corridors.

And George knew what would happen when Brown's defense solicitor heard about it. They'd use it to invalidate the oral confession from the car and Michael Brown would get off the murder charge, get out and they'd pick him up in another year or so for another murder, a second life lost over a slap, maybe, nothing much, maybe.

"When did you last see your brother, Michael?"

The boy shrugged a shoulder, remembering. A flash of panic in his eyes and his courage left him. He covered his face with his battered hands and keened, the breath leaving his chest until there was none left in him. He would confess now, George felt sure, they just had to wait.

But he didn't. Michael Brown breathed in, sudden and loud, a drowning man coming to the surface, and as he did his hands began to slap at himself, scratching at his face, scratching welts on his cheeks and eyelids. Yvonne grabbed his elbows from behind him, pulling his arms back until he couldn't move.

His face was a mess of welts, his eyes wide and chest heaving hard, the breath rasping loud through his throat. George had never seen anything like that; it made him think of an animal panicked at slaughter. He wanted to get out of here.

He hurriedly rolled through the appropriate wording, stopped the tape and waved Monkton out of the room. They didn't speak until they were walking down the corridor and the door was shut.

Monkton spoke first. "What was that all about?" he smirked.

George punched his shoulder, turning Monkton to face him and jabbing a finger at his nose.

"Did you raise your hands o'er that boy?"

Monkton tipped his head, disrespectful, half mocking. "Come on…"

George was furious: "Did you hit the wean when you were bringing him in?"

"As if I'd hit a wean," said Monkton, his flat tone telling George to let it go.

But George had already let it go. He could have asked about it on tape. He had already let it go. What he couldn't let him away with was the lack of deference to a senior officer and Monkton knew it.

Monkton sighed and explained: "It was a restraint, sir. He resisted arrest in the car. He went mental, just like he did then." He looked back down the corridor. "Grabbing at himself, at the headrest and that and we had to restrain him and his hands got bumped." He raised his hands in supplication. "What do you want me to say?"

"I wanted the back-seat confession to be good, for us to only need fingerprints for corroboration and be able to shut the case down. But I'm not getting that, am I, DC Monkton?"

"No, sir," said Monkton as George turned back to the stairs. "But there is a reason why you send us young guys out on a call like that."

George slowed his pace, just a step behind Monkton. The statement hurt his pride. It suggested that George was past his prime, which he was, he knew he was. But it did something else too. It alarmed him. And as he stopped to take the uncomfortable feelings apart—the hurt pride of an older man, usurped, the fear of what Monkton and other young officers understood by their physical prowess—it was then that he saw a scratch on Monkton's neck. It was a deep cut, diagonal, running into his hairline. The hair around it was pinkish, where blood had been crudely washed off. It was proof that the boy had gone for him in the car. But what George saw was an injury from a hand around a neck, a cop kneeling on the chest of a small ill-fed boy in a yellow T-shirt and the boy's hand coming up and scratching the back of the burly cop's neck.

Monkton turned back to him and smiled. "Can I get you a cup of tea, sir?"

George shook his head. "Be back here in ten minutes."

Monkton jogged on down the stairs.

George found Harry in the canteen, eating his pieces, and pulled him aside.

"Sit here," he said, pointing him to a seat in the furthest corner of the canteen.

Harry smiled as he took the seat and laid his Tupperware box in front of him. George sat opposite him, took the Tupperware box by the corner and pulled it away across the table.

"Hey," Harry's eyes followed it, "I'm starving."

"Tell me, minute by minute, what happened when you went to Cleveden to pick up Michael Brown."

Harry looked wary. "Well," he reached for his top pocket, "I've got my notes—"

"Fuck your notes," said George. They both knew the value of notes. Notes were justifications to strangers who had never been punched or bitten or spat at. They were letters for teachers, not a conversation within a family. "Tell me."

Harry and George had always liked each other. They both played bowls, supported the same small football team. If they'd lived near each other and had been closer in age they would have been friends. But they didn't and they weren't.

Harry sat with his hands flat on the table, each a perfect mirror to the other, and looked George in the eye. "I'm telling *you*," he said, meaning "I'm not reporting this or giving evidence." "Just *you*."

"OK," said George.

"Monkton went mental. Stopped the car halfway here, dragged Brown out, screaming at him, 'We could kill you and no one would know,' 'Your brother was worthless scum.' World's well rid, sort of thing." He stopped, looking down. George let him catch up with himself. "It's the wee guy's brother. Dead, know? The wee guy..." Harry got lost in the unhappy memory.

"What started Monkton off?"

Harry looked confused. "I dunno. Kid was crying, he's only fourteen, at the end of the day. Monkton was driving, kept looking in the rear-view and just got more and more annoyed. Dunno."

George tapped his arm with his forefinger. "What did Michael Brown do?"

Harry couldn't look at George. One shoulder rose slowly to his ear. "What could he do?"

George didn't know what to say. Harry was a good man, a good cop. George knew he would have pulled Monkton off the kid and got him back to the station. He knew he would have said a few words to the boy, that he was probably the person who called the staff member in and made sure they got the Yvonne lassie to come from the kids' home and not just use the duty social worker.

"Did he confess to the murder?"

Harry dropped his eyes to the table. "I never heard it."

"Monkton's saying you heard it."

Harry couldn't meet his eye. "I know."

"So when did that first become the story?"

Harry sighed. "When we went to book him. Monkton said it as if we'd both heard it and just looked at me for confirmation. Stared at me until I nodded."

"Aw, for fuck's sake, Harry."

"I'm stupid..." Harry tried to explain. "I just, I kind of thought that..."

But George was aware of his own sins of omission, and it wasn't the first time he'd brushed over irregularities to secure a clean case. He looked up and found Harry staring at the door.

There, on the other side of the room, stood Monkton. He was

watching them. He wasn't angry, or sorry, but he had a look on his face that George had used many times when faced with an accused he found distasteful. It was disgust, or disdain. It was a look that meant the civilian in front of him hadn't the sense to know the damage they had done to the people around them. Suddenly, George wondered if Monkton was a very senior officer sent in to their department to test him. He knew it was a stupid idea but Monkton had authority and George didn't know where it came from.

George had to remind himself that he outranked him. He stood up—he was a little afraid, he could admit to himself that he was—and walked over to him.

"You." He poked Monkton in the chest as he walked past him. "You come with me right now."

They were in a tiny interview room at the back of the station. George had told Monkton to sit but he didn't.

"I'd rather stand."

"I'm not interested in what you'd *rather*, son. Sit-the-fuck-down."

Monkton sat down opposite him. The two men looked at each other.

"You hit that kid."

Monkton smirked and sat back, rolling his eyes like an insolent teenager.

George leaned over the table and shouted, "WHO THE FUCK DO YOU THINK YOU ARE?" He wanted to hit him but didn't. Monkton leaned away in his chair but held his eye. He wasn't scared.

"What if the kid didn't do it, did you even think of that?"

Monkton shook his head. "He did it."

George shouted again, "We don't *know* that yet."

Monkton said quietly, "Aye, we do, George. The prints match."

George didn't understand. "What do you mean 'match'?"

"His prints, the boy's prints, are all over the alley. The kid's prints." He held up his hands, fingers splayed, showing George his palms. "They match the scene."

"They *might*."

"No," said Monkton carefully, "they *do*." And he raised his finger, pointing at the ceiling. "It's a match."

Without speaking George stood up and walked out to the corridor. He shut the door carefully and walked down to the toilet, locking himself in a stall. He couldn't even cry. He sat on the toilet pan, and blinked over and over at the back of the door. It was Sunday. Diana had died. No one was in. None of the admin staff were in. The boy's prints wouldn't get processed until Monday morning.

But Monkton had pointed at the ceiling, meaning it was being decided further up, somewhere. If George decided to pursue it he'd be setting himself in opposition to very powerful people. He'd lose rank, lose his sergeant's pension. George didn't know who Monkton was or who he knew or why he was so confident.

That's when George decided to leave the service and take up his cousin's offer on the paper shop.

13

Robert McMillan had only reached a lower level of consciousness when his stomach lurched violently. He sprang from the bed, looking for something to vomit into and found himself in a strange room. He looked left. He looked right, vaguely aware of a blond Persian carpet and giant double bed. A black tin waste bin appeared in front of his mouth and he emptied himself into it, following it to the ground as it was gently lowered in front of him.

He was on all fours, naked, vomiting green bile out of an empty stomach, unable to stop convulsive retching but suddenly aware of his surroundings. The waste bin was copper, lacquered black but chipped in places so that the copper glinted through. It looked like a military item, like something from the Boer War. At the bottom were the contents of his stomach, a lake of algal water reflecting frothy saliva clouds.

Death. He'd been trying to remember, keep it at the forefront of his mind, but it kept slipping away. Even now his attention was drawn by irrelevant details. The rug below was very fine, silk, pale peach with white and yellow flowers blooming on stems sewn from green and the faintest tint of blue.

"That's it."

The voice was coming from behind him, unfamiliar, soft. And then a hand on his back, low. Too low for his waist. The warmth of a flat palm on his haunches. Though he was still being sick, though his nose was dripping from the force of his vomiting and his eyes were running, he was suddenly horrified by the intimate touch. He shot upright on his knees, his head and eyes roaring hangover objections.

He opened his eyes, blinking to clear the tears, and turned with great effort to look at the figure on his left.

Bright orange pubic hair under a small overhang of belly skin. Troublingly large pink nipples.

The hippie stood with his hands hanging by his sides now, un-selfconscious, watching Robert impassively. "Make sure it goes in the bin," he said softly, looking at the vomit. "The rug's worth thirty thousand pounds."

He turned and padded across the room to the doorway. Robert watched his sagging buttocks until they disappeared down the dim corridor, then swung back to face the bin and threw up again.

A mug of coffee sat on the table in front of Robert, next to a deep Bristol Blue glass with water in it, and a strip of painkillers.

He stared hard at them, trying to keep his line of vision on the table. When he had stopped being sick the first thing he did was stagger across the bedroom and pull his trousers on before follow-ing the sound of the radio into the kitchen. The hippie, however, was still completely bare. He was not in the least bit bothered by being naked in the cold blue light of a cold blue day but sashayed barefoot, stomach out, baggy-arsed, oblivious to being seen.

"Underfloor heating," he said, as if in answer to a question.

It took a moment for Robert to fit it into his head. Underfloor heating. He moved his toes. The slate was warm to touch. It was quite lovely.

He took two pills out of the packet, put them in his mouth and tried to chase them with as little water as possible. They got stuck sideways, the water melting them, and they powdered on the back of his tongue. He managed to swallow some more water but the bitter paracetamol aftertaste hung in his mouth, making the saliva glands in his cheeks yawn.

The hippie came to the table and sat down at right angles to him.

"Do you remember last night?" he said quietly.

Robert didn't. He remembered being in the front room, drunk and sobbing and the hippie being there but not looking at him. Darkness in the pink drawing room. The firelight and another drink being poured. Standing somewhere, somewhere with a low ceiling, by a door. Then he remembered waking up, levitated from the bed by a wave of nausea.

Robert hadn't eaten yesterday. He imagined himself sobbing, telling the hippie everything. Did he? The hippie couldn't know. It was so convoluted, the story, Robert would have talked about the money and the photos of Rose and the SOCA report and that men were coming to kill him. The hippie would have been sickened if he'd told him. And he'd be frightened. He'd have mentioned the police by now.

"You were a bit drunk."

"Was I?" Robert felt sure there must have been hash cakes or pills or something, to make him black out that much. His throat was sore, maybe he had smoked something.

"I need to go," said the hippie.

Robert drank his coffee and the pills kicked in. More remembered snapshots came to him. Falling. A square table with a glass on it.

They'd kill him when they found him here.

The hippie was back at the door to the kitchen, dressed this time. He was wearing a tweed cape with a matching hat and a bizarre pheasant's tail feather sticking backwards out of it. "What time do your friends arrive?"

Robert didn't know what to say. Five? Nine? Tomorrow? What had he said last night? And then finally, why lie? Was the man wearing women's clothes?

"They're not coming. It's just me."

Robert couldn't look at the hippie, stared nervously at his coffee cup, his eyes falling on the blue glass and the hippie's reflection. The face looked warped in the glass, as if he'd had a stroke. Embarrassed, Robert looked back up and said accusingly, "Are you wearing women's clothes?"

"Am I?" The hippie flattened his hands to his stomach and looked down at himself. "Dunno."

"Those are women's clothes."

"OK." He stood straight. "Well-made, anyway."

After a while he heard a door close and moments afterwards felt the cold from outside curl around his toes and realized that the hippie had gone out of a front door. This subterranean flat had its own door.

A growl outside, coming from the back of the house, and Robert looked up to see four fat wheels pass the window. The hem of a tweed cape and a pair of cowboy boots on a quad bike.

Moving carefully, trying to keep his head level, Robert stood up slowly and looked around the room. A large cream-colored Aga, old and chipped with three doors that hung as if they were exhausted. A large pot sitting on top with a wooden spoon through the handle. Next to it a bread board and fresh white bread sitting on its nose to keep the cut side fresh.

His first instinct was to go over and smell the food but his stomach churned at the thought. He should get out of here.

Back in the bedroom he followed the trail of his clothes, shirt by the wardrobe, vest nearer the bed. He found one sock on the blankets and took a guess, feeling under the sheets and finding the other one halfway down. A sudden flash of memory: the two of them in the bed, drunk, were they hugging? Robert sat up. *Hugging? Naked* hugging? Was he remembering that?

No.

He'd imagined that. There were no physical sensations attached to the image. It wasn't a memory. Or was it? No. Or was it? It felt like the image of him sobbing in the front room but it wasn't likely, was it? But his sock was in the bed. The hippie held his hips as he vomited. And the hippie wore women's coats and hats with feathers in them. That wasn't normal but it didn't seem gay when he did it, more like a sartorial mishap.

Cringing, Robert looked at the bed. No. God no, it hadn't happened. Now he was worried that he'd even wondered about it. And then, as if recalling an onerous social obligation, it occurred to him that he was going to be murdered today, his life would end forever, so there was no fucking point worrying about physical contact, hugging, inappropriate or otherwise.

He found his shoes outside the door, one sitting properly, the other on its side. He had everything. Then he looked over at the bin sitting at the side of the dressing table.

It was a beautiful object. The thin light of day filtered in through the low windows and hit the exposed orange copper, just chips here and there on the tar-like enamel. It had a rolled copper brim and was bashed on the side as if someone had kicked it. He walked over to it and looked in.

The hippie had emptied the vomit out and washed it and dried it and put it back where it belonged.

The clothes, the furniture, the house, everything the hippie had was secondhand, someone else's stuff. He was wearing an Edwardian lady's coat, cowboy boots and riding a bad ass, filthy quad bike. He was living in his ancestral castle, inhabiting his own history. Robert wished he could tell him about his father because the hippie, of all people, might understand the suffocating weight of his inheritance.

Robert held his bundle of clothes and went out to the hall. A door sat open to a set of stone stairs leading up inside the castle. He stepped outside the little underground flat. Shutting the door, he heard the lock snap behind him. He immediately felt colder.

He put his foot on the first step and found it there, waiting for him: the awareness of his own death.

14

The circular portico in front of the high court was busy with smokers. All of the cases started at ten prompt and everyone was anxious to get as much nicotine into their bloodstream as they could before they went in. Gowned QCs stood in small groups, smoking quietly next to the families of accused and the families of the wronged who all smoked with their eyes down, avoiding contact with one another. Whatever their differences, there was a consensus of shame in the smoking area.

Wheatly dropped Morrow in the car park. She scanned for Atholl's face as she walked from the car park. She expected to see him. She didn't know if he smoked, she had supposed that he would. She was looking for him, reading the faces, when a small white rectangle passed the very outer scope of her vision. She stopped, turned and saw a white van pulling into the salt market traffic. Wheatly hadn't mentioned the reg number. He was drawing out behind her and she flagged him down.

"That reg," she said. "Did you get anything on it?"

"No record. Just a guy called Stepper."

She looked to the corner but the van was gone. "Find out what you can about him for when I get back," she said and walked away.

White vans were so common, it was easy to get paranoid. Still, her mind reeled through a penciled list: Brown's people, gun-toting school-age nutters. Danny's people, smiley, photograph-of-mum liar sharks. Suspicious loan givers. Angry roof repairers short of work. It wasn't a list of suspects, she realized, it was a list of worries.

She passed the glass wall and glanced into the lobby. The two armed officers were there, as yet without their weapons but still intimidating in their full black kit and ten-mile stares. They wouldn't bring their guns out until the lobby cleared when Brown would be whisked in around the corner.

McCarthy was there already, sitting on a bench, facing the door, the MobileID bag between his feet. He must have been watching for her for a while and gave a delighted smile and a cheery wee wave to her. He flushed, embarrassed, and dropped his hand.

Morrow went through the revolving doors and looked for him again, smiling at him and giving him the sort of wave she'd give the babies on a carousel. They grinned at each other.

She was behind a very old man in the security queue. He gave off the smell of coal tar soap. She could see the back of his neck, the slash tracks of a thousand skyward glances. He had a poly-thene bag with him. Dexie the security guard rooted through it with a pen, increasingly puzzled.

"I'm sorry, sir, what are these?" Dexie was an American ex-serviceman whose wife was from Hamilton. He had American teeth, looked jarringly healthy in the company of Glaswegians, a full head taller and broad on the chest. Because of his accent and confident demeanor Morrow always felt as if she was an unwitting player in an oddly boring TV show when he was there.

The old man was explaining the notion of novenas to Dexie.

"Prayer cards?" said Dexie, not much better off than before he asked.

"Not exactly," said the soapy gentleman, about to launch into a further theological exploration of the issue.

"Are you selling them?" asked Dexie. Morrow knew Dexie. He was smart and he didn't need to know this, it wasn't a gun, it wasn't a bomb, but he had the sort of distance a tourist has, knew he'd get the antsy queue in on time and was interested.

"Certainly not *selling* them—"

Dexie interrupted, "Don't give them out or leave them lying around, sir." He put the man's bag of prayers through to the other side of the metal detection arch and waved him along.

"How are you today, ma'am?"

"Very well, Dexie, how are you?"

"Busy."

Morrow shrugged her coat off, laid it in the plastic tray, emptied her pockets into another tray with her phones and pocket change. Dexie pushed them along the rollers into the X-ray machine. She opened her handbag for him to look in and he took it from her, waved her through the arch and handed her bag back to her.

He told her she should have a nice day, and she ordered him to do the same.

"Actually, Dexie," she hung back, keeping him from the next security risk, "is Anton Atholl in yet?"

"Well, ma'am..." She should go to reception but Dexie looked over there and saw the size of the queue. "Um." He looked back at her. "Yeah. I don't know where he is though. I believe he's in court four today."

"I know he is. He's cross-examining me. Thanks, Dexie, I'll find him."

McCarthy stood waiting for her on the other side. "Brought it." He held up the large square bag.

"Great." She looked up and saw Anton Atholl coming down the stairs with another lawyer, both wigged and gowned, talking seriously.

She told McCarthy to wait and walked over to meet Atholl at the bottom of the stairs, remembering the beguiling lightness of yesterday's interaction, wary of his charm. She needn't have bothered. He was very hungover, she could tell by the angle of his neck. He was trying not to move his head.

Morrow had had just two glasses of wine last night and she didn't feel one hundred percent. She'd even left most of the second glass in case the boys were up all night, which they weren't. She'd had a hangover once. It was a long time ago, before she joined the police, a simple miscalculation of lagers over an evening. She'd felt sick and headachy for an entire day. But as Atholl looked up at her she knew her sore head many years ago bore no relation to what he was feeling now.

"Good send-off?"

He tried to smile and then thought better of it. "Mr. McMillan would have enjoyed it, I think."

"Hope they didn't keep you up too late?"

"No, no, no. Some of us went on to a private club." He smiled at the man next to him, as though it had been his idea, but the other lawyer looked back at him vacantly. "Stayed there until the wee small hours. Great night. Go down in history. 'Good night, sweet prince' and all that."

He was overembellishing. Morrow thought maybe it was a bit of a grim night after all. He looked a bit sad. "And what can I aid you with today?"

His studied pomposity was a defense, she thought, a way of fending people off. "I need to ask you something."

Atholl nodded goodbye to the other lawyer and led Morrow to a bench under the high window. He sat next to her, just a little too close, his thigh almost touching hers. He smelled a little stale. Morrow moved away.

"We need to MobileID your client. We found his prints at a scene of a crime that happened a few days ago."

Atholl frowned. "He was in prison."

"That's why we need to MobileID him."

Atholl sat up, looked away from her. He thought about it for a minute and then gave an odd little laugh. "What sort of scene?"

"A murder."

He harrumphed, thought again, and turned back to face her without moving his head on his neck. "Brown may not agree to it. You can only insist if he's been charged with a fresh offense."

She was sure Atholl's reluctance was feigned.

"I think he will agree. I think he knows this is coming." She stood up with the window to her back so that the cruel morning light was on Atholl's face, making him flinch. "I think *you* knew this was coming."

"I didn't." Atholl said it so simply she almost believed him. She was a little stumped.

"OK, ask him if we can," she said. "See how surprised he is."

She was walking away to the witness room but found Atholl at her back. "DI Morrow," he said, flinching because he'd moved too quickly. "Michael Brown's really ill."

She made a disbelieving face.

"Crohn's disease," he said quietly. "Pretty advanced. Do you know what Crohn's is?"

"It's a gut thing?"

"A terrible 'gut thing.'"

"Well, don't ask me to be sympathetic to him just because he's—"

"I'm not asking for sympathy." Atholl's accent had changed, he was whispering and sounded sincere. "Just saying: I don't think he's a scheming mastermind. He wasn't getting any treatment when he was out. He's got open sores all over his shins, he can hardly walk across the cell to use the toilet. D'you know what I'm saying? *That's not it*, is what I'm saying..." Atholl shrugged. "Never mind. I'll ask him."

Morrow watched him walk away, carefully keeping his head level. She could have countered with the Cyprus villa, but then they'd know Interpol was feeding them information about the Dutch lawyer's banking transactions.

The tannoy announced that the case was about to start.

"You wait here until we get word," she told McCarthy. "Might be a while though."

"Sure," he said lightly, "I can wait."

As Morrow walked down the back corridor it occurred to her suddenly that they might be planning to sell the Cyprus villa to pay for his defense. She could be looking at it from completely the wrong angle. She flicked her warrant card at the guard on the door and went into the witness waiting room. She organized herself, turning her phones to silent, getting her notes out of her bag and ready in case she needed to refer to them, folding her coat nicely on the chair. She could leave that there, she thought, hearing the call of the macer and the scrape of chairs as the court rose for the judge.

She stood ready behind the door, an actor waiting for a cue. She thought about Atholl asking whether she knew what he was saying or not saying. She couldn't even guess what that was about.

The door opened and the macer invited her into the court. Morrow took the stairs down. She had worn the right shoes this time, flats with a soft sole. She didn't attract much attention: the jury were familiar with her now, Brown knew how she was going to be and Atholl was busy with his papers. She took the chance to look around.

Michael Brown was so white he looked almost silver. He had lost weight and was staring at the floor in front of him. Atholl was gathering his folder together.

The macer, she noticed, was looking at Atholl, smiling a little, fond and skeptical. Then the macer turned her attention to Morrow, reminded her that she was still under oath and placed a note on the witness-dock shelf in front of her. It was a creamy bit of paper, folded, with *FAO DI Morrow* written on it in black ink pen. The writing was fat and gorgeous and she knew immediately it was Atholl's.

He gathered his folders, went to the stand, put them down and paled dramatically. He hesitated, opened the top file and suddenly the color returned to his face as he rallied. "DI Morrow." He looked up and smiled, gorgeous. "How are we today?"

He meant to wrong-foot her.

"Fine." She smiled back. "How are you?"

The jury tittered, the macer relaxed and the game began again.

It took no more than thirty minutes for her to finish giving evidence. She was dismissed, took the stairs down and then up to the witness room, taking her bag with her this time. Dr. Peter Heder, the fingerprint expert, was waiting in the witness room. Pete was a big, bearded man, a worrier, whose benefit was his expertise rather than calm presentation style. He hurried to his feet, cheek twitching.

"DI Morrow, hello."

"Hi, Pete."

He looked past her, anxious. "All right, out there?"

"Fine. Nothing to worry about."

Pete watched the door. Morrow picked up her coat, walked out into the lobby and opened the note the macer had given her.

There, in a beautiful italic hand, Atholl had written

DI Morrow:
Mr. Brown says "No,"
AA

The message made no sense.

"Ma'am?"

It made no sense.

"Are we going round to the holding cells, ma'am?" McCarthy was standing in front of her, holding the MobileID bag.

"No." She put the note in her pocket. "Office."

She needed a bit of quiet to think about it properly. They walked together to the car park just outside the front doors. McCarthy unlocked the car and got in. Morrow followed suit.

They drove in silence to the office. Morrow watched out of the window, at the city, towards the wasteland of the east, through the new Dalmarnock road.

She was having to roll right back: she had assumed that the murder was a setup to get Brown off the new charges but the match they had on the guns was good. She knew they were good. Did she? The whole history of the case had to be reviewed. As she went back through the evidence and events she wondered how she had managed to end up at a dead end this solid, with no spurs, no dog legs, there seemed to have been no point at which she had made a faulty decision, or even made a decision.

"There's a van..." muttered McCarthy.

She wasn't listening. She was drawing the events as a mind map: they arrested Brown on fingerprint evidence. Took his prints, got a match with his CRO number. A high-confidence match, the database said. Charged him. Straight to custody. While in prison the same prints appeared near a dead man at a recent site. It wasn't her case. She didn't need to bring it up now. He refused to give a fresh set of prints that would confirm the match.

As McCarthy drew up into the car park behind the police station it occurred to her that Atholl would be bringing the prints up during the fingerprint evidence. She should have stayed.

"Shall I just put this back?" asked McCarthy, reaching back into the well of the back seat for the MobileID bag.

"Yeah," she said, unsettled and pulling out her phone. "Put it away, maybe."

She got out and stood in the car park, scrolling through her numbers. She knew it was in there somewhere. She found it and called Pete Heder's number.

He might still be giving evidence. She glanced at her watch. Ten minutes to lunch for the court. Pete could have his phone on him and when she heard it ring out she imagined him panicking on the witness stand, patting his pockets and apologizing.

He answered, and she could hear that he was outside.

"Pete Heder?"

"Alex Morrow, is that you?"

"Aye, just a quick question, Pete: did anything strange come up on the stand today?"

"No. Straightforward ID, point by point comparison site and ten-prints. A palm print. Nothing unusual."

"OK. Thanks very much. Bye."

"No probl—"

But she'd hung up. She didn't want to interrupt her train of thought.

McCarthy was gone when she looked around. He must have gone in.

She walked slowly up the ramp to the back bar where Mike, the desk sergeant, was sitting quietly behind a round glass window around the computer terminals.

"DS Harkins."

"DI Morrow." He stood up, ready for a bit of banter. "How are we today?"

"Mike, give us a look at the ten-prints logbook, would you?"

He straightened up. "For today?"

"No, for Michael Brown's date of arrest." She scribbled it down and handed it over.

Mike read it. "That's in the storeroom, ma'am." He saw the blank look on her face. "I'll go and get it."

He went off, using his keys to get into the storeroom. Morrow looked over at the LiveScan fingerprint machine around the back of the desk. It looked like an arcade game: the screen was at eye level, bulky, not especially pleasant to look at. They had to replace the screen a while ago when a junkie head-butted it. Next to it sat a spray bottle of disinfectant, plastic gloves and wipes. She remembered Brown standing in front of it, she'd walked through the back bar when he was having his prints taken.

She stood in the quiet, watching the monitors, listening to quiet shifting from the cells. She looked at the blackboard: two in custody. Quiet day.

Mike came back with a black logbook and put it on the desk in front of her, his hand on top. "Have to check it here."

"Can't take it to my office?"

"No," he said. "Logbook has to stay here."

She flicked through it to the right date, followed the column down to the time of day, around ten, and found his entry timed at ten twenty-three a.m. She found the job reference number next to Michael Brown's name and jotted it down in her notebook. She slid the log back across to Harkins.

"Thanks, Mike."

She slipped into the CID wing, went into her office and switched on her computer, logging in and typing in the job reference number for the set of prints they had taken that day.

The computer took her straight to the National Fingerprint Form.

Morrow remembered when these had to be filled out by hand. It was substantially the same form as then but with a few extra fields. Michael Brown had signed it at the bottom. She looked closer. The criminal record number had been entered by the arresting officer—they had the number on the warrant. The prints were the same.

She went to his criminal record and looked up the history of who had accessed it and when. She reread it four times. She came back out and went in again, thinking she must have made a mistake, but the results were the same: Wainwright's division had never accessed Michael Brown's criminal record.

She checked again. In the past two years Brown's fingerprint record hadn't been accessed by anyone but her division.

She sat back. Wainwright wouldn't be lying, he was straight, she was sure. But she'd never have believed Harris was bent either. She stopped, took a breath, felt a little bit sick. Not again. She couldn't report a fellow officer again. They'd picked her because they knew that. They knew she was half ruined anyway, so they'd picked her.

No. That was crap. Morrow splayed her hands on the desk to steady her thoughts. If Wainwright was in Brown's pay, if it was a simple attempt to muddy the value of the fingerprints on the guns in his garden then Brown would have agreed to the rescan. Unless he and Atholl were waiting to bring it up on appeal, but that was clumsy and unlikely to work: they'd be taking a chance.

Looking for something, anything, else, she typed in "Brown, Michael" to the search engine of the Scottish Police Computer.

Seven files came up, each with a distinct history. Wainwright had accessed the fifth one. She was afraid to open it in case she was wrong, shut her eyes, said a vague prayer and clicked. The database holding unidentified scene of crime finger-marks linked Brown, Michael to Wainwright's case.

It was a different Michael Brown.

Relieved, she opened Wainwright's file on Brown. He had been charged with the murder of his older brother Pinkie when he was fourteen and found guilty. He got life.

She opened the photo of him. It was Michael Brown as a young man, front and side. He had a yellow T-shirt on and glared into the camera. The record gave his height, weight, age. It showed the set of prints taken from him at the point of arrest and a serious-case number that she recognized from the last four digits, the date of his brother's murder.

She made a note of the charging station code, and the rank and name of the officer who had signed the form verifying that he was identifying the exhibit: DC Harry McMahon.

Then she sat back and thought through the implications. Michael Brown, the man she had spent three months interviewing, had two criminal records and, apparently, four hands. Two of those hands had touched guns and hidden them in his garden. Someone else's hands had killed his brother when Michael Brown was fourteen. He'd been set up.

If she dug this up now it would be professional suicide for her: it would cost a fortune to reinvestigate, Brown would have to be released from prison immediately because he wouldn't have a safe murder conviction or a life sentence hanging over him anymore and, worse, Alex Morrow would be pursuing another corruption scandal on the force. Whoever set Brown up would be fifteen years further into their career than her. It could be anyone.

15

Julius McMillan had picked this site for his law practice because of the back door. The front of the office was unremarkable: a shop window with his name picked out in gold letters and all the usual solicitors' stickers: legal aid, personal injury. The door was kept painted, the window kept clean and the doorstep brushed, but all of his business came in through the back door.

The first time Rose came here was ten years ago. She was fresh out of prison and though she was nineteen, she'd never been in a professional office before. She remembered hanging back in the doorway, looking around as Mr. McMillan checked the answer-phone and Mrs. Tait's list of "to dos" and "dones." She was blown away by it: the desks, the staplers, the printers, the computer, all the stuff he owned, the sheer volume of *things*. He didn't act rich though. Didn't even seem to notice all of this stuff. Rose left prison with a bin bag and that was only half-full.

She'd come in the back way then and it hadn't changed much.

The back court was a square fortress: surrounded on all four sides by blocks of rotting tenements: small flats owned privately in a rough area. If a housing association had owned them there would always have been the danger of them renovating the back court. If the area had been better, the population more stable, the space in the middle could have been developed as allotments, a swing park, or even a car park. None of that had happened.

The ground was muddy and broken up. The old brick midden in the center was listing, tipsy. Different windows were broken but it was more or less the same as the first time.

The back court could be entered through two openings in each wall around the square. The police couldn't watch every entrance: it would have cost two polis all day on each wall. They could have asked a friendly shopkeeper to train a camera on the doorways, watch who went in, but the locals saw who went in and knew they were not to be crossed.

Rose walked over the muddy ground, keeping to the side of the midden, skirting the side of a wall and veering off suddenly to the near close. Taking the keys from her pocket, she used them on a door so inauspicious it might lead to a coal cellar. She slipped in and shut the door behind her, reaching over to punch the code for the alarm. 0883. Rose's birthday. The alarm beeped twice.

She stood still in the dark. The smell of him. The air a bitter tang, tar radiating off the walls. Rose didn't like the smell of smoke but she liked it here: the sour, kind edge of it like a sin, forgiven.

She shut her eyes tight, shaking her head, shedding heart-softening memories. She had things to do here. She couldn't leave the children with Francine for too long.

In the front office the white blinds on the windows lent a twilight to the room. A reception desk, never manned since Mrs. Tait retired three years ago. She took out the keys from the key cupboard and unlocked the gray filing cabinet, pulling each of the drawers out one by one. Nothing in any of them. Checking for stray documents on the floor of each one, she pushed the hanging folders to the back, to the front. Nothing. She shut them and locked the cabinet before moving on to the desk. Nothing in the drawers there either. Either he had emptied everything recently or else the money was the only business he had last been involved in. He didn't seem to have been defending anyone.

She took the keys and fitted them in the locked office door. Pulling the door open she dredged a waft of Julius's unique smell from the sealed room. She stood still for a moment, ambushed, trying not to breathe, waiting for the air on either side of the door to equalize.

She felt his smell, particles settling on her, bits of his skin on her skin, in her nose, trapped on eyelashes, settling like invisible snow in her hair. She wanted it to go on forever. But it didn't. The sensation of closeness evaporated, her mind drifted.

She opened her eyes and felt inside for the light switch. Click. It was a harsh sun he lived under, strip lights behind ceiling grilles that didn't soften it at all.

Mr. McMillan didn't care about nice furniture, his eyes were always on the middle distance. The desk and chairs he had lived with day after day were perfunctory, as good as they needed to be for their function and not a bit better. A wall chart day planner on the wall behind looked industrial, red and black, a felt-tip hung on a frayed string next to it. Most days were marked with a symbol: a triangle, a star, a square or a dash. The markings stopped from the evening his lungs collapsed.

Her eyes had adjusted properly now and she looked at the floor. Nothing there except for a Biro. The sight of it winded Rose. It was where it was dropped that caught her: on the floor under the desk, where his hand had been when she arrived, where he lay when she called the ambulance and let them in the front door to take him away. Aziz Balfour. She knew it was him before she saw the bruise on his hand, before he tried to explain, because his sticker was on the planner, a red star. And she knew Dawood was the yellow rectangle before him, both in the six thirty p.m. time slot. They must have seen each other. Aziz screamed it at her: he *saw* Dawood. Up in the Red Road, in the burning wind and dark, he screamed that he'd met Dawood coming out of Julius's office, did they know what sort of man this was? He saw Dawood and was offended by the sight of him. That was his excuse for shoving Julius.

She blinked, forced herself to look away from the Biro, back to the office, fighting the tightness in her chin, in her chest, the stinging in her eyes.

Julius McMillan might just have dragged himself next door, holding on to walls as he needed to at the end. She could hear his labored breathing scraping through his throat and nose, each breath in a miracle of will, loud and defiant. He had been so ill for so long, they had all got used to his health being precarious, but none of them expected him to actually die.

She looked back at the pen and tenderness engulfed her. Julius McMillan at a door to an interview room, a fug of smoke was the first thing she noticed about him, his neat yellowed fingernails and the certainty of his handshake.

Hello, Rose, I'm Mr. McMillan. I know what has happened and I, alone, will not turn away. You will be a child for them and only I will know. You can be yourself with me.

When Rose first saw McMillan she didn't take him for a kind man. Even now, she didn't think he was a kind man but he had been good to her. And yet, at the last minute, he chose Robert over her. He'd sent Robert to the office, not her. Atholl was wrong, Julius didn't love her. He didn't trust her in the end. He let her run the money deliveries to the couriers, he let her check his numbers and know his business, but he only loved Robert. In the end it was Robert he had sent down here with the code. He was wrong to trust him. Robert had let his father down, submitted a SOCA report. It was too much for him, they had kept him protected. They'd done the job too well. Julius didn't love her or choose her in the end but she loved him.

Mr. McMillan became the receptacle for all her fiery loyalties and she loved him still.

Rose shut the office door, checked that it was locked from the inside. She glanced around the room and under the desk, worried that someone was hiding. Silly, but she didn't want to get locked in down there. You could die down there.

Opening the small door at the back of the office, she bent, climbing into a corridor to the old coal cellar.

The seven steps led down to a low room, just tall enough to stand up in, lower since Mr McMillan took it over because he'd had it lined in concrete. The cold settled in here like damp fog at the ankles. Set into the concrete on the back wall was the safe. Big enough to get a man into, he used to say. Rose took the handle, turned it down and it opened. Papers on one shelf. Below, leather-bound books. The books he would have wanted the Inland Revenue or the Law Society to find if they raided his office. There was usually cash in there, eight or ten thou, a distraction in case of burglars or cops. Robert or Dawood must have taken it.

She took the binders out and laid them carefully on the floor, took the cold steel shelf out and laid it next to them. She put one foot in and felt along the ceiling of the safe. It was a fake roof. Her fingers slid along the searing cold to the back edge, found the rim and slid it to the left, to the junction with the side. A small button, almost flush with the back wall, she had to feel for it. She took her hand away quickly and waited, counting slowly to eight. She reached back in and pressed again.

The back wall slid slowly to the right, into the concrete wall.

Holding both walls of the safe Rose stepped in, stooping down the short low corridor to a crawl space below the pavement. Bright white motion lights flicked on inside. This room was warm, dry and warm because of the next-door launderette's ventilation shaft running next to it.

A flimsy hotel safe, concreted low down on the wall, with a re-settable four-digit code. It was nothing special. She remembered herself and McMillan laughing at the suggestion of a biotech safe with thumbprint or retinal lock. The salesman didn't understand what was funny about it. The people they were hiding things from wouldn't flinch from cutting off a hand or taking an eye if they needed it. No, said McMillan, no, it's just a small one for the house. Best defense against attack was to give them what they wanted. Danegeld, he called it. They didn't need a great safe, they needed a secret safe.

Rose sat cross-legged on the bare concrete in front of the safe. The code could be reset by anyone, with just a simple press of a hash button. Robert had reset it. She knew before she even tried that none of their birthdays would work, not the kids', not hers, not Robert's own, not Julius's. She tried the date of Julius's death. She tried the hour of his death. Nothing. Could be anything. It probably was anything. Random numbers. But random numbers chosen by Robert. She needed to think like Robert, at the moment he set the safe lock.

He had sent the SOCA report. He wanted the police to come here, get into the safe and find everything.

The police. 0999. No. 9990. Didn't work either. 9999. The door fell open in front of her.

She laughed softly to herself, surprised, triumphant even. She pulled the door wide.

All the shrink-wrapped cash was gone. Disappointing. Robert had reported the money but had also taken it. How like him. He had left his MacBook Air inside, doubtless with the SOCA report saved on it and a melancholy letter about doing the right thing. She took the laptop out. Underneath it was a slim volume, leather-bound, the first half filled with Mr. McMillan's writing, entries in Biro, the pages watered and wavy from the press of his pen. She lifted it out, not looking at the numbers, just running her fingers over the impressions left by him. She shut her eyes, braille-reading his marks. When she opened them again she saw something unexpected at the bottom of the safe.

An envelope. Old. The self-adhesive strip yellow with age. The paper felt crisp to the touch. She let her fingers linger on the edge of it for a moment, unsure about looking inside. This was the back safe. Whatever was in there, it wasn't good or innocent. She wasted time looking at the wall, feeling the tickle of paper on her fingertips. She shouldn't look really.

But she did. She took the old envelope and felt inside with scissored fingers. Not paper. Photos. Old ones, thick ones, not on printer paper. Thick, square with a border around them and a bit at the bottom for writing on. Self-developing film. Polaroids, she thought they were called. There were three of them. They spilled into her lap, facedown. She looked at the black backs for a minute, hands flat on the skin-warm floor, her tongue worrying her molars. She took a deep breath, held it in and turned them over.

The pictures were of her.

16

Wheatly got up from his desk as Morrow came out to the corridor. "Ma'am?"

"Yes?"

"Ma'am, I wasn't sure at the time but come and see this." He waved to her to follow him to his desk. He had a still from the car park CCTV streamed into his desktop. A grainy picture showed the front of a small white van parked across the road. The license plate was readable.

She looked at him for an explanation.

"The van's registered to a private individual, Matthew Stepper. He works for newspapers."

She looked at the screen. "And it's outside here right now?"

"Aye."

Morrow and McCarthy stood on the pavement outside the station. They watched the white van wobble, rain bouncing off the roof. They were both trying hard not to laugh. Whoever was inside was pretending they weren't but every time they moved the entire body shifted. They watched for a while, uncertain they could speak without howling, and then finally Morrow banged on the side.

"We can see you moving in there. Come out."

Hissing whispers inside, there must be two of them. Then someone moved again, down to the front, looking out of the windscreen. Morrow and McCarthy moved back so they couldn't see them.

The van wobbled as the person retreated into the back.

"Are you doing lengths in there?" shouted Morrow. She and McCarthy had a good laugh, got it out.

The movement stopped. They waited. Slowly, as if the people inside were sitting down, having a think, the van tilted towards a back corner.

McCarthy knocked this time. "Come out or we'll impound the vehicle."

After a short while the back door clicked and opened. A sheepish man, short, balding, in denims and a knitted jumper, clambered out into the road. He looked worried. They looked back into the van. He was alone.

"Who were you talking to in there?" asked Morrow.

He touched the phone in his pocket. "My editor."

"You're a journalist?"

"I'm a photographer." He looked pleased about that, but then maybe remembered that he wasn't actually a photographer. "Well, a researcher. But a photographer, really."

"What was your editor saying?"

The man smiled sheepishly. "Don't get out of the van."

Morrow looked back at the vehicle. It was a rusty, tumbledown mess but unobtrusive. She flicked a finger at it. "You want to lock that up and we'll go into the station for a chat?"

He looked terrified. "Can't we do it here? Work's hard to come by, I've got another two jobs this afternoon and if I miss them..."

She felt for him and he hadn't broken any laws. "We can do it here if you just straightforward tell us—"

"Tell you *anything*." He sounded sincere.

"What paper are you working for?"

"*Scottish Daily News*."

"Who's the editor you were talking to?"

He rolled his chin at a far wall, thinking it through. It was printed in the front of the paper, there wasn't any point in lying about it.

"OK, pal." Morrow took his elbow firmly. "We can hold you for six hours, we're going in."

"No." He shook it free. "No, not into the station, please. Alan Donovan. Alan Donovan."

"Who are you watching?"

"Y—" He stopped himself but then said it. "You." He was looking at Morrow.

"What's the story?"

"Your brother. Danny McGrath." He held his hands up imploringly. "Look, I just got the photography job, I don't know *anything*, I mean literally *anything* about this. Nothing."

"Donovan called you and gave you the job?"

"Yeah. Said your brother's a big gangster, follow her, see if you can snap them together. This"—he gave her a USB stick—"this is all I got."

He pressed it into her hand.

She was blushing, she knew she was, but she managed to keep her voice steady. "OK, Stepper, we found out who you were from your van plates. We've got your license plate, name and home address." She jabbed at him with her finger, hesitated, unsure what exactly she should threaten him with. The press were pernickety about threats. They weren't like other people, you couldn't tell them to fuck off or they'd print it. "So...off you go."

She and McCarthy stood shoulder to shoulder and watched

him get in the front of the van, embarrassed, smiling. He started the engine and drove away.

McCarthy looked at her. It was awkward. "That's weird. It's not a secret about your brother, everyone knows."

It was Brown. He'd tipped off the papers, trying to discredit her for the appeal. It had been done before: he'd probably suggest she was working for her brother, that Brown and Danny were rivals in some way. But it was too sophisticated a move for Brown, someone else was suggesting it, she felt sure. Atholl, maybe.

Morrow didn't know what to say. "It's not about knowing, though. It's about how it looks. Bosses just want rid when you get that messy. *Who*'s tipping them off is the better question."

Back at Morrow's desk they looked through the USB files. JPEGS, photos of Danny outside her house, giving her the photo, Morrow outside the station, getting into her own car, Danny with sidekicks, young guys who looked a bit like him, copied his shaven head, his casual tracksuits.

McCarthy sat next to her. She could tell he didn't know what to say.

"Do you know these guys he's with?" she asked, pointing to a gathering of four: Danny with an older guy, Asian-looking, smartly dressed, and next to them two young thugs, one with a big scar running from his lip up to his eye.

"I know the scar. Pokey Mulligan."

Pokey was slang for prison.

"He got a long record?"

McCarthy shrugged. "Just his name. Assaults. Does it to order now. And the Asian guy. I think that's Dawood McMann."

Morrow had heard of him. Dawood was shifty, everyone knew that, but he seemed to have straightened out in the past decade or so. Opened a string of highly successful sports shops. Gave a lot of money to charity. She wouldn't think Danny knew him.

She sat back heavily against her office chair. "Let's go and see Donovan."

Morrow's knowledge about the declining fortunes of the press was informed ambiently, from jokes on *The Simpsons*, from rumors about the Met involvement in the phone-hacking inquiry down south.

The Met's inquiry into blatant phone hacking had been started and abandoned several times and each time it arrived at the conclusion that no one had done nothing, so on your way. Shortly after each finding of utter blamelessness a senior officer had been given a well-paid column in one of the newspapers under investigation, or a club membership, or a horse. Even without a glimpse at the evidence it was obvious to Morrow that a recurrent investigation meant there was something in it. And if some of the journalists were hacking voice-mail accounts, in a competitive market, with staff transferring from paper to paper, they were probably all doing it. Every police force had corruption issues, but Strathclyde's were over giant bags of greasy bank notes, not the fripperies of social status. It seemed more honest to Morrow, somehow.

So she knew the newspaper industry was in a bad way but quite how bad really came home to her when they walked into the office. This was a daily national paper yet the open-plan newsroom had no more than eight desks, only four of them occupied.

While the receptionist was showing them into Donovan's office Morrow asked if everyone else was out.

"No," said the receptionist and walked over to a glass door, opening it and walking in. They followed her and she left without a word, dumping them in the presence of Alan Donovan, editor of the *Scottish Daily News*.

He was a small man but sat, pert as a nipple, behind his desk. He looked at McCarthy. "DI Alex Morrow?"

"I'm Morrow," she said.

"Yes." He turned to look at her as if he knew that she was a woman all along, and a lot more besides. He plainly knew nothing. "Hello." He waited for her to say something else.

"What's going on, Mr. Donovan?"

"In what way?"

They stared at each other for a moment longer. She half expected him to offer her a column.

"You asked a journalist to follow me and take pictures of me at my work."

"Did I?" His eyebrows rose slowly.

She couldn't help but smile at that. She licked her lips, straightened her face and began again. "I believe you were looking for information about me. Could I help you with that?"

Donovan leaned back in his chair, crossed his legs. As if the pose wasn't studied enough he picked up a pen and examined it closely. She half wished she hadn't brought McCarthy because they were both a little giggly. She hardly dared catch his eye.

"DI Morrow, what would your bosses say if they knew that your brother was Danny McGrath?"

"They do know."

He flinched at that, a single blink, and examined the pen again. "How do they know?"

"I told them."

"Everybody knows," said McCarthy. "Ask anyone in our division. You could stand at the door at a shift change and ask. We all know."

"You can print it if you want..." It would be a disaster for her if they did. The senior ranks still read the newspapers. They were of that generation.

"We may very well do just that." He looked uncomfortable. "If it's not a secret, why are you here?"

Morrow stood at the window. "It's a bit thin, isn't it, as an operation? I thought there would be teams of people working here."

"There used to be. Not anymore. Technology."

"Technology ate the other journalists?"

He smiled ruefully at that. "In a manner of speaking. It made for more efficient work practices, more of the work got outsourced. Newspapers were fantastically inefficient in the old days."

"Outsourced?" said Morrow, looking out into the open-plan office. "They're introducing that in policing."

Donovan stood up and came over to her side, looking out with her. He looked a little sad but shrugged. "You should do it. It saved us a fortune. Why pay a full wage with pensions and benefits when you can pay for services delivered? Service industries never go on the sick for weeks at a time. They just deliver."

"What sort of services are outsourced?"

"Printing, distribution, financial services, a lot of our art work is outsourced now. We used to have a whole art department. They were a nightmare. Staff of ten and barely two were ever in. They were all taking time off to set up shows and teach. Ridiculous."

She turned to him, quite close now. "See, Donovan, the reason I'm here is that I'm involved in a complicated case with some very sneaky characters. It's at a pitch now..." She was careful not to mention the court because she knew he'd find out it was Michael Brown. "It makes me wonder if the timing of this is related to that in any way. I mean, when I walked in here, you plainly had no idea who I am. I wonder if this sudden interest in me is related to that case?"

"I don't know anything about any case you're involved in investigating."

She had guessed right: Donovan knew nothing about Brown being in court.

"What I mean is, who prompted you to follow me?"

He raised his eyebrows again. "I would hardly be any kind of journalist if I revealed my sources."

Morrow nodded. "Yes. For us the problem of outsourcing is integrity. We're powerful, got access to information. If we outsource it how can we hold people to account? Do we then need another body to watch them? Aren't we just creating another level of bureaucracy? You know? Places to lose papers. Places to make massive mistakes."

She smiled at him but Donovan just looked puzzled.

"Were you looked at for phone hacking?"

He paled and licked his lips.

She looked out into the room again. "Not that any outsourced mistakes would be malicious. People make mistakes. But sometimes with outsourcing, there can be a willful blindness, reckless ness. Take you, for example. Someone might give you a juicy tip, say it comes from a manipulative source with interests in other cases. You pursue it, willfully. Maybe it could change the course of a case. Bad men get out. People die." She looked at Donovan and found him sweating. "I'm surprised no one mentioned you in the phone-hacking inquiry, you do cover a lot of celebrity news."

Morrow and McCarthy sat in the car, stopped at a red light. She glanced at him. He looked quite frightened.

"You all right, McCarthy?"

He nodded but he clearly wasn't.

"What's on your mind?"

He kept his eyes on the lights. "What the hell's going on, boss? Who is David Monkton?"

Morrow didn't know what to tell him. She had never heard of him either.

17

Robert was in the pink drawing room. There were no traces of last night, no empty glasses, no full or empty bottles. The hippie must have moved them. Was the rental of the castle serviced? Robert couldn't remember.

He had pulled an armchair up to the window and sat looking out at the sea, keeping a watch on the driveway. He tutted at his naïveté: they wouldn't come up the driveway. That wasn't how death came. Death seeped through cracks, burst down doors, stormed beds and punctured walls. Death didn't take a minicab from the station. Still, he couldn't stop himself watching for it.

The painkillers had kicked in, the headache and sickness had retreated, mustering forces in his core as they waited for the medication to leave his system. He wasn't actively in pain but he was smelly and trembling. He felt sticky. His balls were itchy. He was too sad to wash. Sometimes, he was too sad to even scratch his balls. He just sat there and suffered it.

He blinked and the sharp precognition of death receded like the sea on the beach. He saw himself getting lost in details of what was outside the window, how smelly he was, how soon he could take more pills. He was getting caught up in the petty details of day to day.

Abruptly, he imagined someone standing behind him with a gun to his head and he thought suddenly that "my balls are itchy" wasn't the last thought he wanted to have.

That brought him back to himself.

I am going to die, he thought. I am going to die today, probably. He resolved to get ready for it but had to acknowledge how slippery it was, how hard it was to stay focused.

The task then was to manage to stay focused, somehow, to remain aware of what was happening. And then another thought came to him: what good was it remaining focused on the fact that he was about to die? It wouldn't get him ready for it, wouldn't make it hurt less or stop him sobbing at the end and begging.

The questions baffled him. He tried to backtrack to yesterday, when he wasn't hungover and felt sure that he knew what he was doing. He thought they would have followed him here but it was nearly lunchtime and he was still sitting at a window.

He thought he'd be dead by now. Where were they?

He imagined them then, two men in a car, driving off the ferry. He saw them following the licorice strip of road over the hills, around the inland lochs, down through the boggy land by the sea and through forests. He saw them slowing on the winding single track road, pulling over in passing places, letting locals know they were strangers by raising a full hand in thank you instead of the thankful finger-raise used by accustomed locals.

Or maybe the person sent to kill him was on this island, creeping inexorably across a hill towards him right now.

But maybe they weren't coming because they didn't know where he was. In which case he could sit at the window for a year, waiting.

Annoyed at the thought, Robert scratched his balls and then, buoyed by the achievement, he stood up. They might not know where he was. It hadn't even occurred to him. He'd paid for everything with cash, not credit cards, he'd told no one. He even found the castle in a printed catalog lying around the house and called from a pay phone.

No one knew where he was. The SOCA report would be with the police, it would be leaked by now, the police were as leaky as a sieve, and whoever his father was in business with would be after him.

They'd check Robert's old firm, his colleagues at the firm, see who he was close to. Robert wished he was back there, fighting with the other junior partners, falling out with the secretaries, being overlooked for promotion. It seemed a golden time now. He'd left with great ceremony, leaving to take over his father's firm. He remembered thinking as he left that *now* he'd be happy.

The pictures of Rose came into his head and winded him. He sat back down. She looked the same in the photos. Her face was recognizably her. She even had her hair pulled back in a high ponytail. She was crying in one of them. Her face impassive but tears dropping off her nose as she leaned forward. He could tell she was young. She hardly had any pubic hair.

When he took them out of the safe and looked at them Robert threw them across the room. He scurried to the opposite wall and clung to it. Did his father take those photographs? Did his father masturbate to them? No one would masturbate to them, they were terrifying. But then you never knew what people wanted to see. When he saw them Robert was so mesmerized by her face that he didn't see the context. It was a small girl, naked in a group of looming men, dark men, some laughing, some leering. But Robert being Robert only saw Rose in the pictures. Rose crying. Rose looking up at a face, frightened. Rose smiling in one of them as a man fingered her. The rooms were anonymous. There was drink.

These were the things people did when the lights were out, when no one was watching.

I cannot fix this, he thought, in the low womb of the safe room, as he held the warm wall. I cannot fix this on my own. He had seen the books. Why did his father have those pictures of Rose?

Rose was almost a sister to Robert. She was in prison, he was at school. She had accidentally killed a man who tried to abuse her, his father told him. They went to visit her. And Julius and Robert stayed loyal to her, differentiating themselves from those sorts of men.

Robert visited her in prison with his father. On the way there, for the first visit, Robert half hoped he'd fancy her but he didn't. Later he thought that they were too much alike but that wasn't true, really. They just didn't fancy each other. He accepted her the way family do: without too much appraisal, without assessing her. She was theirs and when she became their nanny Robert felt that it was right and proper and was delighted she and Francine got on so well, with Francine being always a little bit delicate even before she got ill. Like his mother: Margery was always a little bit ill.

But to see her in the photos, that made him ferocious about her. He wanted to wrap himself around her, small Rose, and protect her from these terrible men. He was prepared to ruin himself, his family, his father's reputation, if it meant bringing these men down too. He would do that for Rose. So he called the police and did what they told him: fill out the form.

He sat at the window of the castle and felt slightly better again, remembering how honorable he was being, how different from the men in the picture. He was going to let them kill him for Rose. He stood up, thinking he might go for a shit, trying to remember where the toilets were, and then he saw him: the hippie was in the field below the castle, trundling across it on his quad bike. He stopped, took a small bag of grain from under his cape and emptied it onto the ground. Then he drove a few yards away and watched the geese gather around and eat it.

The geese were chalk white, bigger than a city dweller like himself would have supposed. The hippie folded his arms under his cape and watched them. Even from here Robert could see that he was smiling. And then two men at the distant end of the field, beyond the fence, waving him over. The hippie looking at them, seeing them, staying on his bike and trundling over to them and Robert was gripped by horror as he saw him approach them in their dark clothes, faces obscured by woolly hats pulled low. He couldn't see the hippie's face but felt he was still smiling and the men were smiling, Robert could see flashes of teeth, they were smiling as he approached them and one of them had his hand in his pocket.

They chatted. The hippie tucked his hands into his cape, a woman's cape for fuck's sake. And then one of the men took his hands out of his pocket as Robert watched, holding his breath, and he offered the hippie a chewing gum. The hippie shook his head, took his hands out and drove back across the field. The men turned and walked on.

They were out for a walk.

Robert fell back from the window. He couldn't let them kill the hippie. He just couldn't let them. Robert was going to have to leave the castle.

Feeling much, much better, Robert walked up over the crest of the hill and found the sea laid out before him like a silver picnic blanket. To the left a steep drop led to the white sanded beach and the castle overlooking it. To the right soft green hills showed the decaying foundations of an abandoned village, one of those decaying crossword puzzles left by the clearances. The sharp wet wind whipped at his hair. Seagulls hovered over the sea. In front of him the land dropped away into the water.

Robert was wearing his office suit, city shoes and a one pound plastic cagoule he'd found in the boot of his car. Unfortunately, he'd stepped in a puddle as he came out of the house and his feet were wet, his toes numb with the cold now and the material on his shins was damp, sticking to him, making his skin numb on his bony shins. He felt wonderful. The rough terrain, the wind and noise and the screams of the seagulls, the intermittent rain and brutal blasts of sunshine all tore him from his father's burden of guilt, from Rose's tortured childhood and those circles of men, took him from faceless men talking to the hippie and thoughts of his children and left him in the moment. He had climbed up here on his hands and knees, scrabbled over scree, got his loafer stuck in a hollow full of mud. And he stood tall now on the ancient land-scape, looking out at a sea that didn't know or care that he existed.

He looked over at the village. Ankle high stumps of founda-tions that were once homes to generations. They had been run off their land, victims of an injustice, bigger than he had suffered, bigger than a room full of men and small, naked Rose. The build-ings had been left and had decayed back into the soil and now it didn't really matter anymore. He smiled and walked towards them. His shoes were squelching horribly, there seemed to be more water in them than out of them and he thought about taking them off to empty them and promised himself that he would when he got over there. He hurried up the hill, anticipating a little shelter from the wind. The native Highland people knew where to build, it would be a sheltered place for a village.

It wasn't sheltered at all. At the first square of foundation stones he found the wind harder than the hilltop he had come from. He stepped over the little wall, into the house, and tried to imagine what it would have been like. Very small. Tiny room. He felt nothing, tried to evoke some awe in himself: he tried to imagine a whole family, six kids and grandparents too living in this tiny room. But he wasn't sure if it was a house. It could have been a dunny, for all he knew. Or a storeroom. He didn't know how they lived back then. He circled the space. Six children and two parents and two grandparents couldn't fit in this room, actually. It must be a storeroom.

He moved on to the next square, stepped inside and tried to reimagine the whole thing there. Why were there two grandparents? he thought. There should be four grandparents, but even just the two were too many. But maybe some grandparents would have died, at sea or of colds or something. He was pondering this when he stepped out of the imagined room.

His foot, expecting but not finding the ground where it was supposed to be, dropped suddenly away from him into a hole, overbalancing him so that he twisted and fell and landed on his face, on a big stone lying on the ground.

Robert lay in the wet grass, groaning, his cheekbone still on the offending stone. His mind flailed as he tried to think of someone to blame, the tourist board, the Highlanders, gravity. And then, at the same time as he became aware of the futility of blaming anyone for what was essentially a mishap, he became aware of the dull pain in his ankle and the tingling in his numb toes. He sat up and looked at the foot that had gone down the hole. He peeled up his wet trouser leg. The ankle looked raw in the bright light, raw and a bit chubby. And then as he watched, moving his toes, knowing it wasn't broken, the ankle got fatter and fatter.

A seagull landed near him, eyeing him as though he might be a felled lamb. It looked fucking enormous, tipping its big, ugly head at him, getting the measure of him. Robert picked up a stone and threw it, missing. The seagull was unperturbed.

"Fuck off!" shouted Robert, but it didn't.

He felt wetness on his face and reached up, took his hand away and saw blood. Really quite a lot of blood. It was coming from his cheek. He needed a mirror and looked around as if there might be one lying somewhere in the wet grass pitted with sheep shit.

The seagull was watching him. Maybe it had smelled the blood before he saw it. No, wait, that was vultures. It was eyeing him still, tipping and untipping its head as if working out which part of him to eat first. Robert felt foolish, at a disadvantage. He had a massive gash on his face the seagull knew more about than he did.

Then he had an idea. Sitting on the muddy ground with only one fully functioning ankle and blood dripping onto the plastic cagoule that was sticking to him like cellophane now, he took out his mobile, turned it on, touched the icon for the camera and took a photograph of his face. There. He could see it now. It wasn't even that bad. Just a bit of split skin on his cheek.

He smirked over at the seagull but it was pecking at the ground. It opened its wings and flew straight out to sea.

Holding on to the low wall for support, Robert carefully extracted his grotesque ankle out of the hole and pulled the trouser leg back down over it. He bent his good leg under him and stood up, keeping the bad ankle off the ground until he was upright. If he couldn't get down the hippie might be killed in his place. Then he tried it. Not too bad. He could get back down on his own. It was a little bit painful when his weight was on it. He'd have to go slow but it wasn't too bad at all.

On the first step he felt the phone vibrate once, twice, three voice-message alerts. Uncle Dawood. Without even looking at it he reached into his pocket and turned the phone off again and carried on his way.

18

Johnstone was not a destination. Morrow and McCarthy took the turn off the motorway to Paisley, checking the GPS every so often, worried they might drive through it and not notice.

A low town on the outskirts of Paisley, Johnstone had houses as small as a cramped inner-city area, two-up two-downs, with windows as small as factory gate hovels. The inhabitants were inexplicably proud of their town though. While checking ex-DC Harry McMahon's address McCarthy found the house sale— he'd only just moved there. It was a moderate price for Glasgow but, being in Johnstone, they were expecting a mansion.

It wasn't a mansion but abutted a golf course. The detached house had a drive and a square of orderly grass at the front. It looked identical to its neighbors, new and neat. Whatever Harry McMahon had been doing for the past seven years since leaving the police, he'd had a bit of luck at it.

They parked in the street and walked up the drive, past a four-year-old blue Honda. McCarthy knocked on the front door as Morrow looked in the windows. Neat net curtains in the shallow

oriel window by the door. Two ornaments and a framed photograph facing into the room. She could see the floors were wood
laminate, giving the front room an orange glow.

The door was answered by a tall man in his late forties, smart
hair, clean white shirt tucked into ironed jeans. Morrow smiled:
she would have known he was an ex-cop if she passed him in a supermarket.

"Hello," he said, "what can I do you for?"

"Harry McMahon?" She showed him her card.

"Oh, aye." He read her card. "DI Alexandra Morrow. How are
you?"

They'd never met but there was that easy sense of camaraderie
that came with a common value system.

"I'm dealing with a case that touches on an old one of yours.
Can I come in and speak to you?"

"Ah, come away in, both," he said, looking pleased.

The hallway was tidy and devoid of fripperies. A skateboard
stood on its nose against the wall, the messy, tagged design on it a
stark contrast to the sterile white walls and clean wooden floor.

"You a skateboarder?" she said.

Harry nodded, acknowledging the joke. "One of my boys."

Morrow looked around for signs of them. "Do they not live
with you?"

Harry laughed at that. "No, we're just a very tidy family. Come
in." To McCarthy, he said, "Didn't catch your name."

McCarthy introduced himself. They shook hands and then
McMahon seemed to remember that he'd forgotten to shake with
Morrow so he did that and asked them for their coats. He hung
them up in the tidiest understairs cupboard Morrow had ever
seen.

Harry waved them into a sunny kitchen looking out on a garden
that was a square of perfect green ending abruptly in a tall fence. At

one side stood a pine summerhouse, the two large front windows with double glazed doors in the middle. The doors were shut.

"If that was my shed," McCarthy said, pointing at it, "it'd be crammed with bits of motorcycles. All that patio bit"—he looked at the honey-colored flagstones leading to it—"would be stained with oil."

"Oh, aye." McMahon looked out at it. "My missus is a fiend for the tidiness. Don't get me wrong, I'm tidy myself but she's mad for it." He seemed quite pleased about that. "Would you like a cuppa?"

Normally they wouldn't take a cup of tea from someone they were questioning. But Harry was an ex-cop and he understood perfectly the grades of intimacy involved in accepting.

McCarthy looked at Morrow for permission. "Lovely," she said.

As McMahon boiled the kettle and got out cups from the cupboard they talked about mutual acquaintances, about now senior officers McMahon had done his training with and about the politics of the single force. He had not a bit of bitterness about the force; it was nice to hear, encouraging to still-serving officers.

"You seemed to have done quite well since you left," said Morrow as he put the mugs of tea on the completely empty kitchen table.

"Lucky," he said. "Please sit down." He went to the cupboard and took some biscuits out of a plastic box, filed next to another one with cereal in it. "Left at just the right time. Got my pension, still fit to work, job market was buoyant. We've been very lucky."

He came back to the table with a plate of biscuits. They were cheap chocolate chip cookies, an unbranded version of biscuits that were pretty cheap anyway. Morrow looked at her tea and saw it was weak, that the milk in it was thin and must have been skimmed.

"So what is it you do now, Harry?"

"Heard of 'Information Solutions'?"

"No."

"Well," he tipped his head to her, "you will. You'll likely be working for them at some point in the future. They're an investigations firm that work all over Scotland. Really, it's a loose network of firms but we all work together. It means I can call Ullapool and get a company's offices looked at in an afternoon by someone else, report back to the client within the day. It's good. It works."

"Is it not all divorce stuff?"

"No. Precognitions, statements, that sort of thing. The divorce stuff is rare enough. Not very salubrious but it's better than missing pets. Makes you work like a bastard at your own marriage, anyway."

"And it pays?"

He shook his head, he didn't really want to talk about that. "It's fine. But they recruit ex-cops. When you leave the force they'll get in touch, probably. You'll get a letter and they'll see if you want some work or just to register for the future. Very organized."

"That's nice to know," said McCarthy and then winced when he remembered that Morrow was there. It was bad form to let on that he'd been having doubts. Morrow let it go.

"So, Harry," she said, not wanting to drink the weak tea, "this case."

"Oh aye." He turned to her. "So, what year are we in?"

"Nineteen ninety-seven. It was a murder—"

"Done enough of them."

"A stabbing, two young guys, Michael Brown killed his brother."

"Hm, trying to remember..." He looked over her head, into the garden, and took a bite of his biscuit. Harry knew exactly which case she was talking about, she could tell. He was looking into the garden shed as if he wished himself in there. "Nineteen ninety-seven..."

"In the lane off Sauchiehall Street. Body found in the morning. Michael Brown was in Cleveden at the time, that's where you picked him up—"

"Oh!" He was trying to act surprised but instead looked scared. He was an awful actor. "The night Diana died."

"Was it?"

"Yeah. Was it?" He searched her face.

"Well," said Morrow, "what do you remember about it?"

"Nothing, nothing, nothing." He was sitting bolt upright in his chair. "Well!" he said, slightly too loud. "Let's see. Hm. Diana died that night. The boy was found dead in the lane..."

"Down by ChipsPakoraKebab," nodded Morrow, trying to help him out.

"Yes! Down the lane, there, and hm, let's see." He raised a hand to his chin as if he was trying to think. "Ah, hm."

McCarthy couldn't take it anymore. "Don't," he pleaded quietly.

McMahon didn't speak then. He sipped his tea, his eyes flicking about above the rim. Then he put his cup down and reached for another biscuit.

They sat around the circular table, three spokes on a wheel. All of them knew that something had happened to make the case memorable. Wee guys stabbed each other all the time in Glasgow. Morrow guessed it was a bad thing that had impressed it on McMahon's mind. He wouldn't remember a case from fourteen years ago otherwise. But McMahon wasn't used to lying. She suspected that he hated having to do it, that was why he was so bad at it.

He was chewing through the biscuit as if trying to plug his mouth shut.

"That was the worst attempt at a fib I've ever seen," she said to McCarthy and he smiled at McMahon.

Harry looked relieved and rolled his eyes. "Shit," he said, "I'm just not..."

They were all smiling now and Harry relaxed a little, now he knew that they weren't going to push him into a corner.

"Is that why you left the force?" smiled Morrow.

"No." He took another biscuit. "But it is why I'm self-employed. You can't talk to business folk the way we do, do you know that? They start crying and all that..."

He looked at the table, puzzled. They were both glad to know that his transition hadn't been entirely unproblematic.

"OK, Harry, here it is: I'm going to assume you do remember the case?"

He blinked a yes.

"And that something unusual happened in that case?"

Another blink.

"Maybe something you don't want to talk about?"

Blink.

She nodded at the table. "Something with fingerprints?"

He looked confused and gave a little head shake.

"Not fingerprints?"

"No. I don't know anything about that."

"Your name is down as having taken them."

"I didn't."

"Who did?"

He paled.

"OK." She held up a hand. "Now we're not after any old buddies of yours from the force, that's not what we're interested in at all. It's the fingerprints from that case that we're concerned about."

"I don't know anything about that. I wasn't there when the prints got took."

The good thing about interviewing a bad liar was that Morrow knew he was telling the truth. "Who would know about that?"

"George Gamerro. He was my DS at the time."

"And where's he now?"

"Stirling. He's got a paper shop out there in Bridge of Allan."

"OK." She stood up. "You've been great, Harry."

He saw them out to the hall and got their coats from the cupboard, holding Morrow's open for her to slip into. "You're not supposed to do this for women anymore," he said as she put her arms in.

"Aren't you?"

"PC and that," said Harry. "My missus likes it though."

"I think it's slapping us on the arse and not promoting us you're not supposed to do," said Morrow. It sounded a bit harsh but Harry smiled at it.

"Oh," he said, "OK. You sound like my daughter. She thinks I'm a caveman."

Morrow held out her hand and shook his warmly. "Nice to meet you, DC McMahon."

He shook their hands and smiled and then reached for the door. He didn't open it though but turned back. "Would you do me a favor? Please don't mention that you were here. Not to George. Not to anyone."

19

Rose held her paper coffee cup and leaned sideways, so that part of her face was obscured by the plastic plant. She didn't want to be seen by anyone. She couldn't go home. Robert had seen those photos of her. Robert knew who she really was now. She couldn't stand that. And she knew why Anton Atholl hadn't re ported them all this time.

He must have loved you. Julius kept her close because she kept Anton Atholl quiet. That was why he kept her. He didn't love her. He wasn't her father. She was useful. More than useful. They couldn't have run the business without Atholl keeping quiet. They'd always known he was the one weak spot.

He loved you.

She wanted to kill Atholl. She wanted him annihilated. Not to kill him but for him to be gone, wiped off the face. She couldn't kill anyone again. She just knew she couldn't, and she couldn't think straight because she had Aileen Wuornos's chicken in her head.

She shut her eyes and was back to the night she heard about the chicken.

Late, two or three in the morning, sitting in Francine's immaculate living room on the gold striped sofa with pale blue cushions. Rose was holding Hamish, rocking him as he cried a thin, exhausted wail. He had colic. The living room was the furthest place in the house from Robert and Francine's bedroom.

She had the TV on to keep her awake, the subtitles on and the noise down and she came across a documentary about the American serial killer Aileen Wuornos. She was a prostitute. She'd killed six or seven men and now they were going to kill her. She was an ugly woman and a liar. They proved that she was a liar. She made faces into the camera, wore orange, looked dirty.

Hamish began to settle a little, Rose had given him some drops of medicine and he got drowsy. She wondered if maybe she could take a chance and put him down. She was distracted, walking back and forth with him on her shoulder, savoring the small weight of him, his nuzzling into her neck.

On the telly they were saying that Wuornos's father killed himself in prison. He was in for raping and trying to kill a seven-year-old girl. That was what caught Rose's attention, the mention of the father, and she realized that they were going back into her childhood, showing where she was from. Rose rarely heard stories like her own. It piqued her interest.

The father left the family two months before Wuornos was born. Then her nineteen-year-old mother left and Wuornos and her brother went to live with their grandparents.

Hamish was asleep. In the twilight living room, Rose looked for the remote to turn the telly off.

The grandfather was an alcoholic. He raped Wuornos and lent her out to his friends. She got pregnant by one of them. Rose couldn't see the remote. She usually left it on the sofa. Wuornos had the baby and gave it away. When she was fifteen she left home and went to live in a wood nearby. Rose was looking for the remote by the sofa and thinking that Wuornos must have come from somewhere warm, to live in woods, that Michigan must be a nice warm place. Wuornos was whoring for money and food and when she came back into the town she used to hang around a house that belonged to a local pedo.

Rose stopped looking for the remote then. She began to watch the TV.

They interviewed people who had been kids back then and lived in the town. They all hung around there. They knew he was a pedo, they knew he was after them, but they went to his house anyway. He let them in and gave them food. He gave them beer and cigarettes. Rose saw herself at the door of the shack on TV, as if she had been in that house. She felt disgust and hated herself. She told the other kids she went there for beer and cigarettes, but that wasn't why she went there. She went because he paid her attention. He told her she was special, that she meant the world to him. He looked at her and saw her. That's why she was there, not for money or beer, not to save herself from the cold streets of Glasgow, but because he cared whether she was there or not. The things he gave her were a cover, because more shameful than fucking rooms full of old men was the need for someone.

Rose stood in front of the big TV, in the midnight twilight, with Hamish on her shoulder and cried for herself back then. She hadn't thought about it for ten years.

A hard-faced woman talked about the pedo's house, where things were and how dirty it was. Then she told the story of the chick.

The pedo kept chickens. The chickens laid eggs. He used to get the children to crack open fertilized eggs before they were ready to hatch. The chicks weren't ready yet, not ready to come out. He'd make them watch the chicks struggle, trying to breathe, try to stand.

Rose couldn't remember whether they had shown a chick doing that, struggling, but she could see it. She could see it clearly: a broken egg on a table. In the background a man's face watching, smiling as a featherless chick tried to stand on unformed bones, its skin thin and blue, huge eyes bulging. They died, of course. Of course, they died. And the man made the children watch them die.

Robert knew about her. When he came home, the house would no longer be safe. It wouldn't be separate. It would be like everywhere else, then.

So Rose sat in the most anonymous place she could think of, a city center Starbucks. She hid among the shifting sands of customers coming and going, the sameness of the cups and the sticky floor and sugar-freckled tables and waited for the thought to go.

A chick and a broken egg. Not a yellow fluffy Easter chick, plump and full of promise. A featherless creature, blue skinned, staggering on a table. The picture made her feel sick. The picture made her want to bring her fist down on the chick, smash it and smear its soft bones and thin, stupid skin, its watery blood, over the table.

She wiped her hand on her leg, cleaning imaginary guts on her thigh. She couldn't go home yet.

Outside, in the pedestrian street, shoppers hurried by in groups and singles. Rose watched their ankles, hating them. They had real people they belonged to. Real families and friends and they hated them, probably. They weren't making themselves part of the family by giving a service, they weren't being left outside the door of the Art Club to come in later.

Julius must have loved you, Atholl had said at the funeral. He must have *loved* you. But he didn't. Julius used her to shut Atholl up. And in the end, at the very end, he broke the bond between them and told Robert about the back safe, told him the code, as if nothing they had built together mattered.

He was snide, Atholl. A snide shit. She knew exactly what he meant now. Julius loved having her around. She was so useful to him, in more ways than taking care of his business or running his errands or watching out for Robert and keeping him clean. Feeling angry was better than the sad sickness. She was able to look up and see something other than the chick or the photographs.

A woman was sitting at a far table, alone. She still had a woolly hat on, even though she was indoors, and was absentmindedly arranging and rearranging the sugar strip packets into rows on the table in front of her. Her hand movements were jerky, her mouth hanging open and her shirt was buttoned up wrong, the spare button gaping above her heart. She reached slowly into her bag and pulled out a small bottle of antiseptic gel, a clear bottle with a pump action dispenser at the top. Pumping with a nervous finger, she squeezed out two measures and rubbed them on her hands, rubbing too long. Then she put the bottle away again.

Rose watched her from half inside the plant and shut her eyes. She wasn't doing that. She wasn't a nutter trying to clean herself in a café. She wasn't that bad.

She lifted her drink to her mouth but remembered the chick again just as the coffee sloshed onto her lips. She couldn't take anything in her mouth. She put the full cup back down and wiped her mouth with her sleeve.

The disgust shuddered through her. Who took those photos of her? It didn't matter. Wasn't McMillan, she knew that. Wasn't even about her. It was about them, the men in the pictures. She was just a body. Couldn't even see her face in one of them. But their faces were clear. No flash. Maybe they didn't know the pictures existed. Atholl must have known though. That's why he said there was nothing in the safe. He must have always known the pictures existed.

Without the photo Rose would never have remembered Atholl

from back then. It would have been a party of drunk men, Sammy bringing her in, the men, one by one, taking her next door—it was usually in a separate room but not always. It would just have been a party among many parties. She didn't look at faces.

Atholl knew though. Every time they spoke to each other, he must have seen that photograph the way she was seeing the chick in her head. She held her breath for a moment, certain she was going to vomit.

She held it.

She held it.

She let it out and found herself looking at a table of laughing teenagers, at a mother with a baby, at a man in a suit jacket eating a massive cake. They didn't give a fuck. No one gave a fuck. Somewhere in the city right now a child was being fucked by someone and they were all here eating cakes and drinking coffee and chewing biscuits. Chewing and salivating and swallowing, sugar and cream and chocolate and coffee.

They didn't give a fuck but they wanted to hear about it, afterwards. They'd crowd around the telly and listen to wizened old women talk about way back then and how different things were. They listened to people who overcame it, became a film star or a chess champion. That's all they'd listen to, successes, survivors, because it meant they could keep eating and drinking and sitting around complaining about their husbands and housing and shoes and the government.

The woman with hand gel was not a film star or a champion anything. Rose wasn't a champion anything. No one wanted to hear that. She took a breath, saw the chick, featherless, staggering on soft bones, its eyes so bulbous the eyelids couldn't cover them. She saw the chick stagger and fall, felt the air through its ill-formed feathers as it tumbled to its side.

Now Rose looked across the generic café, the sticky café with fake leather seats and windows running with condensation, she looked across and saw that chick again, only now it wasn't a nameless stranger from a warm place in America she saw, laying his head on the table, grinning as he watched the struggling chick fight and die. It was Julius.

It was Julius. And he didn't love her, he wasn't her friend. He had used her all this time. He never touched her but he'd used her just the same and he didn't love her. But she had loved him.

A phone rang; she heard the buzz buzz before she connected it to her own phone. Probably Francine, weak, asking where she was.

Rose took the phone out of her pocket and looked at it. But it wasn't Francine. It was exactly who she didn't want to talk to. It was BB—code for Anton Atholl.

She looked at the phone and let it ring again, unsure whether she should answer, because she wasn't certain she could speak. Fuck him, she thought and answered.

"Is that you?" he asked.

"Hm," she said, hoping for news of Robert.

"Need to see you."

"No."

"It's imp—"

She hung up and turned her phone off. Across the room she saw the nutter woman with her shirt done up wrong. She had the small bottle in her hand again. She was pumping the alcohol rub out into her palm with a nervous jerky motion. Rose could smell it.

Rose was at her side suddenly. The smell from the hand rub was knife sharp, clean. She said, "Sorry, can I have some?"

The woman looked up at her and blinked slowly. "Sure."

She was drawling, her lips moist, but Rose looked away from her face, looked away from her shirt and her chest where the wrongly matched buttons collided, gaping at her heart.

She pumped the bottle four times into her left hand and curled her fingers around the sacred contents of her palm.

"Thanks." She retreated back to her coat and drink.

Under the table, where no one could see what she was doing or how odd she was being, Rose rubbed the alcohol all over her hands, felt it burn off the dirt and the filth. She lifted her hands above the table and shut her eyes and rubbed it into her face.

She sat still, eyes shut, feeling the dirt evaporate into the air.

She couldn't do it again. She couldn't kill Atholl. But she couldn't let him live either.

20

The shops in Bridge of Allan were modest and functional: co-op supermarket and chemist, but the shops in between were florists and card shops, gift shops and country wear. George Gamerro's paper shop was at the far end of the main street.

The students at the nearby university were gathering at a fish and chip shop, the sort of Italian café that would have done good business in north London but here it wasn't retro mock-up but the real thing. A felt-tipped sign leaned forehead first into the window, faded letters boasting *Scotland's best fish tea*. The students stood outside in groups, eating steaming chips, scarved and jumpered, their skin impossibly good and clear with the air of bright futures around them. McCarthy parked the car outside the shop.

"Tell you what," said Morrow, "why don't you wait here and let me go in alone?"

It wasn't what they were supposed to do but they both understood that a cop would know the rules, would know that a single cop would need corroboration. She thought Gamerro was more likely to talk if she went in alone.

"Sure?" said McCarthy.

Morrow wasn't sure. She looked at the paper shop for a moment, wondering whether she was employing a clever technique or just desperate. She felt as if she was trying to trap herself, trick herself into doing the right thing. If Michael Brown didn't kill his brother then his whole history should have been different. He shouldn't have been given a life sentence, shouldn't have been out on license, shouldn't be back in prison now. She was trudging towards an expensive retrial of a dead case and the release of a ruined, unsympathetic man who would be rearrested within a year and tried for something else, at a time of upheaval, when only the budget keepers and company men would feature in the future.

"Dunno..."

They sat for a while, Morrow pulling apart and fitting together her career suicide, McCarthy awaiting her decision.

Students passed them, heading back to the uni campus. Morrow looked at the shop.

The windows were covered in adverts for different papers. A huge black and white skyline of Glasgow covered one whole window and outside stood a bin sponsored by an ice cream company and a newspaper stand from a paper.

"To hell with it," she said finally. "Wait here."

It was dark inside the shop. It took a moment for Morrow's eye to adjust. A chubby young woman was serving, leaning heavily on the countertop and reading a celebrity magazine. She had very pink lipstick on and chewed gum. She glanced up as Morrow came in, long enough to see that she wasn't a child, unlikely to shoplift, and went back to her reading.

"Excuse me," said Morrow, "I'm looking for George Gamerro?"

The girl looked her over. "What for?"

"I need to talk to him."

She nodded. "Selling something?"

"No, I'm an old pal from the police."

"Oh." She brightened at that. "Hang on." She shuffled out from behind the counter and took two steps to a door at the back of the shop. She opened it into a narrow cupboard, crammed with crates of pop and boxes of crisps, shelves reaching right up to the ceiling. The nearest wall was taken up with a narrow wooden staircase, steep as a ladder, that led up to a hole in the ceiling.

The girl kept her eyes on the shop and shouted up into the hole, "Hey, Granda! GRANDA!"

A thump upstairs made her smile at Morrow. "He's annoyed now. Watch this: GRANDA!"

Another thump was followed by a series of muttered curses and the girl laughed softly to herself. "He'll be spitting now." She went back to the counter, leaving Morrow at the bottom of the steps.

A foot dropped through the hole, then another, feeling gingerly for the step. George Gamerro looked enormous as he climbed down from the small hole. When he finally stood in front of her Morrow could see that he was enormous. Tall as the door and muscled, still, despite his age. His face looked old, a craggy map of wrinkles and skin tags but his body was still spritely. He stood like an old school polis, shoulders back, hands comfortably by his side, feet planted firmly on at-ease legs.

"Hello?" he said, looming like a giant in the tiny cupboard.

Morrow put her hand out. "George Gamerro? I'm DI Alex Morrow."

George looked wary. He looked at her hand but didn't take it. "From Strathclyde?"

She smiled. "How did you know that?"

He didn't return her smile. "What are you doing here, on your own?"

Morrow had meant it to be friendly and informal, her being here without a colleague. "I, um, my neighbor's in the car outside. Can we talk to you?"

George put his hands in his pockets. "Why's he in the car?" he whispered, looking over her head to the door. A twitch on his chin expressed the panic he was feeling. "Who is it?"

"Who do you think it is?" She wanted him to say a name, tell her who it was that he was so afraid of, but he heard it as a threat.

He looked her in the eye and snarled, "What if I don't come?"

She shook her head, trying to backtrack. "That would be fine. I came in on my own because I thought it would be more friendly, you being an ex-DS, but clearly it's not come over like that at all…"

George kept the snarl on his mouth but his eyes told her he doubted himself, that he was afraid of who, or what, was in the street, that he was too old for this now.

Unbidden, she put her hand on his forearm. "Gamerro, come and have a fish tea with me and my DS. And don't worry: I'm buying."

The middle-aged café owner was plump, plain and clearly very fond of Gamerro. She saw him from behind the counter and came out to greet him warmly, wiping her hands on her pinny as she pushed through the queue to get to him. She led him to a table for four, explaining to the usurped customers in the queue that Gamerro, Morrow and McCarthy had a reservation.

She asked after his wife, after the shop, good business? How's Holly? Gamerro said she was in the shop now and the café owner rolled her eyes. Her grandchildren wouldn't work in the café, she said, too busy at university. It was an underhand dig at George and Morrow found herself smarting for him.

They ordered three fish teas and drinks: a pot of tea for Morrow and McCarthy, a drink of milk for George. The woman left, a smirk at the side of her mouth.

George saw the annoyance on Morrow's face and smiled at it. She could see then that he was a handsome big man and a warm man. He said that Mrs. Fratini was very proud that her grandweans were at university. She brought it up with everyone. The drinks were brought over by a hassled waitress, along with three sets of knives and forks swaddled in paper napkins left at the end of the table.

"So," George dropped his eyes to the table, "what station are you from?"

"London Road, CID," said McCarthy.

"Ah," said George.

"George, we've got a guy called Michael Brown in court right now. His first arrest, the one you were involved in—"

"Don't remember that."

"You don't remember? Young guy, arrested for stabbing his brother, killing him in a lane off Sauchiehall Street?"

"No."

"It was the night Diana died."

He knew then that the lie was ridiculous. Everyone remembered where they were the night Diana died. They even remembered if there was nothing to remember. George struggled for a moment.

"I wasn't involved in the *arrest*," he said definitely.

She looked up. "What?"

George had his hands up at her. "Not the arrest. I wasn't involved in the arrest."

"You were the superior officer."

George chopped carefully at the table with the side of his hand, head tilted as if walking into a headwind. "I supervised the questioning of Michael Brown but I did *not* participate in the processing of Michael Brown upon his arrest. That would be the responsibility of the officers who brought him in and processed him at the bar."

He was talking to them as if they were defense counsel. No one wanted the mess to land in their lap and the mess centered around the arrest.

"You weren't there when he was brought into the booking bar?"

"No."

"Did you check out the paperwork afterwards?"

"No."

"Did you witness the fingerprints being taken—"

"No!" George flinched.

She could see why McMahon had asked them not to mention his name.

Three plates of fish and chips arrived, served by the hassled waitress without a word. She put her hand in her pocket and took out several sachets of ketchup, dropping them on the table and winking at George who smiled back.

When she was gone he explained, "They used to leave them on the tables but the students would come in and lift them. Now you have to pay for them. She's being nice, given us them for free."

They all three looked over at the waitress and smiled their thank-yous, as if she had sent them over a bottle of champagne. They took their cutlery and ate. All the surfaces in the café were hard: steel and marble and stone floors made the room noisy enough for the silence between them not to hang too heavily. The room was an odd shape, the takeaway ice cream counter at an angle to the door, the fish and chips counter at yet another angle.

Morrow ate the fish and chips and reflected that if the sign in the window was true, a tea of fish and chips was finished in Scotland.

Of a sudden the noise abated, the lunchtime rush began to thin and the waitresses began to clear and wipe tables, scraping the remains of the plates into a bin, stacking the crockery on a trolley.

George and McCarthy cleaned their plates and saw that Morrow had given in halfway through.

"Not like it, ma'am?"

"Nah," said Morrow. "I always think I'll like a fish tea but it's a bit greasy for me." She looked at her plate. "You wanting it?"

"Oh, aye." He swapped his clean plate for hers.

She saw George smiling at that and grinned back. "Skinny as a stick," she said of McCarthy.

"Not for want of trying," said McCarthy, through a mouthful.

Morrow poured them a second cup of tea each as George drained his glass of milk.

"I don't want to ask you anything that puts you on the spot, George."

He nodded solemnly and chewed his bottom lip. "What's the problem, then?"

She thought about how to frame it: whoever killed Pinkie Brown has done it again, Michael Brown's hands got out of prison; all of it was too much information. For all she knew Gamerro was acting shifty because he was part of something. He certainly knew something, maybe not everything, and whatever it was he was scared about it.

"Where can I find out what happened when Michael Brown was arrested?"

"Have you looked on the arrest sheet?"

McCarthy chewed the last mouthful of battered fish. Morrow looked around and spoke quietly. "I've assumed the paperwork will all be in order."

"You're probably right."

"Won't tell me much."

"True."

"Even if it does have pertinent information in there it would be hard to pry out. If there was an irregularity, in my experience, the person responsible will have been careful to make sure their name isn't found on it."

"I suppose."

McCarthy was looking at the counter. "Do I have time for an ice cream?"

On the counter there sat a plaster statue of an outsized silver cup with a giant scoop covered in raspberry sauce, a wafer at the back like a Spanish dancer's hair comb.

"Aye," said Morrow, "go on up and order one."

He got up, was three steps away across the room when Morrow heard George mutter a name she had heard before.

She glared at him. "Say it again."

George looked across the room, frightened, and said it more clearly. "Monkton."

"Thank you." She squeezed his forearm, just a little too hard, and got up, pulling her purse out of her bag.

She was paying across the counter when McCarthy saw her and said, "Can I still get an ice cream?"

"If you can drive at seventy while eating a double nugget."

21

Rose let herself in this time. It wasn't late at night, it was teatime and the cushioned hush she was used to in Lonely Mansions was replaced by dulled thumps and muffled shouts, the suggestions of washing machine hums and televisions. She kept her head down, walking up the stairs to Atholl's flat on the third floor.

The block of flats looked out over the River Clyde. No river views were wasted on the communal stairs. The developers could charge extra for them, so the river views were saved for the flats. The stair windows looked out over the street.

Rose was halfway up the third flight of steps when she heard a door opening on the floor below. She flattened herself to the wall and stayed still and listened as the door closed, the lock slipped shut. She heard a faint *tss tss* from headphones as the person padded downstairs and opened the door to the street. She waited until she was sure they were gone. Then she slipped up the remaining steps to Atholl's door.

She had a key because they were renting the flat for him. Part of McMillan's deal with Atholl. He called it a retainer, for future legal work. Rose couldn't remember the last time Atholl had done any official work for them. If it was a reciprocal arrangement she couldn't see what they were getting back.

She let herself into the empty hall and shut the door behind her. The flat was still and dark. She stood in the hallway and listened, heard the river slither past through an open window, heard a kid shout in the street.

She didn't think about what she was doing. She didn't think about what she had done. She just stood in the hall, hands in her pockets, and waited for Atholl to come home.

It only took an hour.

Atholl arrived home with a lot of fanfare. The front door opened, a bag was dropped, Atholl was grunting, short of breath from climbing the stairs.

He dropped a briefcase in the hall and carefully hugged an off-sales bag to his chest as he shut the door behind him, enveloping himself in the darkness. He turned in to the dim hall and then he saw her.

He started, the bag slipped. He grabbed the bottom of it, catching the glass vodka bottle but not the carton of orange juice, which slid out of the plastic bag and bounced on the floor, corner first. It didn't burst. He looked from her to the bashed carton, attempted a smile.

Rose didn't smile back.

"Hello, Rose."

He reached for the hall light but stayed his hand when she whispered, "I was in the safe."

He changed his mind when she said that, preferring the dark. He dropped eyes to the floor, the bottle slid down his torso and landed with a thud on the carpet. She could see his tongue moving in his mouth, rehearsing excuses. His chin quivered.

She hissed, "I will beat you to fucking death, right here in your hall, if you dare cry, Atholl."

"Ah, yes, I called you..." He was crying, his eyes were crying, but he tried to change the subject. "Because I know where Robert is. He turned his phone on."

Everything he said was a trap. That wasn't what he had wanted to tell her. He must have known she was checking iCloud and would find out anyway. He'd called her about something else. He was talking as if he had summoned her here, giving out teasers, prompts for her to ask him things. She didn't rise to it.

"Want to know where he is?" he said brightly.

His eyes though, just the eyes, were dying of sorrow. He dropped his chin to his chest and looked at the vodka bottle lying on the hall floor. It lay on its side like a dead chick. The light was behind her, coming from over the river, catching the sequins dropping from his eyes, tumbling through the air and being swallowed by the carpet.

Atholl bent down slowly and picked up the bottle by the neck, holding it in front of himself, muttering, "A light refreshment, perhaps, before we go in for dinner..."

He stumbled towards her, veering left into the front room. Rose stepped back to let him pass.

He dropped into the armchair as she came in through the doorway. Tears rolled down his face as he unscrewed the bottle lid with a sharp metallic scratch.

"Actually," he told the bottle, "that would be lovely, thank you. So much."

He put it to his lips, tipped it back and the light from the window caught the swirl of vodka, lighting it blue like liquid tears.

He dropped the bottle, his eyes rolled back in ecstasy and his shoulders loosened.

Rose watched him, herself expressionless, listening to her own shallow breathing. Atholl fell to staring at the bottle he was clutching on his knee. His sad eyes brimmed again, tears trembling. Then he looked at her and said in a small voice, "Rose, I didn't know you, then."

"But you know me now."

His voice was very small now. "Are you here to kill me?"

"Why would you think that?"

"You killed Aziz Balfour, Rose, I know that."

She was shocked, her thoughts tumbled over each other: how could he possibly know? There was no one else who knew Aziz had hit Julius and made him fall so heavily his lungs collapsed. No one had seen her with Aziz, no one. No motive, no witnesses. He couldn't possibly know that.

Suddenly furious with him, Rose pulled her hands out of her hoodie pockets. In each one she held a plastic bottle of paracetamol. She stepped forward, put both of them on the side table and stepped away.

Atholl looked at them. Then he looked at her, confused.

She didn't know how to say it: I cannot suffer you to live. I cannot breathe air that you have breathed. You are all of them, Sammy and Wuornos and her father and the man with the chickens.

"Why would I?" he asked.

"If I kill you they'll want to know why. They'll dig. They'll find the photo. If you kill yourself they'll say you did it because you missed your wife and kids. You choose."

Atholl looked at the pill bottles for a long time. She saw him think himself into the future, see his sons remember him one way, then the other. He was trying not to cry but she didn't think it was because he would be dead soon. She felt he was half-relieved about that. He was trying not to cry because he had meant well and his life had been a bit crap; he was crying for himself. He took a deep breath and addressed the pills:

"I did an inquest: these take four days to kill you," he said.

"Often asymptomatic for the first twenty-four hours...then... liver failure."

He looked at them. He looked at his vodka and she knew he was thinking about washing them down. He looked from the bottle of pills to the vodka, rehearsing the back-and-forth of an overdose.

He looked at the pills and began to cry again. "If I take them will you burn that photograph?"

She had scratched her own face off in the photograph. When she got here, before he arrived, she had tucked the photo carefully behind the cleaning products in Atholl's kitchen cupboard. She wanted it found after he died.

"Yes."

"Promise me?" High voice, childlike inflection.

"I promise I'll burn it." She wouldn't.

He looked at the bottles again.

"Go on," she said, reassuringly.

"Rose," he had lost his breath to tears now, "I never, I swear, *never* did anything like that again. It was a one-off." But he had spent a lifetime listening to excuses for crimes and he knew there were none that really meant anything.

She kept her eyes on the pills. "It's done now, Anton. You take 'em."

He looked at her, asking if it would hurt, telling her he was afraid.

She wouldn't reassure him, said nothing but gave a fraction of a nod at the bottle of pills on his left. Following her eye, Atholl reached over and took the first bottle, holding it strangely, thumb on the bottom, finger on the top, looking at it as if it was an exotic species. He glanced back at her.

"Promise you'll burn it?"

"I promise."

His face twitched a grateful smile. Then he pinched the tag for the plastic seal around the neck, pinkie out, as if he was availing himself of a tiny delicacy. He turned the bottle as he undid the strip. Still holding it strangely, as if he didn't want to touch the sides, he pressed and turned the clicking lid until it came off.

He sat with the bottle of pills in his left hand, a finger under the bottle, another over the open top, as if he found her so disgusting he couldn't bear to touch the bottle where she had touched it.

She nodded him on and he lifted the pills, holding her eye, and tipped them into his mouth, chewing them like Tic Tacs. They were bitter. He grued at the taste and undid his bottle lid, again the sharp metallic grind. The sound took her back to the Red Road flats, to the wind and the sensation of a knife grinding through skin. She'd been sick, almost passed out over Aziz's body. She'd held on to a girder to stop herself falling.

Now she felt sick again. She wanted to run forward and slap them out of his mouth. She felt the breath go out of her but she didn't move. This was different. This was harder. This wasn't business.

Atholl held her eye and lifted the vodka bottle, drinking down a solid swallow of jagged little pills, his eyes rolled back and she felt the scratch at her own throat. Keeping his eyes shut he lifted the bottle of pills and took another mouthful, chewing less purposefully this time, mechanically. He dropped the empty pill bottle and drank again from the vodka.

He opened his eyes and seemed suddenly calm and restful. He glanced at the second bottle of pills and Rose nodded. He took the lid off, holding it as before and, balking but persisting, chewed another mouthful, washing it down.

He smacked his lips and looked at her. "You know, I'm getting quite drunk here. I might go to hospital, have my stomach pumped if I'm alone. Will you stay with me this evening? Stop me from changing my mind?"

Rose shook her head. She didn't think he would change his mind. Part of him wanted this too. She looked at the pill bottle in his hand and realized that she was feeling better, cleaner. She thought she could face going home now.

She realized suddenly that he wasn't sorrowful anymore. The alcohol had hit his mood and shifted it sideways. His eyes narrowed slowly and she saw a flash of the mean man who would tuck a terrified fourteen-year-old in front of other men. She was glad she had stayed for this.

"Rose, what is hell?" He took another mouthful of pills and raised his eyebrows in a question. She waited for him to finish chewing, expecting a cracker joke.

"Hell, my dear," he paused to grimace, "is unanswered questions."

He rolled his snow-coated tongue to the front of his mouth, scraping the powdery white onto his teeth in a paracetamol snow-drift. Then he lifted the bottle and washed it down.

"Do you believe in an afterlife, Atholl?"

He shrugged, struggling to keep it down. "D'you?"

"Used to."

He smacked his lips and grinned at her. "When I called you earlier, it wasn't about Robert. I called to warn you that the police have found..."

They stared at each other. In the street below a man shouted for a dog. They stared at each other for a full minute, Atholl smiling gently. Rose realized that she had stopped breathing.

She was the first to snap. "Found *what*?"

Atholl took a breath, grinned and burst out laughing. He dropped the second paracetamol bottle onto the carpet. It rolled towards her.

"The police found *what*?"

Atholl laughed again, then flinched suddenly at the realization of what he was doing. Panic in his eyes, horror, and his eyes bulged as if he might throw up, but he didn't. She held on to the doorway to stop herself storming over, hitting him. One hard jostle might make him sick it all up.

Atholl smiled and his eyes shut for a long time.

She wouldn't beg him. She wouldn't burn the photograph either.

"If you're not dead in three days' time I'll kill you."

He didn't answer.

Deciding to leave, she pushed herself off the wall. Atholl looked up at her. A white froth was forming at the corner of his mouth.

She was facing the door when she heard him muttering behind her. She reached for the door handle, stepped out and shut it behind her. She was in the hall before the words Anton Atholl had said assembled in her ear.

See you down there.

22

The street was dark outside the glass-walled office where people sat working at computers in gray cubicles. The investment firm seemed to have a late-night culture, because it was almost eight o'clock and fewer than half the desks were empty.

Mina Balfour was in charge of this floor. Reception must have warned her that they were coming because she stood to meet Morrow and DC Daniel at the door to her prestigious glass cubicle. She looked more than seven months pregnant, but that was because she was so slim and tall. When she stood her thin frame bulged out at a ridiculous angle, like a Hollywood actress with a pregnancy prosthetic. She wore a sharp business suit jacket, not a maternity one, and a pencil skirt. She had long, impossibly sleek black hair, reaching almost to her thighs, glinting under the bright ceiling lights.

She stepped across the room to open the door for them, graceful in impressive heels that were three inches high and thin as a string.

Up closer Morrow could see that Mina was pretty, not beautiful, and wore an extraordinary amount of makeup. Red slashes of blusher, a deep solid foundation, glossy purple lipstick and black eyeliner that might have been applied with crayon. She held the door as she introduced herself and shook their hands, serious, listening carefully as they introduced themselves, nodding formally, and inviting them to her desk.

"I've really only got about twenty minutes and then I need to be on a conference call to New York," she said, almost for the benefit of the plebs around her who didn't have a glass office of their own. "So if we could keep this short..."

She let the door fall shut and retook her seat, waving them to chairs that backed onto the workers. Her own chair, Morrow noticed, faced out into the office like a warder's.

Morrow started by saying, "Mina, I'm amazed you're still at work, after all you've been through."

"I like to keep going." Mina's eyes flicked to the floor outside.

"I'm so sorry about your husband."

She ground her teeth at that, licked her tight top lip and then looked hard at Morrow. "It's very nice of you to come here to tell me that." She was clearly furious.

"The reason I'm here is that I can't get any sense of what Aziz was like from the file—"

"Sorry, no sorry." Mina pointed a fast finger from one to the other. "Who are you two? I met a guy called Wainwright and he told me he was investigating Aziz's death."

Daniel looked at Morrow.

"He is," said Morrow carefully. "But fingerprints that we picked up from the scene have also come up in a case I'm investigating—"

"Are you Wainwright's subordinate?"

"No."

"His boss?"

"No. I have equal rank with DI Wainwright but I work in another division."

That seemed to please her. "So, there's two DIs working on it?"

"Yes. And two divisions."

She nodded for a moment, taking it in, her tongue flicking behind her teeth.

"What sort of work do you do here, Mina?"

"Pensions fund management."

"Financial services?"

"We're the Scottish division of a big company down south."

"Is that what you've always done?"

"Since I left uni, yes. I studied accountancy but didn't fancy it for a career."

"What's your maiden name?"

"Ibrahim."

"Of the Queen's Park Ibrahims?"

"No." Mina was firm but smirked a little. "The *Lenzie* Ibrahims."

Lenzie. nice area, middle class, quiet. Morrow gave her a little smile back. "Quite different."

Mina seemed a little surprised that Morrow understood the difference. The Queen's Park Ibrahims were rascals. Morrow had never heard of the Ibrahims from Lenzie so it was a safe bet that they were good-living people: lawyers, accountants, keepers of lawns and washers of cars, attendees at private school parent councils.

"Yes," Mina gave her the full smile, "*quite* different." Her teeth had been straightened and capped. Morrow saw Mina then as the Glasgow princess that she was. Morrow had been at school on the south side, with boys who dreamed of girls like Mina but settled for girls like her.

"How did you meet Aziz?"

Mina circled her right shoulder in a shrug that was anything but a shrug. "Family."

"He knew your family?"

She rolled her eyes in a fond reproach. "Ziz knew *everyone*." But she remembered him then, and her chest jolted forward as though she had been slapped on the back, and she froze, blinking hard, struggling to breathe in.

Morrow realized why Mina had so much makeup on: she had been repairing it over and over during the day. When she spoke again her voice was hoarse. "He was a nice guy, know what I mean? Real one-off. Funny guy…"

Then the weight of sorrow came over her and she sat exhausted, hands limp on the table. Morrow tried to move her mind on. "Can you tell me about his work?"

"Yeah, he was doing good work, raising money, event organizing in the community, big-money events. He knew everybody and everybody loved him. Very gregarious…" She broke off, slumping again.

"What was the charity for?"

"Uh, raising money for the people made homeless by the earthquakes, '05 and '08. They're still living in tents, a lot of them. No water, stuff like that, you know. People were happy to give it to him. They'd already given a lot of money but Ziz knew none of it was getting there. It's so corrupt over there but Ziz had ways of getting the money into the country without going through the formal channels. Government creams off half of it. People knew the money they were giving would actually get there, and not be financing blocks of luxury flats in Dubai for the military."

Mina had clearly said this before, possibly to Wainwright, and didn't expect it to attract any interest. She stopped, lifted a bottle of sparkling water from her desk.

"What *ways*?"

Mina swallowed, keeping her eyes on the office. "Auch, you know, networks, family, safe ways. People trusted him."

"Did he use hundi men?"

Mina stopped still. Eyes flicking about the office floor outside. "Well, I mean, I don't know..."

"You don't know what hundi is or who the men are?"

"I don't know any of that ."

Morrow cleared her throat and wriggled forward on her chair a little. "I understand," she said confidentially, "why people would do that. I know the banks aren't safe and the exchange rate... well, but you have to understand, Mina, that these are heavy people. The amount of cash they deal in, it makes them vulnerable and they can't afford to be vulnerable so they buy guns and charities aren't the only people who use them—"

"*I know that.*"

"No, I don't think you do. I don't think you do know how hundi men make money or who they're involved with. I think Aziz did know, or he found out, and maybe that's why he was killed."

Mina broke eye contact and tipped slowly back in the chair, chin to the ceiling, tipping back in the chair as if her pregnant stomach was rising out of her. Thinking she was having an attack or a stroke, Morrow and Daniel were on their feet, standing over her. But she was crying, tears running down her temples. She looked up at Morrow, rolled her fingers over her face. "Mascara," she whispered, taking a tissue from her sleeve and dabbing watery black from her hairline. It took a while to stop.

Morrow stood over her like a benign dentist. "Mina, I am awful sorry."

"Will you please stop saying my bloody name," whispered Mina. "You're doing my fucking head in."

"Sorry," said Morrow and then realized that was probably pretty annoying as well. "I'll sit down."

Mina managed to sit up, cupping her stomach. "You got kids?"

Morrow nodded. "Twins."

Mina was impressed and stroked her belly. "'Kin' hell. You must have felt like a monster."

"I actually was a monster," said Morrow. "Towards the end I was as wide as I was tall."

Mina snorted a smile and with a spark of terror in her eyes added, "They OK?"

"They're brilliant."

"I worry, you know, because, it's not good." She pointed at her tear-stained face, almost crying again.

If she had been another woman Morrow would have squeezed her hand and told a sugary lie, said everything would be all right and having a baby was nothing. Instead she said what she knew to be true.

"We see a lot of hair-raising stuff in this job. You're a nice woman from a good family. That baby's luckier than most."

Mina nodded at her computer. "Not living in a tent..."

"Can't you get some more time off?"

"Not in this economic climate," whispered Mina. "I don't dare. You've got no idea what the private sector's like, and I'm going to be a single parent. I'm due maternity off this company and I'm getting it at this level. Give them any excuse..."

Morrow nodded. "Tell me about the hundi men Aziz dealt with. I'm not going to leave you vulnerable. We're just after the men that killed him."

"You'll keep my name out of it?"

"Your name wouldn't come into it. We're investigating a murder."

Mina hesitated. "A wee lawyer called Julius McMillan handled all the money. I'm only telling you because he died."

"I know he did."

"Like, a week ago, of natural causes."

"I know, I know Julius McMillan died."

"I always knew when Ziz had been there because he came home stinking of fags and I was like "You're *stinking!*" "

"When did he last see McMillan?"

Mina slumped in her chair. "The night before he died. He had three big bags of money when he went out. Came home without them. *Stinking,*" She stared at her desk top, lost in it for a minute. "Stinking. Upset. He'd seen someone there... Outside. He had a fight with McMillan about it... He was upset. His hand was hurt... said he banged it off the desk but I didn't believe that. Ziz don't mind confrontation. Something else had happened."

"What did you think happened to his hand?"

"I thought he punched Dawood."

Morrow held her breath. "Dawood McMann?"

"Yeah."

"He met him at McMillan's?"

Mina looked at her. "Aye. Dodgy Dawood. Mr. Glasgow. Ziz was ranting about him for a day." She sat up, calmer now. "Dawood's shops are a cover, but you know that." Morrow didn't, actually. "He brings in drugs from Pakistan. Everybody knows that. The carnage he causes back home, the people they fund to keep the channels open. Pakistan could be a rich country, you know, a safe country. All over the world, they've raised enough money to build three houses for every single family made homeless by the earthquakes but they're still living in tents, children dying of cold and hunger. It's bastards like Dawood who let that happen. But you can't prove it because he never touches anything, someone else holds the money, someone else holds the drugs, the guns, the everything. Every time you get someone it's another monkey running errands for him. Ziz didn't want the money he'd raised being part of that."

216 · denise mina

"So he got in a punch-up with Dawood and then what happened?"

"I thought nothing had happened." She shrugged. "Next day he got a call from McMillan's office, there was a problem with the access code. It was late at night, we didn't know McMillan was dead already. Ziz went to meet someone in his office. He never came home."

"The office is quite near the Red Road flats, isn't it?"

"Yeah." She smiled sadly. "He looked out at it from his window. Saw the hard hats and the yellow vests they all wore. He used to say if that was in Pakistan families would be living in it." She looked up. "You seen the state of it?"

"Yeah, went up it."

"Bloody hell."

"Yeah. Terrifying. Thought I might need airlifted off."

"Wouldn't bother Ziz."

"No?"

"Nah, he was part of the rescue effort in 2008. He'd climbed through collapsed buildings and everything."

"They said he ran up there and someone followed him."

"Yeah, he'd be trying to get away. Wouldn't think they'd be brave enough to follow him."

"But they did."

Mina nodded slowly at her desk. "They did."

Out in the car Morrow checked her phone and found a voice mail from Anton Atholl. He sounded drunk. "I have something important to tell you. Please meet me for breakfast," he said, "seven a.m. in Le Pain Provençal in Argyle Street." He pronounced the café's name in a thick, guttural French accent.

23

Rose stood at the window, stirring a pot of spaghetti hoops with a wooden spoon. Behind her, sitting across from each other at the table, the children were playing a game of Guess Who?

She knew what she was doing with the toast and the spaghetti hoops, feeding them comfort food because she wanted to be comforted herself. Normally she disapproved of those fat nannies who crammed cakes and biscuits and sweeties into their children's mouths, who coaxed them quiet with the promise of what they themselves wanted. A sit-down. A DVD holiday. But it was all right. It was all right to do that sometimes. She was using a pot instead of the microwave, dirtying it and stirring to make herself feel as if it was any effort at all. It was a nice pot, a little round-bellied one that looked homely and well used, to add to the lie she was telling herself.

Hoops on toast. No nutrition in them. At least beans were a vegetable. The children were delighted. So delighted they weren't even fighting about Guess Who? yet.

She looked at the window and caught her own eye, flinching

at the sight of herself. She began to stir faster. An avocado bath. Fast breathing in a pissy alleyway. She shut her eyes tight and held her breath. They were coming thick and fast now. Worse and worse. Dust on her face in the Red Road, in her nose and ears and hair. She opened her eyes. The sauce was sticking to the side, drying and turning a deep bloody red. Her stomach lurched but she managed not to react to it. She reached down carefully and turned off the gas burner.

The fight had begun behind her. Jessica and Angus were arguing with Hamish about their question, hair, it's got hair and the hair had sick in it, dried sick in it and he was fucking her anyway though she had been sick in her hair and she was trying to tell him she'd been sick but he just kept pumping into her, nudging her up the dirty, the dirty bed, and she could see her childish hands on the bed, Jessica hands, kids' hands and the stupid cheap ring Sammy'd given her out of a cracker or something.

A sudden physical twitch made her flick the spoon, unbalancing the pot on the stove, tipping it onto its fat little side and spilling the hoops all over the hard-to-clean stove top.

"Ships!" She reached into it, burning her fingers. "Ships!"

The children fell silent behind her, all their attention on her suddenly.

She was crying, she couldn't turn around to them now.

"Oh, dear," she said, raising her hands in a pantomime. "Oh dear me. Now I've spilled a little bit." But her voice was wrong and strained and cracked and they knew something was very wrong. "Oh, ships."

Tears running down her face she reached into the heat and picked the burning hoops up with her fingers, dropping them back in the pan. The heat clung to the hot sugary sauce, sticking to her fingers, scalding and merciless. A rifle shot of toast bouncing out of the Dualit made her jump and she stood sobbing at the cooker.

Even in prison she hadn't had this, these ambushing thoughts and visions. In prison, after the first short panicking while, she knew where she was to go and at what time, where she was to sleep and at what time and she was numb mostly. No one touched her. She was visited and she knew that soon it would all end and she would be looked after by Julius McMillan. She was offered counseling and said no because she had Mr McMillan and it was all right, that was taken care of. She was taken care of. Now there was no one between her and herself. She raised her burning hand to her face and held it, the red sauce colder now but still burning enough to feel right and she pressed it to her tender eyelids and the softness of her lips. She stood and burned and sobbed at the stove, hardly knowing where she was or what age.

A hand on her arm, small and calm. Come on, said a wee voice, come on. It might have been herself that led her across to the sink. There now, she said to herself, it's OK. She thought it might be herself because she did say those things, come on and there now, she said those things. And then a tap came on, not in a frantic gush but calmly. She opened her eyes and saw the water was as cold and clean as baptism water. Her hand was held beneath the water by smaller hands and the soreness was washed away. There now, come on. The burny sauce was washed away and then she was bent down over the sink and the small hand scooped the water to her, to wash away the red and the burn. There now, there.

A tea towel to dab dry her eyelids. Dab dab. Dab dab. She opened her eyes again, just a little, and saw that it wasn't herself but Jessica and Jessica was afraid for her and sad for her and worried. She wasn't playing at being kind, Rose had seen her do that, standing next to a crying girl at a party, touching her casually, implicating herself in the drama without feeling it. She was feeling this but Rose didn't want her to. Rose wanted more for her than this chipping away. She wanted her to stay selfish and casual and not know these other things.

"Is it because Grandma said wait outside?"

"Eh?"

"At the funeral, is it 'cause Grandma said wait and come in after us? Hamish said that was rude, didn't you, Hamish?"

Hamish sat at the table, hands stiff in his lap, and nodded solemnly.

"He said you'd be upset about that because it was rude and insulting. Because you're our servant but also our family member and Grandma was insulting about it."

Rose stood up and took the towel from Jessica's hand. "Yes," she said, folding it carefully though she knew it would have to go in the wash. "Yes," she folded order into it, restoring order, "I was insulted."

"I want to kick Grandma in the penis," said Hamish with venom.

"That's not a nice thing to say," muttered Rose.

"Anyway, she doesn't have a penis," said Jessica.

"No, I know." Hamish read Rose's face again. "She's a monster."

Rose ordered them to set the table, charging Hamish with the cutlery and napkins, Jessica with the glasses and Angus with the plates. She made what she could of the hoops that were left. She spread extra butter on the toast, as if that would make up for the small stack of spaghetti on each plate, and grated a little bland cheese for a bowl in the center of the table.

They sat down together and Hamish, with great solemnity, led them in the grace she had taught them: We're grateful for the food we eat and thank you for the comfy seat.

Rose's plate was empty and she saw them noticing. "I'm not that hungry," she said.

"But *we* have to eat, even if we're not hungry," objected Angus but Jessica hushed him.

They sat on their best behavior, quietly using cutlery, remembering halfway through to tuck the napkins into their collars. They didn't even beg for straws for their drinks.

Rose sat slumped in front of her empty plate, her mind on Atholl eating the tablets. He knew about Aziz, what she had done, and the police must know about Aziz.

She felt the world closing around her, coming to get her, and she didn't give a fuck.

24

Robert sat at the kitchen table with his foot up on a chair. His ankle didn't hurt when it was up, it tingled, the skin sort of fizzed, but that was because it was stretched over the puffy flesh. He sat looking at the cold Aga in the dark kitchen, calculating. It took about one hour to drive to the castle from the ferry terminal, the last ferry had been due to arrive an hour and a bit ago. He had been sitting at the table, in full view of the window, waiting every moment for a blinding white light in his left eye, a jolt in his left temple, the one nearest the French doors. He had sat there for a long time and now the mug he was clutching was cold and his fingertips were sore from holding on so tight. He peeled them off, flattened his hands to the table and considered for the first time in days the possibility that he might not die.

He had turned his phone on again, knowing that the reception was patchy here in the shadow of the mountains and knowing that as he came down the hill, slow and hobbling, his phone was picking up emails and texts and voice mails. He hadn't looked at them but he knew the phone was giving and receiving. They could track him through the phone, they knew where he was and they hadn't come.

He went back to the why. The SOCA report and the dark night in intensive care with his father. He honestly thought Julius had opened up to him in those last hours. He thought it was the morphine or some other end-of-life chemical excreted by the body as it began to shut down. Near-death visions of tunnels of light were supposed to be chemical. Maybe deathbed confessions were too. Robert wished he'd waited outside the room. He wished the frail liver-spotted hand had found nothing there when it crawled across the carefully folded sheet for the touch of a loved one.

He was in the room with his father because he was trying to feel something for the old man. They had never connected, not really. It was a source of regret to Robert that his father's eyes always slipped his, that he never made it to sports days or for birthday parties or his brief, subordinate role in the school football team. All his life he had thought his father regretted Margery, felt guilty and helpless that the wife he had chosen was clinically depressed and spent all her time in bed or sipping wine in front of the television. That's what Robert would have felt if he was Julius. Now he could see that Julius had avoided him because he was even less of a prize than Margery.

The back of a bony hand, a purple lake with a yellow shore under the skin around the cannula into his vein. Julius had tried to pull it out when he got into recovery and they had taped it on with shiny waterproof plastic tape, winding it around his palm so tight that it caught the skin and folded it over. His yellow smoker's pinch still gave off a faint smell of tar as the fingers walked their way across the sheet and took Robert's outstretched hand.

Robert was trying to feel something, devastation, some loss. He was embarrassed at how little he felt for the man. When the staff consoled him with hollow pleasantries he dropped his eyes and nodded. A very difficult time, yes. Keep hoping, he knows you're here, yes. Make sure you get enough sleep, yes.

So he sat by the bed with his own cold heart, hoping his emotions were in there somewhere and he would be feeling big things shortly. Then came the hand, crawling towards him like the sea coming in, and the dry lips trying to move under the oxygen mask.

Robert slipped his hand underneath Julius's and they held each other. Well, as much as the tight tape around Julius's palm would allow. He could really only keep his hand straight but the tips of his fingers curled down as if he was trying to communicate the intention of a tight, meaningful squeeze. Robert's hand looked meaty and pink against his father's dry bones. The hand reminded him of Francine choosing a canteen of cutlery for their wedding list. This set is made of a softer metal, said whoever-it-was in the department store. It does mark, yes, so that every occasion the canteen is used for leaves a mark on the set, a memory of each event. I don't want that, said Francine. I want them to look new all the time. What about those ones? Julius's hand had scars and folds and wrinkles, knuckles poking through freckles, crosshatched, weathered skin.

The blue lips moved inside the mask, *bub bub bub*. As if from nowhere Julius's left hand rose from the far side of the bed and dropped onto the mask, pausing there, an exhausted climber on a summit. The hand squeezed the soft mask, gripping it and yanking it to the side, half off Julius's mouth. The elastic band around the back of his head made full removal impossible. Robert stood up, still holding the hand, and leaned over.

The hiss of the oxygen into the mask made his eyes water. He turned his face away, leaning his ear to the lips.

I love you, son. That was what he expected, as if Julius would have sat through the same heartwarming romcoms

Francine favored and would know the script. Instead, "The back safe. Remember: left-hand corner of the safe at the back. Button. Press—"

Julius stopped. Thinking he might be passing out, Robert lifted the mask to put it over his face again but Julius's left hand batted it away.

"Left-hand corner right at the back. Reach in. Press once. Wait for a count of eight, press again. The code: *your birthday*."

Robert looked at his father. Julius hadn't even opened his eyes He seemed still now. Tentatively, Robert lifted the mask and put it back over his father's mouth and as he did Julius said the line, the three syllables: I love you.

Robert fell back into his seat. He hadn't expected it. After all this time, and all this distance between them, he began to sob and covered his face and just then all the alarms went off and the staff ran in. Robert ended up against the wall and somehow, by inches, in the corridor. And then again by inches in the café downstairs, drinking tea and waiting for news from the emergency surgical ward. It was two fifteen a.m. when they called down for him. Bad news, I'm afraid.

Robert didn't even really remember going to the office. He wasn't there and then he was there. They told him to go and get some sleep but he was afraid to go home because he knew he would sleep, soundly, untroubled. He stayed awake, feeling sure that dizzy with tiredness was about as close to really upset as he would get.

The safe. The button. The back of the safe swung open into a small lighted corridor.

Climbing in, Robert was certain that he would find the usual sort of things lawyers kept in their safe: disputed papers, some bits of evidence relating to old cases that they didn't want anyone else ever to find but needed to keep. Some jewelry for safekeeping because of the value or because it was stolen and couldn't be sold, maybe some cash. But there had to be something special in Julius's safe because it was a second safe, a secret safe. And because Julius had built this room for it, under the street.

It was a crappy little safe. He typed in the first four digits of his birthday. It didn't open. He tried the last four, the middle four, nothing worked. Stumped, he sat back. Why did his father send him here? And then he realized. He felt sick with jealousy when he realized. His father's eyes were shut when he said I love you. He was almost unconscious. Those last words were not for Robert. He thought he was talking to Rose.

Weeping softly, Robert reached forwards and typed in the last four digits of Rose's birth date. The door fell open.

He covered his face and cried. Always something between them, Rose and Julius. Always something. He chose Rose over Robert time after time.

Finally he stopped crying, not because he was less sad about it, but because he ran out of energy. He pulled the safe door open and looked in.

Bricks of cash, shrink-wrapped. A solid square of them. If each brick had five grand in it, he remembered thinking, even if they had ten grand in them, there were only eight of them. It was a very small safe. He took them out and found, underneath, a bright red double entry cash book, the worn cardboard cover held shut with a thick elastic band. The spine was facing him, the edge bald gray cardboard. He took it out and opened it at the last page that had writing on it.

Six columns: a name, all Indian or Pakistani probably, his father knew a lot of the Pakistan community here. Then a number: 40, 20, 0.9. The name of a city, he recognized some of them: Quetta, Karachi, Rawalpindi. Then a long number in a column headed *Access Code*, half letters, half numbers. The next column had nothing but two or three letters, many of them recurring. Then, in the final column, a cross or tick, added later in different pens. The total was added up at the bottom of the number columns on each page with a plus or minus underneath. All scored out. Total paid.

Robert flicked through the book. Month by month, going back many years, fifteen or so years. All the pages were half filled out and the increasingly exorbitant sums were paid at the bottom of the page. Over the years whoever-that-was had paid vast sums of money to the owner of the book.

Robert looked at the writing: it was Julius's hand, starting in pencil, changing to Biro sometimes, then fountain pen as the numbers got bigger. Sometimes he introduced a red Biro for the final summing up. Sometimes he stayed with the fountain pen. Towards the last ten pages the writing got less certain, less firm. Back to pencil, faint scratches. He had been ill before the fall. They knew his health was precarious.

Robert dropped the book to his lap. It wasn't good, whatever it was. Not at all good. His father had been sending money to Pakistan, informally, illegally. What did Julius want Rose to do with it?

Robert realized then: Julius wanted Rose to burn the ledger. The payments were illegal payment and Rose had known about it all along. She knew and he didn't. Julius chose her, to tell her, involve her and not Robert.

Why always her? Was she more dependable than Robert? Smarter than him? Or because they were involved in something more than illegal, something venal that Robert would never agree to. He had always been honest, and ethical and honorable. Had they not? He was contemplating whys when he looked up and saw a small envelope on the floor of the safe.

Idly, he reached in and lifted it out, thinking about the book while he took out the pictures. He saw then that they were involved in things he could never be a part of. Blackmail, hateful business. Robert was better than that. He was a better person than that. He couldn't believe they had sunk so low. It was from this high ground that he had phoned the police, was put through to the Serious and Organised Crime Agency and a woman who told him in a bored voice that the only way to report the illegal movement of money, the only way, was to fill out the form and email it in.

Remembering that moment, the photos in his hand, the breath stuck in his chest, put him back in the cold kitchen in Mull. Remembering the images made him pull his foot off the chair and stamp it on the ground. Weedily, but still a stamp to bring back the pain.

He was wincing at it, his eyes shut tight, realizing that he had been here for over an hour, hoping that when he opened his eyes he would stop seeing that image of Rose's young face.

The hippie at the window made Robert jump. He was up too close to the glass, his whole face framed by one of the small panes like a grotesque picture.

Seeing that he had startled Robert, the hippie raised a hand in greeting. It filled another pane.

"Come in," said Robert, gesturing in case he couldn't hear.

He came in through the French doors, bringing with him a blast of cold from outside. He sat down at the table, looking at Robert's ankle.

"Ouch," he said.

"What *is* your name?" said Robert, sounding short-tempered because he was in pain.

"Oh." He looked at the ankle again. "Simon."

Robert held his hand out and they shook. "Hello, Simon."

"Yeah." Simon pointed at the fat ankle, back on the chair again. "Ouch. And your face."

"I went for a walk and fell."

"Oh."

It was getting dark in the kitchen. Suddenly it was the time when someone should have put on the light. Simon stood up and put his hat on.

"Come up the hill on the quad bike? For a smoke? Tide's coming in, the dolphins'll be out soon. We can see them up there."

Robert smiled. It sounded like a great idea. "Is there room on the bike?"

Simon walked off to the corridor. "Jumpers."

The rain was off and the sun was setting, a burning orange shimmer on a navy blue horizon. They sat on plastic sheeting on the ground, Michelin men in their many jumpers. The island of Coll was silhouetted on the horizon, deep black with white lights at the shore, sparse enough to be earthbound stars.

The wind was fierce up here though. No trees grew this far up. The hill was bald green grass defiantly swishing back and forth. Simon had parked the quad bike twenty feet away, in a rocky corner. The wind, he said, pointing up the hill, could knock it over when they weren't sitting on it. It could roll all the way down the hill. They walked and hopped the rest of the way, into the wind, faces tight against it.

A wind so sharp, thought Robert, it could strip a soul of original sin.

Now his swollen ankle was out in front of him, resting high on a rock. He took the spliff from Simon's hand, cupping the red tip to stop the wind blowing it out, and took a drag. It scratched down through his throat, a pain familiar from last night. He remembered smoking downstairs now, at least his throat remembered. That was what had happened. He'd been very drunk and blacked out and smoked some weed or something and didn't know and that was why it all seemed so muddled and crazy.

Simon was sitting cross-legged, hands tucked inside his tweed cape. He was watching the water for the dolphins to break. His hair was pulled back, ponytail thin as a rat's tail. The wind held it horizontal with his shoulder, whipping his face sometimes. He'd taken his hat off for safekeeping.

Robert felt the burning warm flood through him, felt the tingle in his swollen ankle change to a sensation of warmth, a tickle on his skin. He imagined the skin stretching wide, wide, wide over a balloon, so wide the pores were the size of Biro tips, comical. He thought of Hamish and Angus as men, holding his ankle as he died and seeing the marks of this particular adventure on his skin. It made him feel nice. He missed them, his kids. He missed Jessica.

Simon leaned forward, touching the ground with his forehead as if he was bowing to the setting sun, making Robert smile. But he stayed down, his forehead on plastic.

"YOU'RE AGILE," shouted Robert over the sound of the wind.

And then, as if to prove his point, Simon stayed there, absolutely still.

"SIMON: I SAID 'YOU'RE VERY AGILE.'"

He must do yoga, thought Robert, noticing the black shadow creeping out from under Simon's face.

"DO YOU DO—" A sudden flash of blinding, brilliant white light blotted out the world as the bullet passed through Robert's head. He didn't even have time to wonder before he fell sideways, facedown on Simon's back, bleeding onto him.

25

Through the gloomy blue morning Morrow ran, crouching, under heavy fire from the rain until she reached the coffee shop doorway. She was up far too early to feel altogether well and was proactively angry with Atholl. He probably wouldn't be there, she felt, might not even remember calling her. Even if he was it was presumptuous, asking her to come at this hour, as if she had no calls on her time but the summoning of an earl.

The place was only technically open. Through the glass door she could see staff dressed in stiff white aprons, one handing metal trays of defrosted raw croissants over the counter to another. They had ovens behind the counter and pumped the smell of fresh baking out into the street to bait passersby. The furniture was French rustic, scrubbed pine tables and stone floors, so ill suited to the mucky damp of Glasgow as to seem almost sarcastic.

She opened the door and stepped in to glares from the staff, their morning faces as raw as the pastry.

Atholl was slumped in a far corner, watching the door for her. He looked as if he was between two worlds: one side in a warm

Provençal kitchen, the other stuck to the rain-warped window. His eyes were unfocused, redder than usual, and he looked as if he had brushed his hair, perhaps for her, which she found ominous. He saw her, raised his chin and tried to smile but couldn't pull it off. He raised a greeting hand instead.

Hungover. She worked her away around the empty seats to his table, remembering Brian offering her another glass of market research wine the night before and how they'd decided they both actually wanted a cup of tea instead. She was ready for a rant at Atholl if he'd forgotten why he'd asked her here.

He tried to stand up to meet her but his knee buckled and he dropped back in his chair.

"You been out for a run already?" she said.

His smile worked this time. "Come rain or shine. Old army habit."

She sat down opposite him, shedding her wet coat, wondering why she liked him at all.

Atholl had a small pile of creamy yellow vellum envelopes on the table, sealed and face down, square like invitations, not business letters. The color of the envelopes matched the whites of his eyes, yellow and so dry she could see the grainy texture of his eyeballs.

"God, you look terrible." She noticed her accent was more succinct than normal. "Have you even been to bed?"

Atholl gave a queasy smile. "I seem to have contracted a stomach bug, I think. I've been ill..."

They weren't in court. They weren't even in the building and she felt that maybe she could just say it. "You need to stop drinking. It's killing you; I feel like I'm actually watching it happen."

He grinned.

"What's funny about that?"

Then he gave a wheezy laugh.

"Heard it before?" She leaned over the table at him. "A hundred times, I know, but I can see your eyeballs drying out, for pity's sake."

Atholl chortled to himself, wiping the rough wooden table back and forth. "Ah, Alex Morrow." He looked up at her. "Alex. Alexandra." His eyes weren't dry anymore, they were damp but he didn't look sad. Morrow met his stare and, for a moment all too fleeting, read there the course of a relationship they might have had if things had been different: laughs and fights and an ocean of tenderness. She remembered Brian suddenly and dropped her gaze to the table.

Atholl reached his hand into her field of vision and let it sit on the table. She didn't move. His hand slithered back to his side.

"Coffee?"

"Aye," she said in her own voice, "go on then."

Atholl raised his hand to a server behind the counter and the man put the tray down. "No," called Atholl, "no need to come over. Coffee for two, please."

"Pot of coffee, sir?"

"Yes, please."

"Would you like some breakfast?" asked the waiter. "Organic pastries? Granola? French orange juice?"

Morrow saw Atholl's eyes stray to a tray of uncooked dough and he bit his lip and shook his head. "Just coffee."

The waiter went to get it and Atholl turned his attention back to her. He had his work face on. "Anyway, good morning and thank you for coming."

She was glad. "What can I do for you?"

"Well," Atholl hesitated, "uh, a couple of things..."

His mind seemed to stray then. He looked out of the window and reached for the letters on the table in front of him.

Morrow thought of Brian, how she'd had to negotiate a change of shifts with the boys to get here.

"Atholl, what is it you want to tell me?"

"Yes," he said and drifted, blinking at the table. His skin looked a little blue.

"Are you on medication?" she said, aware that it was a question she had asked often, usually of people on charges.

Atholl leaned his head against the glass. His hair stuck to the condensation as he slipped down the pane.

"I wouldn't tell anybody," she assured him.

The waiter came over with cups and a jug of hot milk. As he set them down and went back to get the coffeepot, Morrow reflected that Atholl didn't seem irrational but preoccupied by a fluid stream of private thoughts.

The coffee arrived and the waiter poured them a cup each, retreating back to the counter. Morrow poured herself some milk.

"It's nice to see you out of court." He said it with such solemnity it might well have been what he'd brought her here to say.

He smiled into his cup as he splashed milk into his coffee and added two rough lumps of brown sugar from the bowl. "Where did you grow up, DI Morrow? Originally?"

"Southside." She didn't want to go into that. "You?"

"Wiltshire."

She could tell that he didn't either.

He gave a wry smile. "We're not the same, are we?"

"Polar opposites." Morrow lifted her cup to her mouth and drank. The coffee was thick and chocolaty.

She raised her eyes and saw that Atholl was crying. Not sobbing, his breath hadn't changed at all, but thin tears oiled from his eyes. He took a beautiful linen hankie from his hip pocket and dabbed them dry.

"Epiphora," he told her. "My doctors are doing their utmost."

He was lying. That might well be what watering eyes were

called, but Atholl said the word as if his mouth had never been around it before. She wanted suddenly to get very far away from him.

"Why did you ask me here?"

He took a deep, uneven breath. "Michael Brown has agreed to see you this morning and give you his prints again."

"He changed his mind?"

Atholl gave a deep nod to the table.

"When did Brown tell you that?" They didn't let prisoners meet their counsel as they left court and Brown couldn't have phoned him last night. He certainly hadn't seen him this morning.

Atholl shook his head. He was giving her nothing.

"Why did you ask me here three hours before the start of your working day?"

He drained his coffee as he thought of a lie. "Thought it might be nice to meet for breakfast..."

His eye condition kicked in again but he didn't bring out the hankie. He smiled miserably at his cup as a bin van passed slowly outside, washing the window with orange hazard lights.

"Where I grew up..." His eyebrows rose. "...Very leafy. Married. Followed my wife up here...Went to the bar..." It felt as if he was trying to tell her his life story but he hated it, as if they were on an ill-conceived first date, early in the morning, under brutal light, tears dripping from his chin.

She stood up. "So, that was lovely coffee."

He looked up at her, hopeless and haggard. "I think you'll do the right thing."

Morrow stood over him. Atholl was drunk, she decided. He was one of those drunks who topped up, so used to covering up their inebriation that you wouldn't know they were pissed until they plowed their car into schoolchildren at a bus stop.

"Alex, I don't think you'd make the mistakes I've made."

"I need to go." She lifted her coat and bag.

"I'd like you to come to my house."

"I'd better go," she said. "I'll see you in the holding cells in a couple of hours."

"Sure." He picked up one of the envelopes. "An invitation. For you."

He held it out imploringly. It had her name and station address written in the same beautiful hand as the note about Brown's fingerprints. Morrow didn't want it. She only took it because refusing would start another conversation. She dropped it in her bag.

"Whatever you hear about me..." he said, his self-pity in full, glorious flower.

Morrow stood over him, furious. She wanted to call him a cheeky bastard. She wanted to say that she wasn't impressed that he was an earl, that she had a lovely man and two beautiful kids that she could drown in the sight of, tell him to take a flying fuck to himself. But she had been open with work contacts before and it never played out well.

"Goodbye," he said simply.

She left and was out in the rainy street before she had her coat on. She stood in the doorway struggling with the last arm, rain falling in sheets on the pedestrian precinct in front of her.

She hated Atholl for flirting with her, for the implied slight on Brian, for being drunk and calling her here so early in the morning. And now she was tired, bad-tempered and had to meet him again in two fucking hours with Michael fucking Brown trying to pull his cock out at her.

Walking to her car, she took out her phone to call Riddell and left a message saying that they were getting Brown's prints this morning. The case against him from 1997 was unsafe. Could he notify the Fiscal that Brown's license might be revoked so they could decide what to do about it? He'd log the time of the call. She'd get points for that anyway.

As she dropped the phone back in the bag she saw the corner of Atholl's envelope. She wanted to drop the party invite in the bin.

26

Atholl didn't turn up. Morrow and McCarthy were waiting to get into the holding cells with the MobileID machine, standing in the chairless reception area, when a guard came through and asked them where they thought they were going.

"We're booked in to fingerprint Michael Brown."

"Have you got his CRO number?"

Morrow didn't have his record on her, or his number. "No, we're meeting Anton Atholl and he's taking us in. Atholl's his counsel."

He nodded and disappeared into the back office again. Morrow and McCarthy looked at each other. It was odd. Atholl should have been here by now and he should have informed the front desk before they arrived too.

The guard came back. He wanted to see their warrant cards. He took their station number and went back into the office, locking the door between them and watching through a small window as he called the number to check up on them. Satisfied at their identities, he reached below the window and was suddenly lit up by a computer screen.

"Something's gone wrong here," he said, reading the screen.

"Yeah," said Morrow, "Atholl was supposed to be here with Brown. They're on in court four in twenty-five minutes."

"We've got Brown downstairs," the guard told his screen, "but we haven't got Atholl."

"Has he told you we're coming?"

"No," said the guard as he typed something in. "It's not logged..."

They looked at each other across the desk and Morrow realized that she wasn't getting in.

"McCarthy, you wait here," she said and went back out to the rain, pulling her collar up as she ducked through the two locked doors next to the loading bay. She had to look up at the camera both times, show her face and wait for the door to buzz.

Back on the street, thoroughly wet, she walked around the corner to the scrum of smokers and pushed through to the doors.

Dexie let her jump the queue. He hadn't seen Atholl this morning, nor had the receptionist, a plump man of infinite patience. Seeing how desperate she was he called up to the chambers and waited on the line until someone answered. Atholl wasn't there either. He now had ten minutes before the case started.

Morrow didn't know what else to do. She was standing, wondering how the hell she was going to tell Riddell that she'd made a mistake, when she saw the solicitor who had sat with Atholl coming out of the toilets in the dark corridor under the stairs.

"Excuse me?" She hurried over. "Excuse me, d'you remember me?"

The woman looked at her, wary at first but then relaxing when she realized it was a polis. "Yes."

"Atholl asked me to meet him at the entrance to the holding cells this morning."

"Atholl's not coming in, we're getting a continuation."

She said it so languidly Morrow wanted to kick her shins. "Why's he not coming in?"

"He's sick."

Morrow imagined him asleep on his desk. "We need to finger-print Brown this morning," she said. "Atholl authorized it. Will you come with us?"

They couldn't do it if he didn't have counsel with him and the solicitor could easily have said no. She didn't seem to be aware of that though. "Did Atholl say—"

"Atholl said to meet him at the entrance to the holding cells. Michael Brown *wants* us to fingerprint him again."

"OK," she said. "Well, I'll meet you up there." And she shuffled off to a door at the back of the court.

Morrow hurried out through the main door, back through the rain, around the corner and again gave her face and warrant card to the cameras on the holding-cell entrances. Her hair was plastered to her head when she got back to McCarthy's side.

She only realized she was breathless when the solicitor showed up in the back office with the guard.

He lifted a flap on the reception desk and came through to them.

"OK," he said. "I'm going to have to direct you back through to the main entrance for a security check. Wait at the reception desk and Mrs. Toner will come and collect you from there."

"*Back?*" said Morrow.

"We don't have an X-ray machine and you can't bring equipment in here in case it's a bomb." He held a hand up to the exit. She knew it was the voice he used on prisoners: expressionless, slightly too loud, leaving no room for negotiation.

Morrow and McCarthy went out into the rain, through the two doors, around the corner and into the now empty lobby of the high court. Dexie waved them through, x-raying the MobileID bag and glancing at the screen for the contents. He opened it and looked through, poking down the side with a pencil, before flapping the lid shut and handing it to McCarthy.

Dexie smiled. "Last time I saw a mobile that old a nun was using it."

McCarthy smiled back but the joke was lost on Morrow.

They stood at the reception desk and Morrow dabbed at her hair with a paper tissue as they waited. A screen hanging from the ceiling like a flight departures board detailed which cases were in session: *HMA v. Hancock*—Assault with intent to injury: in session; *HMA v. Mullolo*—Robbery: in session; *HMA v. Brown*—continued.

They waited. Morrow's eyes strayed to the lettered frieze around the room. Some of the letters were carved deeper than others, some of the letters were bigger. Quite suddenly she realized that the frieze didn't say:

TURNS OF SPEECH RIDDLES;

She had read it with half an eye before, grouping words together, distorting as she forced a pattern from them. Read properly the frieze said:

SHE UNDERSTANDS TURNS OF SPEECH AND THE SOLUTIONS OF RIDDLES;

"What is that?" she asked the receptionist.

The receptionist looked up. "That's from the Wisdom of Solomon. You know, in the Bible."

Morrow didn't know it, but she read it now:

SHE KNOWS THE THINGS OF OLD AND INFERS THE THINGS TO COME;

She looked down and saw Finchley coming out of court four with his briefcase. He stopped when he saw her, his mouth falling open a little. He put his head down and came over, shaking both their hands.

"Continuation?" said Morrow.

"Atholl's in hospital."

Her first thought was that she was glad but she berated herself and lied, "Oh no, that's awful."

"Liver failure. Quite serious. They took him in an hour ago."

"But I met him for breakfast this morning," said Morrow. "In that French coffee place just as they opened."

"What for?" asked Finchley, suspicious.

"About another case." She could see he didn't believe her but she couldn't let the Fiscal's office know the Brown case might fall apart until it did. "Which hospital is he in?"

"The Royal."

"Oh dear."

Finchley moistened his lips. "Another case?"

She'd have to call him in an hour or so and tell him she was a liar. She didn't want to lay it on too thick. She sort of hummed.

Finchley nodded at her, narrowed his lips and walked away thoughtfully.

Atholl's solicitor passed him in the corridor under the stairs, coming towards them.

"Ready?"

Morrow and McCarthy followed her, heading for the heart of the building. Security was tight. They had to pass through three separate sets of locked doors and down two staircases to get to the holding cells in the basement.

Two guards were on reception, standing in front of a bank of security screens showing fish-eyed views of each and every cell.

The picture definition was dull, the color low. Gray shadows sat on benches, stood by walls. One was standing on his bed, trying to see out of the deep window just under the ceiling.

The solicitor introduced herself to one of the guards, showed her ID, left her bag at the desk and turned back to Morrow, saying she'd only be a minute. "I need to tell him about Atholl anyway."

They watched her progress on the bank of screens as she walked down a corridor, came towards them on another screen, then the top of her head as she waited for the guard to open the door to a cell.

A shadow, Michael Brown, got up from his bed, standing to attention as the guard spoke through a slot in another door. The shadow put his hands out and the guard came into the room, patting him down, finding nothing, ordering him to sit, which he did. The solicitor came in. She spoke for a few minutes, her hands clamped in front of her. Brown looked at the camera. Even in the poor definition of the small screen Morrow could see he was confused. The solicitor backed out of the room and the door was shut again. Brown put his hands to his head and curled over his stomach.

The solicitor appeared at the mouth of the corridor.

"He says Atholl never asked him about fingerprints. This is the first he's heard of it. He wants to know what it's about."

Atholl had never asked him. That meant he hadn't agreed to it, but it also meant he'd never refused in the first place. Morrow didn't know what to make of it.

"That his fingerprints turned up at a murder scene—" The solicitor was amused and incredulous, thinking that they were asking Brown to implicate himself in another murder, until Morrow explained: "This murder was committed *last week*."

The solicitor nodded as she took it in. "Oh."

"We need to clear this up as soon as possible."

"Oh." She thought about it for a minute and then motioned to the guard to take her back through.

Michael Brown was standing up when Morrow and McCarthy came into the cell. Though his fists and jaw were clenched and he raised his chin defiantly at Morrow as she came through the door, she could see that he was wasting away.

"Hello, Michael."

He gave a curt nod.

"How are you? I heard you've been ill."

"Crohn's," he said, sneering.

"Atholl's not well, did you hear?"

"In hospital."

"That's what I heard. This is DC McCarthy, who you've met before."

Brown didn't acknowledge him. "Said it's his liver."

"Yeah, must be painful." She nodded McCarthy to get the fingerprint machine out. "You've known each other for a long time, haven't you?"

"Since I was a wee guy. He defended my first case."

"Yeah, I read that in your notes."

McCarthy had the machine out and turned it on. The fingerprint plate glowed red and Brown muttered, "My brother..." and turned his attention to the machine. "D'ye want me sitting?"

"Whatever suits you, Michael, is fine."

"Think I'll sit down..." He shuffled over to the bed, his steps uncertain, his knees staying bent like an old man's. She felt for him, for the crap life he'd had and his frail condition. He reached behind himself, feeling for the bed, and helped himself down onto it. "So, this murder...?"

"The prints came up as yours, Michael, or something very like yours. We're not that clear, but we need to eliminate you even though there's no way you could have done it."

"So the prints machines are going mental?" He grinned up at her, trying to look cheeky, but his gums were bad, pale and veined, retreating from his teeth. There was no threat about him now and not just because he was ill and twenty pounds thinner. Michael was resigned to his fate now.

"Aye, well, we'll see," she said, allowing him to think they were in trouble.

McCarthy held out the MobileID and instructed Michael to put the thumb of his right hand on first, then his index finger. Thank you. Next the middle finger, now the ring and the pinkie, thank you. And now the left hand.

They were as quick as they could be, though the machine had trouble with Brown's left ring finger. It was slow because it was trying to make a Wi-Fi connection.

"So," said Morrow to Brown, "you must have met Atholl at the height of his powers?"

"How?"

"Back in the late nineties, he was one of the greats, wasn't he?"

"For all the good it did me."

The machine blinked and she tipped forward to read the screen. Connection failed. "Try again," she told McCarthy.

"Who was your solicitor back then?"

"Julius McMillan. He died..."

"Oh, I heard that. Just recently. Shame."

"Aye." Brown was looking at the ground and seemed tired. They should have left. They could get a better connection if they just went upstairs and McCarthy kept looking at Morrow, wondering why she wasn't ordering them out.

"Was that the first time you got your prints taken? Back then?"

"Aye." Brown sounded faint.

"Was it different, then?"

"It was on *paper*. That's how different."

"They took your prints onto cards back then?"

"Aye, there was no computers in the cop shop lobby back then. They did 'em on cards and fed them into the machine."

The tampering would never have shown on the database. The prints were switched before they were fed in.

"Who took those prints, the ones on the cards?"

Brown looked up and met her eye, exhausted but aware that she was asking him something significant. "David Monkton. You ever heard of him?"

"Don't think so."

"Cunt," he said, soft as a sigh.

She remembered the photo of the boy in the dirty T-shirt and looked at Michael now. He would get out. When this came to light they'd throw him out of prison pending a retrial, desperate not to incur further legal liability for the unfair conviction. She could see how ill he was now, and Atholl said he was getting treatment. He'd die out of prison.

The machine declared that it couldn't connect again.

"We better go upstairs for this," said Morrow.

Michael stood for them leaving. "You'll tell me, yeah?" he said, first to Morrow and then turned to the solicitor, afraid to ask a favor of a cop.

"We'll let you know the outcome," said the lawyer.

They backed out of the cell, the guard coming last. He locked the door.

In the time-honored tradition of prison, Brown waited until the door was safely locked before shouting that Morrow was a fucking cunt and he knew where she lived and her weans were cunts and he'd fucking get her.

Morrow stopped and turned back to the door. They had eaten

Michael Brown and now she was going to make them spit him out.

"OK, Michael," she said, a guilty hand on the metal door. "That's fine, pal."

Flummoxed, he paused and called, "See ye later, anyway."

"Aye," she knocked the door gently with the back of her hand, "I'll see ye later."

27

The Royal was a large teaching hospital in what had once been the center of the city. Built next to the squat medieval cathedral, it overshadowed an elaborate Victorian necropolis, where monuments to great men vied with each other in death as they had in life. Now they were towered over by the modern additions to the hospital. It was an architectural shouting match that medical intervention won hands down, the brand new maternity ward, in gray and steel, stealing the light from the dark hill.

Morrow and Daniel went to intensive care and found Atholl's name on a board. The nursing staff wouldn't let them in. Atholl was unconscious. He had been in surgery. He had taken an overdose and the damage to his kidneys was irreparable. The nurse made a solemn face and said that all they could do now was wait. She nodded them to a woman sitting on a nearby chair.

Morrow knew immediately that she was Atholl's wife. The woman was slim with messy, dyed blond hair, green eyes. She was the right age for Anton, self-possessed and swaggeringly informal, dressed in baggy charcoal linen slacks and a short gray

V-neck sweater. She had a ring on her wedding finger with a diamond so big it looked fake.

Mrs. Atholl was red-eyed and curled tight with tension, arms crossed at the elbow, legs crossed and curled around each other. Morrow wondered if she would ever be able to unravel.

She was looking down the corridor toward Atholl's room, a glass-walled box with a curtain half drawn over the windows, the bright white light inside stirred and muddied by the movement of a nurse.

Morrow told Daniel to wait where she was and went over.

"Are you Mrs. Atholl?"

She looked up at Morrow, critically assessed her outfit, wondered if she was having an affair with her husband, dismissed the idea and then said, "Yeah, why, who are you?"

Morrow smiled. "I'm DI Alex Morrow. I was involved in the case he was trying just now."

Mrs. Atholl nodded, shuffled over in the chair to make room for Morrow to sit down next to her.

"You met him for breakfast?" She sounded suspicious.

"Le Pain Provençal at seven a.m. They didn't even have any croissants ready yet."

The wife nodded. "He liked..." The past tense shocked them both. "Anton took the pills yesterday. Did he say anything to you?"

Morrow thought through the awful meeting. "We had coffee. He said I could meet one of his clients. He said he'd made mistakes—"

Mrs. Atholl interjected a "hm'" to shut Morrow up and looked away. "You were friends." She clearly didn't mean "friends" but it was said without rancor.

"Not really."

She turned back, seemed to like that. "Not friends?"

"No, we knew each other from court, he cross-examined me,

and I'd asked him a favor, about the client, and he asked to meet me this morning—"

"When did he ask you?"

"Last night. Very late. Left a message on my phone."

"After he took them." She nodded, seemed to be trying to piece together his last few moments. "They think." Her accent was drawly and English, soft and easy, without all the guttural harshness of Morrow's own.

They suited each other, the wife and the husband. Smart and sharp and charismatic. Anton Atholl had bothered Morrow. He'd made her wonder if she was in danger of having an affair, with him or someone else. It made her feel unsure of herself, as if, without meaning to, she might miss her footing and end up in bed with someone, shattering everything she had with Brian and the boys. But sitting here with Anton's wife, a female version of him, she realized that she had just liked him.

"Mistakes…" muttered his wife.

"Mistakes," echoed Morrow.

They fell into a comfortable quiet, in the hum of beeps and buzz of lights until Morrow asked, "How is he?"

"He's, um…" She blinked hard. "His organs are shutting down one by one. He's not coming out of it. The blessing is he's unconscious." She looked down the corridor again towards his room, craning her neck towards him, pleading for something, a quick death, a miraculous recovery, Morrow couldn't tell. "You got kids?"

Morrow nodded.

"Anton and I have three boys. We separated. The boys are furious with him. I said 'Daddy's taken an overdose' and the oldest said 'good.' What a thing to live with…"

Her hand rose to her face, cupped her mouth, pressing hard on her lips. Morrow wanted to say something comforting but there wasn't anything to say.

"I see kids survive amazing things." It was stupid and banal but Atholl's wife latched on to it.

"Really?"

"Oh, every day." Morrow struggled to think of an example. "Every day."

The wife looked at her, waiting with her for her to think of something useful.

"It's the day-to-day things that do the damage, mostly," said Morrow, unable to deny the desperate woman some trite comfort. "Not the big stuff. Not really."

She nodded to Morrow in the dark. Morrow expected her to be more cynical, more like Atholl. "I suppose so."

She turned back to the room. "His drinking. That's why I asked him to leave. Mood swings. We had a different man living with us every evening. Julius dying didn't help. He was in the ward across the corridor."

"Julius McMillan?"

"Yeah."

"What happened to Julius?"

"Oh." She shook her head softly. "Julius...He smoked like an absolute bastard, he was always on the brink of death, past ten years. If you heard him cough it sounded like oil being struck." She did a fair impression of someone gargling on phlegm but with a comic edge, did it quietly. "Quite disgusting, actually. He fell over and his lungs literally collapsed. No surprise, I don't think. Astonished it hadn't happened before, really."

She turned back to facing the direction of Atholl's room.

"He *fell* and his lungs collapsed?"

"Hm." She looked back at Morrow, clarifying by placing a hand flat on her breastbone. "Fell forwards and his lungs collapsed. They must have been half tar anyway."

"Right?" Morrow tried to envisage a man falling onto his

breastbone without lifting his hands to protect his face. "Did Julius drink too?"

"No."

Atholl's wife still craning to the room, watching for changes while Morrow stared straight into the brutal whiteness of the linen room opposite. She waited until it seemed long enough. "He hasn't woken up, has he? Has he said anything to you?"

The wife blinked hard and shook her head. Her lips twitched and then she said reluctantly, "They don't think he's going to…"

Morrow stood up. "I'm sorry. I liked him."

"So did I," she said wistfully.

Morrow didn't know how to end it and took out her card. "If I can do anything for you."

The wife took the card without looking at it. "Cheers."

Daniel and Morrow buzzed to get into the next-door ward, since they were here anyway. The nurse in charge welcomed them to the desk but refused to answer any questions about Julius McMillan unless she was given written authorization from the hospital management to discuss the case. The consent would have to come through the family, she said. Morrow wasn't that sure she remembered Julius McMillan. She got the impression that the nurse had been on a training program about patient confidentiality and was treating this as an impromptu test.

"We're the police," she said.

Nevertheless, the nurse insisted, whichever agency they claimed to be from. Patients' files were kept centrally and she was not in a position to release details about a patient's care or condition, at this time.

She looked up, crossed her arms and her weight slid defiantly to her hip. A young medic was replacing a file behind her and rolled his eyes at the wall. Not a happy ward.

"Thank you for all your help," said Morrow and left with Daniel in tow.

They were waiting for the lift when the young medic caught up with them. "Going down for a bacon roll," he said and smiled warmly.

He was tall and wiry, wore the blue uniform of an intern: half uniform, half pajamas, industrial press. He stood behind them, nodding and avoiding their eye until they were in the lift and the doors were shut. "What did you want to know about Mr. McMillan?"

Morrow got straight to the point. "He *fell* and his lungs collapsed?"

The medic touched his breastbone with his fingertips, where Atholl's wife had. "Fell onto something, edge of a desk or something. Had a big bruise there." His finger flowered outwards.

"Is that possible?"

"If it struck hard enough, yeah."

He smiled down at them and answered the unspoken question. "My uncle's an officer up in Caithness."

Just then the doors opened and an elderly couple helped each other in. He didn't speak to them again and got out at the canteen without a backward glance.

Morrow was asleep in bed when her phone rang. She had it to her ear before she was fully conscious. It was the night shift at London Road, telling her that Anton Atholl was dead.

She fell back on her pillow and looked at Brian. He was snoring, mouth open, teeth prominent and a double chin under his slack jaw. In the warm dark she reached across the duvet and sat her hand in his, savoring the warmth radiating from his palm.

28

Morrow had briefed the squad and avoided a long chat with Riddell about Michael Brown's unsafe conviction. He'd get out as soon as she explained the mismatched prints but she felt sure it was a death warrant for him. She dodged her boss until he went to a meeting.

Now everyone was working hard. Prints. It was all about fingerprints, because Michael Brown didn't kill his brother and someone else had. They were still out there. She wondered if they'd followed the Michael Brown case, seen him go to prison, heard he'd got out, if they felt anything about it.

She hadn't discussed Atholl's death with anyone, covered it in her briefing to the squad only by mentioning that Brown's case was being continued until they found a replacement counsel. She didn't know how to talk about his death. It was work-related but seemed personal, didn't connect to any investigations.

She was at her desk and the memory came to her mind every so often—Atholl is dead, she thought, and then remembered that it wasn't relevant. In police terms it didn't really matter.

She made herself a coffee, took a quick tour of the squad at their desks, checking their work, seeing what they were doing, who was coming up with what on the car dealership investigation. The day felt formless, as if she couldn't quite get hold of it.

She went back to her office, keeping the door open to stop herself thinking about him. Then she remembered the invitation in her handbag.

She shut her door before taking it out of her bag, sat down at her desk and pushed the computer keyboard to the side

A square yellow vellum envelope, pockmarked with dried rain. Morrow held her mouth and stared at it for a moment. Then she took her hand away, and stared at it for another short while.

Holding the lower edge of the envelope she fitted a Biro into the loose seal and ripped it open, shaking out the card.

His name was embossed in racing green. No qualifications were added underneath, none of his titles. The font was no-nonsense.

She let her eyes rest there for a moment and took a deep breath before reading the handwritten note:

> Dear Detective Inspector Alexandra Morrow,
>
> I do hope you will come to my home. Please pay particular attention to the two discarded bottles of paracetamol. I have tried not to touch the sides or smudge the prints.
>
> I'm sincerely sorry for involving you in this unpleasant business, but I suppose, strictly speaking, murder is your business.
>
> I think you are lovely. I wish I had been a better person.
>
> Faithfully,
> Anton Atholl

It was strange. For a full five minutes she sat there and all she could really see on the letter was the line *I think you are lovely.*

The words rolled around, warming her. He knew he was dying in the café. She wished he had lived, that they had grown old together in the city and bumped into one another over the years. She wished he was alive to worry her.

She sat back from the card. Then she stood up and opened the door to the corridor as McCarthy passed.

"McCarthy." He turned to her. "Get me Anton Atholl's last known address."

He nodded and left.

She stood, leaning against the wall, and looked at the envelope again. There were three letters on the table in the coffeehouse. This was one of them.

McCarthy looked back in. "Ma'am: Wallace Street. Tradeston. South."

"Who do we know in the south?"

"Tamsin Leonard's there now."

"Get her on the phone."

Leonard's pull in the south wasn't quite Wainwright's in the north. Morrow had to wait for permission from her boss's boss before she was allowed into the flat for a look.

It was the perfect flat for a middle-aged man to commit suicide in. It was in the old dock area of the city, a grim quarter of anonymous luxury flats down by the river. Danny used to live across the water from Anton's. Morrow didn't like the area. The flat itself was devoid of furniture. It looked as if he had been squatting. The only chair faced firmly away from the window overlooking the water. A bouquet of empty bottles lay on the floor. The paracetamol bottles were on the carpet: one next to the chair, one by the skirting board.

Morrow had explained that Atholl was an earl and an advocate and had killed himself in strange circumstances. It must have been a quiet day in the south because Leonard's DI had ordered a search of the flat as well as the fingerprinting.

There wasn't much to find: some clothes, a laundry ticket, basic toiletries. No food. No files. No address book. They searched his cupboards and found a Polaroid of Anton Atholl at an orgy. Morrow didn't want to look at it. She found herself squinting away from the image, screwing her eyes up to stop herself seeing it. He wished he had been a better man.

She took a breath, looked out of the window and forced her eyes back to the image.

Atholl and three other men who formed a wall at the back of the picture. Anton was fucking a woman who was bent over towards the camera. Morrow actually mistook her for a boy at first glance: she was so slim she barely had breasts. Then the image resolved in her eye and she saw that it wasn't slimness that made her frame so modest. The woman was a girl and she was very young. Atholl's face was flushed and contorted. The men behind him were out of focus, their faces cut off at the chin, at the nose.

Morrow held her hand up. "That's it," she said to the officer holding the picture for her. "That's fine."

The fingerprints on the bottles of pills were processed while they stood there and sent over to her division: they were only partly Anton's. A separate set, very clear, had been lifted. Morrow knew before McCarthy phoned her that they were a match for those found at the scene of Aziz Balfour's murder.

On the way out the SOCO told her that the prints on the Polaroid were the same as the paracetamol bottle.

She walked slowly down the bare, soulless stairs towards the street, thinking that evidence could be processed in an instant now but it could take her a lifetime to sift through it. She knew so much but she couldn't fit half of it together.

*   *   *

They were driving back to the station when an unknown number called her mobile.

"Hello? Is that DI Morrow?"

"Yeah, who's this?"

"Greta." The woman's voice was hoarse and faint and Morrow didn't recognize it. "From last night?" She paused to sniff hard.

"Sorry," said Morrow, "I don't know—"

"Greta Atholl. Lady Greta Atholl. Anton's wife. I got a letter from him in the post. I thought I should ring…someone."

Anton had written a letter to his wife and one to his sons.

They sat on the work surface at the far side of the kitchen, the envelopes face down, the cards pulled out and read. They lay like dead albino insects on the glinting black granite.

Morrow sat at the table with Greta, staring at them along with her while Daniel lurked in the front room. There were no offers of tea or coffee, no plates of biscuits pressed into the hand. This was a house in shock and Greta moved as if she was afraid of breaking: slowly, carefully, glad to be sitting down.

They had settled at a small table next to French windows into a large well-tended garden where a big lawn was scattered with weather-beaten rugby balls and dog-mauled chew toys. Old trees sheltered the end of the garden, giving it color and texture while the borders died back for the winter.

The house was gorgeous. Big, square and Georgian in the middle of the countryside near Hamilton, close enough to the motorway to effect a quick escape to Edinburgh or Glasgow. Around it were soft wild fields for horses and wildflower meadows.

As they drew up Morrow had imagined Anton and Greta moving in, a handsome couple with their three fine children and a large dog. Greta opened the door to a silent house, took their coats in the carpeted hall and hung them on a coatrack near to toppling with the weight of scarves and blazers and teenagers' coats.

Still the house was silent. They went through to the letters and as they passed different rooms, a telly room, a sitting room, a nice old dining room with a table and ten chairs, she imagined them over the years, buying furniture, curtains and rugs.

But as they sat in the kitchen staring at the letters on the worktop she felt their slow descent into hell and recrimination. Fights and splits and paracetamol. There was hardly a trace of Anton in the house. No coats, no shoes, no overfed dog. It was as if he had only ever been a notion there.

The notes were hardly pertinent to the investigation. In them he told his wife that he had always loved her and that she was too good for him and that he wanted her to forget him and marry again. Tears had mottled the page. The letter to his sons was equally bland but Morrow was glad. Truisms might not give comfort but they wouldn't haunt either.

"Are your boys OK?"

Greta shrugged. "It hasn't really hit them," she said apologetically, and her eyes strayed to the letters on the worktop again.

"Do you want me to take them away?"

Greta nodded.

"I'll give you them back."

"I don't want them back," said Greta.

29

To save themselves the forty-minute round-trip drive to Busby they asked the only independent witness to Michael Brown's 1997 interview to come into the station. As soon as Morrow saw Yvonne McGunn sitting in the reception area at London Road she knew they should have gone to her. Her date of birth on the accompanying adult form put her in her midforties, but illness had rendered her ageless.

She sat with her eyes shut, her face bloated and mottled purple under thin blond hair that needed a wash. Under the hem of her blue flowery dress, her ankles were purple and as swollen as a man's thigh. Black corduroy slippers were fastened with Velcro. She opened her eyes as Morrow came over.

Morrow introduced herself and Wheatly and they shook her swollen hands.

"Yvonne, I'm so sorry for asking you in, I didn't know that you didn't keep well."

Yvonne held up a puffy hand. "I'm all right."

"I'm so sorry. Would you like to come with me, we'll get you home after..."

Morrow left a pause for Yvonne to object but she didn't. She was busy trying to stand up. She bent forward, leaning heavily on her four-footed walking stick as she tried to rock herself up. It was painful to watch. Morrow reached forward to help a couple of times before finally slipping her arm under Yvonne's and nodding Wheatly to the other side. They lifted on three, managing to get her onto her feet. Morrow was left with a sweat-damp hand she didn't know what to do with. Still, it was her left hand. Wheatly had used his right.

Morrow had planned to take her into the interview room upstairs but the lift was two hundred feet away, through a couple of locked doors, and she didn't know how they could possibly manage it. She led her instead to the small, rarely used interview room by the reception desk. There was no tape machine or camera, just a table and four chairs. They sat her in the one nearest the door and took the seats opposite.

"So, Yvonne, you know why you're here?"

Yvonne nodded.

"We wanted to ask you about the night after Diana died, when you were working in the Cleveden House group home and got a call about a young boy—"

"Michael Brown."

"That's right, Michael Brown. You went to Stewart Street police station to act as his accompanying adult. Could you tell us about that?"

"Yes." They looked at each other. "Um, what do you want to know about it?"

"Could you maybe start by telling me what your job was?"

"I was a staff member at Cleveden House. My first job out of college. I trained as a social worker."

"So, who phoned the house?"

"The police. They asked for someone who knew Michael to come down and sit with him, a familiar face."

"And you knew Michael?"

"Really quite well. He was one of the first kids to be admitted to Cleveden House when I first started. Those kids really stay with you, the ones you meet early in the job. I know things have gone bad now but he was a lovely wee person back then, very close to his big brother John. Nickname was Pinkie."

She smiled as she remembered the two boys.

"Why was he called Pinkie?"

"'Cause he had a broken pinkie." She held up her hand, straightening the last two joints of her little finger.

"Why were they in care?"

"I'm not allowed to discuss that."

Morrow liked that. It was a long time ago and Michael Brown was unlikely to sue her for defamation but she was still respectful of him and his history.

"He was a nice guy back then?"

"Lovely." She was adamant. "*Lovely* wee guy. Loved being read to and kids' TV shows. He was kind and cried *a lot*, relied on Pinkie, on John. After he died I didn't see Michael for a long time and then when I read about him, it didn't sound like the same person at all. Weird how someone can change that much. I actually wondered if he'd had a head injury because it didn't sound anything like the wee guy I knew. Very sad."

"So, the day after Diana died…"

"Yeah, so that night the police phoned and we knew they had Michael, that they were asking him about Pinkie's death but we didn't think there would be anything in it. I mean, Michael adored John and he didn't carry knives or anything and he fell apart when they came and told us that he'd been found dead—"

"Were you on when they came and told him?"

"I was. The police came and told us and they asked us to get Michael and bring him to the office. That's why I went to the questioning of Michael, later, because I'd been there when they told him Pinkie was dead."

"How did he react, exactly?"

"Very upset."

"But can you describe where they told him? How they told him?"

"Well," she looked at the ceiling, taking herself back to the time, "Michael came into the office, it was small, quite messy, full of rotas and stuff. Big window so the kids could talk in to you even if you were working. He came in and the two cops were there, full uniform, and they asked him to sit down. He looked a bit worried but he probably thought it was his parents or something, he hadn't seen them for a long time, so he sat down and I remember him looking out into the corridor through the window, a kid came past and he looked out and there was a flash on his face, like hope or joy or something, because I think he thought the kid outside was Pinkie, you know?"

"You don't think he knew Pinkie was dead at this point?"

"No, he didn't."

"So, what are you thinking, that he knew Pinkie was stabbed but not dead?"

"I don't think he knew that either. I've never believed he killed his brother. I was amazed when they found his fingerprints all over the place. If he did it he didn't remember because when they told him Pinkie was dead he just melted. He slid off the chair. I mean, he couldn't take it in. He was in a total daze for the rest of the day. He didn't eat. We made macaroni cheese—he loved that, his favorite—but he didn't eat. I had to sit over him and make him drink water. He was in bits. If he did it, he didn't remember doing it."

"So you don't think he did it?"

"No. Then I was quite naive. Later I got pretty cynical but

I still don't believe it. He loved Pinkie. Pinkie was his parents, you know? Michael could be soft because Pinkie was a hard nut. Pinkie protected him, let him be tearful. He allowed him to be a kid. More than Pinkie got."

"So, on the night Michael was questioned, what happened?"

"Oh, yes, so, the police came and asked if they could talk to Michael. He went in to the station—"

"Wouldn't a social worker have gone in with him?"

"Well, we were shorthanded and couldn't leave the other kids with just two members of staff, it would have been illegal. Believe me, we wanted to go with him but we could hardly say to the police, you'll need to wait until tomorrow because so-and-so's off sick tonight. They billed it as just an informal chat, I mean, we didn't think it was any big deal. There was no way Michael was involved. Next thing we know, Michael's a suspect, can one of us come down and sit in on the interviews."

Morrow nodded. She wished she had a tape recorder now— she needed to clarify everything before they moved on so she would remember. "So, Michael is told the morning afterwards. Then later that day the police come to pick him up for an informal chat, they didn't charge him or read him his rights or anything?"

"No, absolutely not. I was there, in the station, when they read him his rights."

"So, there was some sort of change between picking him up at the home and the station?"

"I was told he'd confessed to one of the cops in the car." She looked skeptical.

"Who told you that?"

"When they phoned, that's what they told us. He'd confessed in the car on the way there."

"Do you know who phoned you to come in?"

"No. I can't remember names. We were all pretty shaken."

"So you got there, to the station, and what happened?"

Yvonne then rolled through the questioning but none of what she said added to anything.

"He had cuts on his hand as well, like he'd hit someone or something. It wasn't entirely peaceful, is what I mean."

Morrow nodded dutifully. "I see. Did you see his prints being taken?"

"No."

"Did he talk to you about that?"

"No."

"Do you remember DC McMahon?"

"Policeman?"

"One of the arresting officers. Big mustache."

"No."

Morrow didn't know what else to ask. She stood up and opened the door to the lobby. "Well, Yvonne, thanks so much for coming in to see us, we can arrange for you to be taken home—"

"I've got a car outside," said Yvonne, turning back to her stick, "it's fine."

"I'm amazed you remember that all so well."

"It was a big night, Diana dying and both the murders."

Morrow grimaced. "You really think she was murdered?"

Yvonne laughed at the misunderstanding. "No, I mean the two murders. There were two murders in Glasgow that night: one outside Turnberry group home, and Pinkie. I didn't mean Diana. I don't give a stuff about that."

"Who else was murdered?"

"Auch, a wee lassie at Turnberry killed her abuser outside the home there. That was a knife as well. Very sad. It wasn't even in the papers. Because of Diana, I suppose."

*   *   *

An hour and a half later Morrow got up from her desk.

The girl charged with the murder outside Turnberry Children's Home on the same night that Pinkie Brown was killed was called Rose Wilson. Morrow had got McCarthy to download and print the court report on the case. Rose Wilson had been represented by Julius McMillan and no evidence was brought in the case, fingerprint or otherwise, because Rose Wilson pleaded guilty.

Her current home address was in Milngavie, a high prestige hamlet to the north of the city, and she shared the address with Robert McMillan, LLB.

30

It was a strange-looking house. The only consistent thing about the facade was the white paint. Morrow and McCarthy stood outside the low gate, looking at the backs of two large matching cars. No one had bothered to put them into the double garage, only twenty feet away, with a roof that matched the attached main house. They sat outside like prize bulls abandoned in a pen.

The house itself was low, with so many features, columns here, stair window there, eaves, ornamental chimneys... the eye couldn't read where the floors were. The entrance door wasn't especially big but was heralded with twin rows of two columns and a path that snaked violently towards it.

"I hate these new builds," said McCarthy, as if they were all like that.

"Nice area though," said Morrow, looking around the street of equally ugly mansions. Three of the five were for sale. "Posh."

"Broke," said McCarthy, his eye on a garish *For Sale* sign next door.

The buzzer was answered by a woman's voice. And a red light blinked on the camera lens.

They introduced themselves and the woman asked them to show their ID to the lens. The gate fell silently off its latch and dropped open.

Swinging it like a field gate, they stepped inside the low wall, onto the gray herringbone path that led to the front door. Doubtless the garden designers had drawn the snaking path to give an illusion of distance from the gate but the grass was bald in strips where the path led off in the wrong direction and Morrow saw a small print in the mud. Children, more than one, judging from the muddy footprints, taking short cuts.

A young woman was standing at the door. Her hair was pulled back in a high ponytail and she had great skin, a good figure swamped by a saggy mustard jumper and UGGs. Her earrings were small gold hoops, and she had on a small gold chain that sat on her collarbone, all very tasteful and upper middle, but Morrow recognized Rose Wilson from her mug shot. She still had the broad round cheekbones and thin lips she'd had as a child. Her forehead was short under her thick black hair.

"Can I help you?"

"Yes." Morrow held out her hand. "I wonder if you can. We're looking for Rose Wilson."

Just a moment's hesitation and then she said, "I'm Rose. Won't you come in." Not a question, a pleasantry, an automatic response. She stepped back and disappeared into the hall. They had no option but to follow her.

It was a big hall, like a small hotel might have. Rose Wilson took their coats and scarves and hung them on hooks in a cupboard. Morrow heard a voice from one of the rooms, a Disney voice, an adult doing a child and asking for something and then an F/X rumble.

"Have you got kids?" She was trying to sound light.

"No, I'm...I'm the nanny here. We've got three: seven, eight and a half and ten."

"Nice ages," said Morrow, looking up the stairs, wondering where the children's mother was.

"Got kids yourself?"

"Twins. One year old."

"Wow," she said languidly, "that must be hard work."

"We're getting there."

Rose waved them across the hall, through a door to a kitchen with a dining room attached. The back wall of the house was made of timber-framed glass panels looking out onto a bland garden. A lawn. A far wall. No features, no toys, no bikes abandoned on their side in the rain. The kitchen was very tidy.

"Tea? Coffee?"

"No thanks," said McCarthy.

Morrow was looking at the cooker. It was strange that everything in the house was immaculately clean but the cooker was smeared with red sauce, wiped up very badly into ridges and swirls. It reminded her of the bloody girl in the mug shots and she wondered if Rose had thought about that when she abandoned the checkered cloth in the sink. She hadn't been cleaning up when the door buzzer went. The spill was dry in parts, on the swiped ridges. She had just stopped cleaning it and dropped the cloth. Maybe they had a cleaning woman and it was her job.

"So, what can I help you with?"

"OK." Morrow turned back to her. "Can we sit down, please, Rose?"

"Sure." They sat around the nose of the dining table and Rose watched their hands, expecting perhaps a form or something. Morrow took a notebook and a pencil out.

"Do you know why we're here?"

"Robert?" She bit her lip hard.

"*Robert?*"

"Have you found him?" Rose's eyes rimmed then and she started to weep, feeling in her jeans pockets for tissues, finding one, drying her eyes. "I'm sorry."

"Robert McMillan?"

"Have you?" She looked at them and realized suddenly that they had no idea what she was talking about.

"We're not here about that. Is Robert missing? Since when?"

"Oh." Her composure was a little compromised by that. "Robert? He went missing, I thought you were here about that..."

"No, no."

"Just, when police officers come to the door..."

"I know," said Morrow. "We're not there to say you've won the lottery, usually, are we?"

Rose laughed, tears still dropping from her eyes. "Sorry."

"When did he go missing?"

"After his dad died." She realized that they might not know. "Sorry, his dad died and then he went missing. Upset."

"Rose, it's Julius I wanted to talk to you about. He was your lawyer a long time ago, wasn't he?" She had never seen shutters come down so fast. Rose sat tall, straight, and her face dropped into neutral. But it was her turn to speak and she did.

"Julius?"

"Yes. When you killed Samuel McCaig?"

"Yes, Julius represented me then, yes."

"And afterwards you stayed in touch?"

"Yes. He visited me in prison. We became very close. Robert was just that bit older than me and his father used to bring him to visit. I came to work for them shortly after I came out."

"You must have liked each other?"

"Very much."

"Like a father?"

"A grandfather." But she seemed to think of something uncomfortable and corrected herself. "A *benefactor*. Like in an old film or something."

Morrow nodded agreeably. "Do you remember the night Diana died?"

Rose blinked. "Of course."

"That was the night you killed Samuel McCaig."

She blinked again, keeping her eyes on the tabletop. "Of course."

"You pleaded guilty. He attacked you. He had a history of attacking girls."

"So I found out. Afterwards."

"Anything else happen that night?"

There wasn't an obvious answer to the question. She looked up. "Diana died?"

"Pinkie Brown died."

As if she had dropped from the sky Rose was back in that alley and her hands were wet and her lips were pressed tight together so nothing could get in there, and her young bones were sore and her backside was aching and she was frozen with terror. But she managed, through tight lips, to mutter, "Who's that?"

"Pinkie Brown. A fourteen-year-old boy in local authority care. He wasn't in your home, he was just up the road in Cleveden. I remember those homes. They used to pal about together, Cleveden and Turnberry, didn't they? When they weren't attacking each other."

"Yeah."

"Hung about in wee gangs, didn't they?"

"Yeah."

"Because they were close by."

"Yeah, yeah, we did. I didn't know Pinkie though."

"Did you ever meet his wee brother, Michael?"

She remembered him, Morrow could see the flash of recognition and then a slump as if she was shrinking down into her hips. "No, I don't...don't remember a wee brother."

Morrow sat back and took a deep breath as if she was telling a story. McCarthy tipped his head, listening. Rose glared at the table.

"The night Diana died was a strange night, for everybody. But here's a really weird thing: within half a mile of each other there are two murders and two children charged with them. Everybody involved—the people charged, the people killed—are all associated with Turnberry and Cleveden. Both of them were killed with knives. Both of them with pretty much the same *type* of knife. One knife is found," she touched Rose's arm, "the one you used—the other one is never found. But—and here's the really weird thing for me—no one ever puts the two murders together."

Rose looked at her dumbly. "Is this about Julius?"

"What do you mean?"

"Did he leave letters or something?"

"I don't know what you mean."

"Why are you here?" Rose was pleading with her and Morrow didn't understand why.

"Michael Brown got life. He's just been done for something else. He'll spend the rest of his life in prison. I need to know if it's right."

Rose scratched her chin. "What's he like?"

"Michael grew up in prison. He got out three years ago and he's back in now. What do you think he's like?"

Rose turned suddenly, to look out of the door. She was worrying about the kids.

"Rose, did they fingerprint you when you were arrested?"

"Course."

"Your prints aren't on file."

She frowned at that. "They should be. They took them."

"Who took them?"

"I don't know, but they took them. I had ink on my fingers for days after, it wouldn't come off..." She rubbed at her fingertips.

"They're not on file. I looked at the set of prints on your record. They're Michael Brown's prints. They match his prints *now*. The old prints, the ones he was charged with his brother's murder with, those aren't his."

Rose curled her fingers into her palms and tried a smile. "How could you tell they're not mine?"

"Because I ran them through the database."

Rose looked her straight in the eye. "Why are you doing this?"

"I'm a police officer."

"It's history," Rose whispered. "What difference does it make?"

A soft buzzing in the hallway startled Rose. She stood up, excusing herself, walking dreamlike to the door.

She stopped there and turned back, opened her mouth to say something but didn't. She went out to the hall. Morrow was on her feet and signaled to McCarthy not to let Rose out of his sight.

Together they went out to the hall and watched Rose answer the buzzer, check the video screen carefully and open the door.

Two tall men filled the doorway. Morrow saw for the first time what death looked like from the inside of a house. The concerned but calm faces, the request to speak to the family. Rose fell back on her heels and turned, jogging up the stairs with her head tucked into her chest. The cops at the door saw Morrow and McCarthy and recognized them.

"What are you doing here?" one of them said, his frown a presage of bad news.

Morrow was explaining that they were just doing a bit of follow-up on an old case when Francine McMillan came to the head of the stairs.

She was beautiful. Slender and willowy with blond hair that verged on silver, pale skin and thin limbed. She was wearing gray silk pajamas and Rose was holding her arm to help her down the stairs. Francine held the banister with the other hand.

Though moving was a struggle for her, she looked up at the assembled cops and gave a little smile and said hello.

She arrived at the foot and looked a little puzzled. "Who's...?"

"Oh," said the visitors, "that's us. Would you like to sit down?"

Francine began the shuffle to the kitchen. "Yes, I think I'd better."

At the doorway she faltered, tried to move on but couldn't. Rose held her elbow and Francine looked at her and they smiled at each other.

Rose looked back to the hall. "Francine has—"

"Parkinson's," said Francine.

Rose smiled at her. "Doorways—"

"I stall," said Francine, managing to lift her right knee high and drop it into the kitchen.

Morrow and McCarthy watched them disappear into the back of the house. They saw Rose sitting Francine carefully down at the table, her eyes never leaving her face, and take a seat next to her. The shadow of the police officers blocked the exit from the kitchen as they took their places on the other side of the table.

They couldn't hear more than a low rumble of a voice delivering the news, an irreversible act of destruction. Francine keeled slowly over the table, her vertebrae a perfect mountain range through the silk. Rose's hand came slowly towards her, landed with gentle mercy on her back and the stripped frame of Francine swayed and collapsed into Rose's arms.

"Maybe we should go," said McCarthy.

Morrow didn't want to but there was nothing they could do. If they had more evidence they would be able to justify arresting Rose Wilson and taking her fingerprints but right now they had nothing. The family had just lost a father. It would look like harassment if they stayed.

"Get the coats," said Morrow.

They were pulling them on, finding their scarves, when Morrow realized that her bag was in the kitchen. Steeling herself, she went back to get it.

Francine was still sobbing into Rose as Morrow picked up her bag, keeping low, as if that would make anything better for anyone. She was on her way out when Rose suddenly pushed Francine off and stood up.

"Dawood killed Robert." Rose was talking to Morrow, not the cops at the table. "It was Dawood."

Francine was pulling Rose by the arm, trying to make her sit down, crying and frightened.

"Dawood McMann?" said Morrow.

"Yes," said Rose. "He had Robert killed because he submitted a report to SOCA."

"SOCA?" said Morrow, wondering how she knew the acronym. "SOCA report? How do you know that?"

Rose looked down into Francine's panicked face. "It's on Robert's laptop. I've got it upstairs. It'll be all right, Francine." Rose gently peeled her arms free from her friend. "It's the only way to get them. They killed Robert. Our Robert."

Francine let her go.

Rose hurried for the stairs and Morrow went after her, keeping after her, trying not to look as if she was chasing.

A SOCA report would confirm where the money was coming from, where it was going to, who the agent was. With a SOCA report they'd be able to find the next level up from Michael Brown and trace the weapons. She followed Rose to the top of the stairs and down a corridor to the right, through a double set of doors into Francine's dark bedroom. Rose slid the double doors on a wardrobe back, dragged an ottoman that stood at the end of the bed over and stood on it, tiptoe-reaching into a high shelf in the wardrobe.

She pulled out a laptop that looked paper-thin. She looked at it. Then she turned and handed it down to Morrow.

"In there," she said. "That's his."

Morrow took it, hugging it to her.

Rose stepped down with one foot and then, as if she was spent, dropped to sit on the stool. All the fight had gone from her. She sat still, hands limp by her sides, staring at the carpet.

Morrow sat on the bed. They stayed there for a long time. Eventually, Morrow spoke.

"Rose, I need to fingerprint you."

"I know. For Aziz. I know."

"And Atholl."

Rose nodded. "And Atholl."

"What happened with Aziz?"

"He punched Julius in the chest. Julius called me, that's how the ambulance found him. His lungs collapsed." She began to sob. "He was on the floor, his eyes were—" She covered her face and fought for breath. "They tried. But it didn't...Next day I called Aziz, said meet me at his office. He ran when he saw me. I can't tell you what was in my mind."

"You had a knife. It's pretty obvious what was in your mind."

She shifted her legs. "I suppose. He ran up the stairs, he thought it was too scary, that I wouldn't follow him. He didn't know me..."

"You were sick afterwards?"

"I was!" She laughed, surprised and still crying. "I was, I was sick! Ridiculous! As if, you know, as if I'd never…before. Stupid."

Morrow watched her crying and laughing at herself. "You ask a lot of yourself."

"It's stupid, being sick for God's sake, I've been in worse…"

Morrow nodded. "We found the photo at Atholl's. The face was scratched out."

Rose flashed her a warning.

"You knew Sammy McCaig, didn't you? That night wasn't the first time you'd met him."

Rose wouldn't look at her.

"I'm saying that because if you tell them that in court they'll take it into consideration."

When Rose spoke her voice was very small. "No. I'm not telling 'em."

"Don't you trust them?"

Rose smiled and looked up through her eyebrows. "I *know* them. I know them *all*. And they know me."

"That's not all you are," said Morrow.

"What they took." She froze then, like Francine in the doorway. She looked up. "Why do you care about Michael Brown? Is he someone you know?"

"No."

"Why then?"

"It was wrong," she said. It was a stupid thing to say. It was wrong to break up this family, to take Rose from Francine, to have Michael Brown released into a world he couldn't handle. It was wrong to hold a child of fourteen to account for the murder of a man who had pimped her out. It was all wrong. Morrow had done it all so that she could sleep at night, so that she could feel like a better person than Riddell and Danny. She longed for some high ground to scramble towards but there wasn't any.

Rose stretched out a leg. "Bet he's a nutcase now, is he?"

"Michael's done all right with a bad hand," lied Morrow. "You've done all right. Francine loves you, she trusts you."

Rose slumped over her knees, tears dripping onto the carpet— she looked ancient and broken. "But it was Julius I loved the best. I loved him. And he didn't love me."

Morrow came down the stairs with Rose and the laptop and found the cops standing there, waiting. Francine was in the games room and had turned the television off to talk to the children. Everyone wanted to get out right now.

"Ma'am," said McCarthy, "quick word. They got a film of two suspects on the ferry to and from Mull."

"Anyone we know?"

"One unknown and Pokey Mulligan."

31

Morrow was not allowed to arrest him. It could fatally compromise the case when it came to court if the defense called her and asked if he was her brother. She wasn't even allowed to attend his arrest. The honor was handed to Wainwright, even though it was her case, her evidence and she had put the whole thing together. But the McMillan case overlapped and it was decided higher up that Wainwright's division was a good fit.

"Are you annoyed?" asked Wainwright as they left the briefing in Peel Street.

"Aye, I'm annoyed. I did all the work." But she was only half-annoyed. The rest of the emotion fizzing up through her knees, making her stomach flutter, was reckless thrill.

"This is like a diabetic giving me a cake," grinned Wainwright. "You can't even have any."

He laughed loudly, bending back, aiming it over her head and Morrow laughed along, thinking about the demolition of the flats in the Gorbals and all her imagined complaints against Danny. He had never harmed her, she had to admit that to herself, and here she was, relishing the explosion.

＊　　　＊　　　＊

The viewing room in Stewart Street was as busy as a pub during an Old Firm match. DCs and DSs crowded in, wasting their piece breaks and after shifts for a glimpse of Danny's interview. Morrow stayed at the back so that she couldn't be watched. Every so often someone would take a chance and turn to glance at her, only to be met by her eye, making them flinch and turn back.

Danny did himself proud. He didn't fight or shout as Michael Brown had. He didn't sneer. He didn't speak more than to acknowledge his name, date of birth and home address. He fell in a straight column to the ground, without smoke or flying debris. There was no glass shower, no blood on the table.

Cheated, the audience began to disperse.

His lawyer answered for him, mostly. He did know Mulligan but Mulligan did not work for him. Danny did not arrange the murder of Robert McMillan and Simon Hume-Laing. He knew nothing about it.

Wainwright presented him with some bits of evidence: the Stepper photos, which proved he'd met Pokey but nothing more; a receipt for a cash payment of petrol bought at the ferry terminal for Mull, found in Danny's car—he had driven them up there but, again, that proved nothing. Morrow knew they were well served with CCTV cameras at ferry terminals and she doubted Danny knew where the cameras were.

Then Wainwright told them that Mulligan was prepared to give evidence in court saying that Danny had paid him to kill Robert. Mulligan had the money and the money could be traced back to Danny through his taxi business. The accountant's fingerprints were on it.

Danny snorted and shifted in his chair. The lawyer glanced sideways at him, anxious, knowing they were off the script now.

"Why would I pay him to kill guys on Mull?" Danny was smirking but she could tell he was nervous.

"Money," said Wainwright.

His laugh was genuine this time, if bitter. "I've got money."

"You've got 3.2 million," said Wainwright.

Danny didn't flinch but his lawyer sat forward. "Where are you getting that number from?"

Wainwright kept his eyes on Danny. "Taxi business turnover last year. Accounts file at Companies House. You're the license owner."

"No," said Danny, "I'm not."

The lawyer leaned forward, trying to sit between them. "And it doesn't answer the question: if he had that much money why would he take money to commission the murder of someone?"

"As a favor to a powerful friend... There's only so many big cars a man can buy. Past a certain point everyone has to start making connections abroad, don't they, Danny? But you've got no connections."

Morrow shut her eyes and held her breath. This was the point at which it could go wrong—all Wainwright had to do was blurt it. But he didn't. He didn't mention Dawood's name.

He shut his file. "I think we'll leave it there just now."

The viewing room had emptied now and Morrow sat alone watching the small screen. Dawood McMann, a wise Solomon, sat at the interview table and conferred with his lawyer in short whispers, deciding who would be going to prison and for how long. He had been promised a non-custodial sentence on the condition that he gave them evidence against a certain number of people amounting to a certain tariff of charges.

Morrow watched Dawood hand them Mulligan, a gang of car thieves, the family of the young guy who had taken her car dealer's Lotus, two other rings of moneylenders out in the east, and Danny. Danny would be going away for a very long time on a conspiracy to murder charge. It was disgusting to watch. Dawood was so calculating, she imagined him asking Danny to arrange Robert McMillan's murder, not to cover up his own activities but as a trap, to get him out of the way so that some acolyte of Dawood's could take the £3.2 million. Three whole areas of the city would be without a dominant influence now. Danny was gone, the trade in stolen cars interrupted, whole ecosystems wiped out. The ensuing scrabble for control of the city would be carnage.

She sat with her arms crossed, examining her conscience, thinking about the Red Road flats collapsing in a cloud of gray dust and rubble. Same mass, different shape, one big mess.

Dawood smiled at his lawyer, their heads inclined towards one another as they decided another fate and Morrow stood up. She wanted to spit at the screen.

Alone in the room, she pulled her coat off a chair so quickly she knocked it over and it fell, banging loudly off the hard floor, and she liked that.

32

Morrow and McCarthy stood in the street and looked up at the office premises for Intelligence Solutions. It was a nice old building in the center of town, next window to a luxury estate agents where the window showed aerial photographs of giant stretches of the Highlands for sale. A mountain range was for sale. By contrast, the private investigator's office was sober and discreet. A brass plaque announced *Intelligence Solutions* but didn't declare the type of investigations undertaken. Morrow had looked at their website on the way here in the car. They highlighted adoption tracing and preemployment screening, evidence gathering and missing persons' investigations. She had called the number listed and got an answer machine, even though it was within office hours. And now it was shut. It seemed odd and unfriendly for a company that was supposed to provide a service.

They went back to the office. As they walked in McCarthy talked about ice cream and how much he liked it while Morrow thought about Harris and how much she missed him. Not for the first time she wondered if she had done the right thing, telling the truth against her interests, but then she remembered that Harris had been found out anyway. McMahon and Gamerro hadn't told the truth at the time and maybe Michael Brown had gone to prison for a vicious crime he didn't commit. They must have seen him the way she did, as a crime about to happen, as an arse who couldn't be trusted, but that didn't give them the right to cover up. They were afraid.

McCarthy went off to the lockers to check his private phone and Morrow, distracted, went through to the CID wing. She said hello and went into her office, put her bag down, checked her messages. She looked out and found Riddell's office door shut. He might be having a meeting.

She was considering whether or not to knock when the door opened and Riddell stood there, smiling back in to someone, hand out to shake. A civilian came out of his office, tall and fat, gold-framed glasses, brown hair, long faced. His clothes were what caught her eye. Jeans and a very good jacket in brown tweed, soft wool and tailored so that it came in at the waist and out at the shoulders. His shoes were brown brogues that looked so sturdy and well polished, they might have served several generations. He was not the sort of civilian they usually saw in London Road and he seemed to have given Riddell some very good news.

"Ah, DI Morrow." Riddell held his hand out to introduce her. "This is David Monkton."

The moment David Monkton turned and met her eye, Morrow knew he was there for her. He held out his hand.

"Alex Morrow, I've heard a lot about you." For a moment she saw disgust flickering behind his eyes but then he gave an almost-blink, half closing his eyes and rolling them up to wipe them clean. When they righted themselves he smiled warmly. "All good, of course."

Like a domino chain she saw suddenly how useful she would be to him: astute and hardworking, center of a network of cops, con-

tacts made through Danny and Harris, even, untouchable reputation. She put out her hand.

"Nice to meet you," she said. "I was just at your office."

"How strange," he said, though she felt he knew that already.
"And I'm at yours."

He laughed then and Riddell laughed too.

"Sir..." Morrow said anxiously.

"Yes," said Riddell, "that other thing is all done. All being interviewed in the north."

Danny and Dawood and Pokey Mulligan sitting in separate interview rooms, being confronted with SOCA reports, with Stepper's photographs and the ferry's CCTV. She had Rose Wilson
to bring in and question and she was glad that she hadn't seen
Riddell to brief him yet. She looked at Monkton and felt that he
would be her high ground.

"They found, um..." Riddell gave a discreet glance at Monkton. "I'll tell you later."

Monkton gave a condescending smile, as though Riddell had
just passed a very important test related to his future employ-
ment.

"Don't let me interfere with police business," he smirked, "I'm
just in for an informal—"

"No, no," said Riddell, "it's just, um." He looked at Morrow.
"It's all, you know, it's good. Ties together. With the other thing."

Riddell smiled at her, Monkton smiled at him, and Morrow
thought about fourteen-year-old Michael Brown's mug shot. No
one cared about that. They were all doing fine.

"DI Morrow, can I speak to you for a moment?"

Monkton was looking at the door to her office, leaning towards
it slightly, and Riddell was following his prompt, craning towards
the door, smiling, glad he had passed and keen to comply. The
sheer pressure of social prompts almost made her ears pop.

"Upstairs?" she said.

Both men looked at her.

Just then Daniel came bumbling out of the incident room, saw them, the group by Morrow's door, Alex looking small in front of the two large men who were standing too close looking down at her angrily.

"Oh," said Daniel, and retreated back into the office, half closing the door.

"Daniel!" Morrow called her out. "Come with me and Mr. Monkton upstairs, please."

Sheepishly smiling at DCI Riddell, Daniel came out, paused and walked to the end of the corridor. The tense silence was filled with the sound of her spectacular thighs rasping against each other.

Monkton turned to Riddell and spoke very calmly. "I won't take long, Kevin."

Riddell looked at Morrow, pleading with her not to piss off his new, best hope. She hadn't known he was thinking about leaving. Monkton looked at her too.

She remembered the photograph of Michael Brown as a boy, dirty yellow T-shirt, eyes cast down, no one in the world to stand up for him and she said, "Upstairs, please, sir."

But Monkton was not going to go. "I don't have time for this."

"You don't know what *this* is."

"I have an appointment with your chief—"

"Mr. Monkton, you had the time to talk to me in my office, let's use that time to speak upstairs."

And she had his elbow and she was guiding him gently towards the door to the stairs and thinking about Danny. Danny in his car staring out at her, Danny's need for her to keep lies alive.

The door was shutting behind her as she and Monkton turned to the stairs and she glimpsed for a moment DCI Riddell standing small and dismayed like a child denied at Christmas.

Alone on the stairs Monkton muttered, "Know about you."

She didn't respond. Interview room 2 was busy, so she took 3 and Daniel came in after her. Monkton sat down quite calmly on the interviewee side of the table, a smirk on his face, hands open on the tabletop as they sat down opposite him and fitted the cassette tapes in and told him he was being filmed.

"I do know the drill," he said.

"Good. Then you'll know this is just an informal chat about some matters arising from a case we've been investigating."

Monkton raised his eyebrows slowly at her, suggesting that there was no case that she could possibly be investigating that he didn't know about.

"David," she said, aware that Daniel was very comfortable in Monkton's presence. "You are the director of Intelligence Solutions, is that right?"

He glanced at the camera in the corner of the room, licked his lips and said yes.

"Can you tell me about your business, and what you do?"

"We are," he addressed the camera, "a private investigations firm. We do many different types of cases, all of which are within the law, I might add"—he took the time to smile at her, then went back to the camera—"from adoption tracing to legacy placement. We also do background checks for prospective employees et cetera."

Then he flashed her the two-hundred-grand smile and waited for the next question.

"Those are all very lovely things," she said. "Now, before you set up the company—"

"Don't you think those things matter to people?" He wasn't looking at the camera now. He was looking at her, eyes hooded behind his expensive glasses, nostrils flared.

A dog leg. A distraction. He was trying to construct a dispute

where she would argue on the tape that putting families back together was bad and he could argue it was good.

"You used to be a policeman, didn't you?"

He saw that it wasn't going to take. He took a breath, smiled.
"One of you, yes."

"Do you remember what you were doing the night Princess
Diana died?"

He did remember it and again tried to derail her. "In Paris?"

"You were in Paris?"

"No." He laughed, light, sparkling. "*She* was in Paris. She died
in Paris. Very sad." And he made a face that told her he was feeling sad and he shook his head to tell the world that it shouldn't
have happened and it made him sad.

"Where were you the next day?" Morrow sounded flat but she
felt righteousness flare in her chest. They were all lying, all of
them, dodging the truth out of fear or self-interest or for a few
quid. But she wasn't.

"I suppose..." He rubbed his chin and looked at the ceiling for
an answer. "I suppose I would have been working."

"As a police officer?"

"As a police officer."

"Where were you stationed?"

"Stewart Street."

"Who was your DS at that time?"

"Hm..." He pretended to try and remember.

"You know, David, most people remember exactly where they
were that night. If you say you don't people might think that
you're lying."

He was pleased with her now because she was providing the
distraction. He smiled at her, this rich and gorgeous man, this
connected man who had the means and the power to grant abso-
lution for almost any transgression.

She blinked and for a second saw Michael Brown, standing up at the same table, handcuffed, fumbling his flaccid cock out of his elasticated trousers to scare and disgust her into looking away from him. And she remembered Brown's face, a mask of terror, fury at his terror and horror at his life.

She opened her eyes, remembering McCarthy using alcohol wipes on that same table to wipe away the tiny flecks of piss Brown had flicked onto it.

"People remember." She had almost forgotten what they were talking about. "Because it was shocking and afterwards everyone talked about where they were when they heard, over and over we tell those stories. Why do we tell those stories? Are we trying to put ourselves into her story? Whatever we do it for, everyone knows where they were, don't they?"

Thinking she was offering him an out Monkton went for it. "Yeah, I don't think I did talk about it—"

"That's not what I'm saying. What I'm saying is that everyone remembers where they were that night."

Monkton nodded, still thinking that she was telling him to come up with a better lie.

"We have clear documentation that shows that you took Michael Brown's fingerprints that night."

"*Michael Brown.*" He squinted at the table, shook his head. "I don't think I remember a Michael Brown..."

"Young boy, fourteen years old. You picked him up at the care home he was living in, Cleveden House."

"No, I don't think I remember..."

"That's odd. Everyone else remembers."

He looked at her, read her face and smiled. "Oh, yes. A young boy."

She realized then that he was expecting her to help him. It hadn't occurred to him that she wanted to arrest him. He thought

she had left a door open for him and he was trusting her to guide
him to it.

"Young, yes," she said. "You took his prints. On paper."

"I did."

"You remember doing that?"

"We did them on cards then."

"The old ten-print sheets."

"That's right, with ink."

"Do you remember taking Brown's prints?"

"I think..."

"Did you switch them with Rose Wilson's?"

Seven seconds passed without Monkton moving or breathing.
Morrow imagined him flipping through a Rolodex of lies until he
settled on:

"Rose who?" The headshake began slowly, gathering speed
and fervor. "I don't—"

"OK." She stood up. "I'm not going to try and jog your memory—"

"I remember Michael Brown." He was panicked. She could see
it in his eyes. He thought he had chosen the wrong lie. "But my
DS that night..."

She sat back down. "George Gamerro."

"Yes." He searched her face for clues. "George Gamerro..."

"It was murder. A care-home boy found dead in an alleyway,
stabbed in the neck. His younger brother was picked up at the
home by you and DC McMahon—"

"Harry." He was quick to get that in, wanted her to know he
knew him.

"Harry McMahon. He works for you now."

"Does he?"

"Don't you know he works for you?"

"We have a massive staff. I don't know everyone."

"So, you picked the kid up and booked him. McMahon was not there when the prints were taken, you were. What happened?"

"What do you mean?"

"They're not Michael Brown's prints."

"Sounds like an administrative error. Possibly?" He was shooting in the dark now. Morrow looked him meaningfully in the eye.

"There are a series, as you're no doubt aware, of procedures to ensure that doesn't happen."

"Is it how they were entered into the system? Maybe?" He read her face and saw that it wasn't that either. "Changed subsequently? It's all been computerized, there could have been a mix-up since. Maybe?"

Morrow had no other questions and nothing else to put to him. She sat, expressionless, and watched him flail. His eyes raced over her face, looking for the open door he was sure she had left him. Monkton could not believe she wasn't helping him.

"McMahon could have switched them? Gamerro? Is that what you're thinking? Or the desk sergeant?"

She sat and looked at him, savored his discomfort as she thought about Brown as a child, a bereaved child made a further casualty because it suited someone somewhere for some reason. Whim, perhaps.

"Who was the desk sergeant that night?" asked Monkton, fishing.

"DS Riddell," she said. Riddell wasn't the desk sergeant but she would show him the tape afterwards, get him onside.

Monkton looked disappointed but resigned to blaming Riddell if that was the door she was leading him through. "Well, if Riddell...I mean this seems to me to be a police matter. I don't see how I can—"

"You switched the prints, Monkton."

Monkton stopped flailing. It would not be picked up on the camera but she could see he was furious with her.

"You did it."

"Why on earth would I do that?"

"For Anton Atholl." His face didn't register an answer. "Julius McMillan." Again nothing. "For Dawood McMann."

There it was. The answer. He'd done it for Dawood. Service industry. Corruption to order.

"Why would I do something like that for Dawood McMann?"

"Money? A favor? That's not my problem but I think you did."

"That's quite an allegation, DI Morrow. Quite an allegation to make about a respected businessman and two of Scotland's leading lawyers."

"Both of whom are dead."

"Both of whom are dead," he conceded.

"They'll probably get the blame then."

Monkton rallied. "Do you honestly think you can just do what you like, say what you like to people because your brother is a gangster? A well-known gangster? A fact that you deliberately kept hidden for years from this force?"

"No, I think I can say it because I'm a cop."

"A cop with a fraudulently acquired crisis loan? How's the roof, Alex?"

She couldn't think straight. A massive staff, he had said, hundreds, maybe. And then there were subcontractors: Stepper and the van was one of them. How on earth could they find that out? They must have access to her medical records, her son's death certificate, results of her smear tests and her mind flicked through every document she ever signed in her life. He was omnipresent and powerful.

At a loss, she said again, "I think you switched them..." But she found her voice diminished.

He didn't need to say anything to her then. He sat back looking offended and crossed his arms.

Her voice stayed small as she said, "Are you trying to intimidate me, Mr. Monkton?"

"Why would I do that?"

"Again, I'm not concerned with motives, just whether or not you are trying to intimidate me. I understand that your firm tipped off the *Daily News* about my half brother being Daniel McGrath."

"Did they?"

"No, *I'm asking you* if they did."

"I don't know if that happened. We're a big firm, we operate all over Scotland. We have, as I said, a massive staff. I don't keep tabs on the individual operations of our operatives, it would be inappropriate to do that—"

She saw a hand knocking on her front door and Brian opening it. She saw a smiling face and a cardboard wine carrier with three bottles of wine. A cheap trick, smoke and mirrors. Brian would have told them about the loan, he was honest. He told them about the loan.

Monkton looked up and found her smiling. Three bottles of wine. She could still taste them. For the price of three bottles of wine. He wasn't omniscient. He was a cheap con. She nearly congratulated him.

"Professionally, do you ever approach people seeking information under false pretenses, Mr. Monkton?"

He shook his head, as if baffled by the notion.

"Someone came to my house and said they were doing market research—"

"Well, that's a very broad term. That doesn't mean they're using it themselves to engage with an actual market."

"Hm."

He changed his stance quite suddenly. "Do you ever think about what you'll do for a job after being on the force?" He smiled. "I found that time quite hard."

"Hm."

Now she had him, and he had her. They could both put their guns down and back off, no harm done and all would continue as normal. He was offering her a job and she could see again how useful she would be to him, and how much he would pay her to be useful.

Her career was dead in the water. She wouldn't get credit for Dawood or Danny or Pokey Mulligan, she wouldn't get credit for shutting down the hundi operation, that would all go to Wainwright. She had cost the Fiscal's office a fortune over the Michael Brown prosecution and now they'd have to revoke his license, retry Rose Wilson for the Pinkie Brown case and they could hardly afford current cases. When the new nationwide force came in they'd stick her in an office doing paperwork. But she could get Monkton. They hated her anyway, she might as well arrest their future employer.

Alex leaned across the table to him. "Mr. Monkton, I think you willfully switched the fingerprints and that led to the wrongful conviction of Michael Brown for his brother's murder."

He was sweating now, panicked as a horse in a burning stall. "Who is Michael Brown to you? Is he your cousin or something? Is he your nephew?"

"And in pursuance of that, Mr. Monkton, I am charging you with perverting the course of justice. I am now going to read you your rights and I'd like you to listen carefully, because they might have changed since your day."

And then she did.

ACKNOWLEDGMENTS

Many thanks to Herr Doktor James Semple, who I now appreciate has really done all the work and not Philip or Gerard who were just stealing his thunder. Also thanks to Herr Doktor for the bucket of methadone.

Again, as ever, fervent thanks to Jon Wood, Peter Robinson, Susan Lamb, Anthony Keates and Angela McMahon for all their help and support. Jemima Forrester is afraid of meringues, so don't give her any as a thank-you from me.

Finally, to my mum, my men, wee and big, and all my beezer pals. I truly am a lucky little bastard.

BACK BAY · READERS' PICK

READING GROUP GUIDE

THE RED ROAD

A NOVEL BY

denise mina

An online version of this reading group guide is available at
littlebrown.com.

A CONVERSATION WITH DENISE MINA

Would you give us a bit of an introduction to yourself, how you got started as an author, and what kind of books you like to work on?

I'm a Scottish woman who lucked out! I started as an incompetent legal academic, doing a PhD in "The Ascription of Mental Illness to Female Offenders." I realized that I'd probably spend the rest of my life trying to get people to listen to the things I'd discovered, and I'm not that pushy. To be an academic you have to really sell yourself, and I'm not the best at that. So I started writing a crime novel with all of the ideas in it, thinking that people would read for the mystery but come across all of the ideas in there. That book was *Garnethill*.

The books I like to work on have pace and take the reader into a different world than they have imagined before. I like heroes and heroines that are unexpected: psychiatric patients, rude women, the fat girl in the office.

I am often struck by the different ways books can be interpreted by who reads them and how they read them. Can you share with us any routines, food or recipes, or favorite books or rituals that help you get into character and prepare to write a book?

Honestly, I've got kids, a lot of elderly relatives, and a man who couldn't find his arse with both hands, so I don't have time for routines or rituals. I just look at the calendar, weep softly, and get on with it. Panic is a good motivator. Working in the morning is good too: there's a period of about two hours just after I've woken up when I don't have a head full of other things, so I often get up a couple of hours before everyone else and work then.

Write the question you would most like to answer in an interview, and then answer it.

"Does being lauded as a writer make you feel like a bit of a phony?"

All the time. I see other writers talk about their work with total certainty and confidence. Maybe they don't feel that way, but I can't even put it on. I always think of Philip Larkin and Ted Hughes. Larkin was constitutionally questioning and Hughes was certain. I feel like Larkin. I wake up a little bit embarrassed. I used to be embarrassed about feeling embarrassed, but now I think of it as the ability to have two feelings at the same time. It's my superpower.

What was the most interesting thing that you've found out while preparing for a book that you'll be working on?

Reading a lot of the research on women who marry men in prison or on death row for *Deception*. The dynamic in those relationships mirrors that between fan and pop star: you can be completely over the top because you'll never meet really; it's the distance that causes the erotic tension. There's a great book about Australian women who married men in prison and followed them after they got out. Terrifying! One guy took all of his wife's teeth out to punish her.

In the past I have visited a blog called Daily Routines and it's all about the schedules of writers and creative people. What does a typical day look like for you and how do you manage a busy schedule?

I get up before the kids and write for one or two hours before they get up. Then an hour and half of nagging, feeding, shouting, walking, and getting everyone to school. Then back to the desk, reread what I've done, decide what I'm going to do today. Batter into it. By about 11 a.m. my concentration is fading and I spend about an hour and a half refusing to admit it has. I check my email, Facebook, Twitter. I empty the dishwasher. I sweep the hall.

Then I give up and have lunch early. Then I come back, work for a bit more, set out the work for the session, and get on with interviews, admin, phone calls, etc. The kids get out of school at three o'clock so I usually think of something great at 2:30, just as I have to set off. Jot it down, go get the kids. Get everyone back home, feed, nag, homework, nag. If I have child care, which is about two afternoons a week, I sit down and work until five.

How jaw-droppingly dull is all of that?

What were your experiences with reading when you were growing up? Was there a pivotal moment in discovering literature when you knew that you wanted to work in the publishing industry in this capacity? In any capacity?

I moved around Europe a lot when I was a kid and didn't really learn to read until I was about eight. I couldn't write until I was nine and wasn't academic at all.

When I was nineteen I went on a girls-gone-wild holiday to Greece with waitresses I worked in a coffee shop with. I honestly thought we were going to look at churches, but, well, there was a misunderstanding of epic proportions. One of the girls had brought these books: *One Hundred Years of Solitude* and *The Master and Margarita*.

I sat on the roof for a solid week and read. Best holiday I've ever had. Best tan too.

I read obsessively after that. I remember reading Zola and Dickens and thinking how wonderful it would be to write a book that would touch someone the way they had touched me.

What's next?

I'm finishing a book just now called *Blood Salt Water*, writing the graphic adaption of *The Girl Who Kicked the Hornet's Nest* (by Stieg Larsson), judging the Baileys Prize for women's literature, editing a graphic novel for the Edinburgh International Book Festival, and doing promotion for a short film I made with my cousins called *Multum in Parvo* (translation: *Much in Little*). The film was a documentary we made of our parents being interviewed about growing up one of fifteen in a four-bedroom house. Then we showed it to the extended family in a cinema in Glasgow and filmed them watching themselves.

This interview was conducted by Nicole Bonia for *Linus's Blanket,* linussblanket.com.

QUESTIONS AND TOPICS
FOR DISCUSSION

1. Michael Brown is introduced to us as an extremely threatening man; Morrow feels uncomfortable just being in the same room with him. How does her (and the reader's) view of him change over the course of the novel? In what sense does the initial fear of Michael play into the scheme of the truly fearsome people who appear in *The Red Road*? Is there anything to be learned from this about how we judge and stereotype criminals?

2. How would you describe Morrow's feelings toward Anton Atholl? Do the interactions between the two of them change or complicate your view of him? Why do you think Mina created the chemistry between them?

3. Do you find Rose Wilson to be a sympathetic character? How does having access to her point of view affect your reading and your assessment of right and wrong in the book?

4. Children figure prominently in this novel, not only in the stories of Rose Wilson and Michael Brown, but in the more peripheral presences of Morrow's twin boys, Robert's three

kids, Atholl's estranged sons, and even the unborn child of the murder victim, Aziz. At one point, thinking of his daughter, Robert remembers the maxim "Give me the child until he is seven, and I will give you the man," a quote that hints at how early our characters are formed. What view of children and childhood do you come away with?

5. There are many villains in this story; they come from different worlds and cause harm in different ways. What or who do you see as the darkest or most dangerous force of evil in the novel, and why?

6. Would you include former detectives Harry McMahon and George Gamerro on the list of villains? Why or why not?

7. After discovering the photograph of herself in Julius's safe, Rose's thoughts keep returning to "Aileen Wuornos's chicken." Why does the television program about Wuornos have such a profound effect on Rose, and what do you make of the details in it that plague her? How do they relate to her own life?

8. Rose's second visit to Atholl's apartment is one of the most brutal and intense scenes in the novel. Do you consider Atholl's suicide a noble or cowardly act? Do you feel any pity for him? Does the fact that he "meant well" and "wished he had been a better man" distinguish him from other corrupt and predatory characters in the novel?

9. When Rose and Morrow finally come face to face, their interaction strays from the expected script between cop and

criminal. What do you think the women see in each other? Do they have anything in common?

10. After solving the case of who killed Pinkie Brown, Morrow experiences a sudden sense of doubt and futility; "It was all wrong. Morrow had done it all so that she could sleep at night, so that she could feel like a better person than Riddell and Danny. She longed for some high ground to scramble towards but there wasn't any." How do you interpret this moment? What does it say about Morrow? About the world she lives in? Do you agree that sleeping at night and feeling superior to others are what motivate her? If not, what does?

ABOUT THE AUTHOR

Denise Mina is the author of *Gods and Beasts, The End of the Wasp Season, Still Midnight, Slip of the Knife, The Dead Hour, Field of Blood, Deception,* and the Garnethill trilogy, the first installment of which won her the John Creasey Memorial Award for best first crime novel. She lives in Glasgow.

...AND THE NEXT ALEX MORROW NOVEL

In *Blood Salt Water,* a missing-person case leads Alex Morrow to investigate the dark underbelly of a seemingly peaceful seaside town. Following is an excerpt from the novel's opening pages.

Alex Morrow was conscious of her mundane happiness. She had the insight unique to those who have known otherwise.

She was slumped on her couch, in a living room scattered with toys, damp towels, all chores pending. She was aware of the warmth, of her kids' good health and how nice the man beside her was. She didn't care about work or the state of the place. She was just where she was.

They had the telly on, half watching the news of wars and fights and crises affecting other people. Mostly, though, they were listening to the baby monitor, waiting for the boys to try something else.

Brian shifted his leg on the footstool they were sharing and his toes touched hers.

She smiled at his foot. "Your day all right?"

"Usual," said Brian. "You?"

"Same." She sipped her tea. "Liars and politics."

"I spent forty minutes answering emails this morning while the boss lectured me about how men can't multitask."

The baby monitor crackled and the light glowed green. It sounded as if the twins were asleep, but that didn't mean they were. They were conspiracy incarnate.

Alex and Brian were listening carefully, not just for naughtiness: baby Danny had a night cough and hair-trigger gag reflex. If they didn't pick him up before a coughing fit set in, he was sick, the bed needed changed, both the boys would be up. They were so attuned that they could tell when a cough was two or three breaths in the future from tiny changes to the depth or rhythm in his breathing.

A small voice on the monitor tried a tentative *Daddy?* The pulsing green light on the baby monitor flared into the red zone.

Brian shouted at the ceiling, "GO. TO. SLEEP."

A pause. A calculation. Alex imagined the twins looking at each other in the dark.

Mumm—

"WHISHT!" Brian sounded stern but he was smiling, "SLEEP."

A woman in Syria sobbed and shouted at the camera. In a flat voice a man explained that her family were in the building at the time. She no longer had faith in the UN.

Alex glanced at the baby monitor. The boys had missed their cue. They must be falling asleep.

The news had finished and they found themselves watching another debate on the independence referendum. A red-faced man in a suit tittered in bitter disbelief as another man spoke. The camera cut to the audience, capturing a woman putting a sweet in her mouth. Unaware she was being watched, she chewed and smiled with delighted surprise, taking the packet out to look at it and offer one to her neighbor.

Brian reached for the remote. "Wish we had some sweeties," he said, switching over.

Alex's phone lit up on the side table. She frowned and looked at it. Unknown. She sat up and answered it.

Was this Alexandra Morrow? This was Shotts prison. They had her number listed as Daniel McGrath's family contact. The officer apologized for phoning so late, but her brother had been attacked and stabbed. He was in hospital. He had been operated on and was in a stable condition. If she wanted to visit him she needed to contact this person in that department of the Scottish Prison Service. Thank you, sorry, and good night.

"What?" asked Brian.

"Danny." She whispered. "Stabbed. He's in hospital."

"Is he okay?"

"Stable."

On TV a smiley man was forecasting a change in the weather. Heavy rain, danger of landslides. Brian's hand found hers across the settee.

"Are you all right, love?"

"Aye," she said, but too high, too fast.

He squeezed her hand, "Want to call the hospital?"

"I forgot to ask which hospital it is. I'll call tomorrow."

They lay shoulder to shoulder in bed. Lazy tears oiled from Alex's eyes, running into her hair at the temples.

The dark room was lit kelp green by the baby monitor. An undulating ocean of sound filled the room, the ebb and swell of the boys' breathing. Brian waited for a wave to crash before he spoke.

"You crying?"

She waited for the next pause and whispered back, "A bit."

"I'm sure he's okay."

She wasn't crying because she was worried about him. She was crying because Danny, once again, had robbed her of the delusion of nobility. In the moment just after the news, before Brian spoke,

Alex had wished her brother dead with a fervor that was almost sexual. Not because he was a bad man, she wasn't wishing him dead for the good of the world. She wished her brother dead because he made her uncomfortable. He was an obligation she did not want to meet. It was mealy, malevolent, and she didn't want to know it about herself.

Brian whispered in the green dark, "Never going to be over, is it?" She didn't answer.

They shouldn't even have her number. Danny must have given it to them, even though her division had been instrumental in arresting him. She tried to think of another motive; he was shaming her by giving them her as a contact. He was implicating himself in her life. He was tainting her. But none of it rang true. It was another lie. She was trying to vitiate her own guilt. Danny had given her number because she was all he had. She had all of this, Brian, the twins, her job, everything. But she was all that Danny had, and she didn't want him.

She lay still, listening to the wash of the twins' breathing. They were trying to synchronize: one would snuffle, the other stumble over an exhalation, correcting themselves, trying to meet as completely as they had in the womb, but failing. Always failing.